CW01501962

# ACKNOWLEDGMENTS

It goes without saying that to produce anything worthwhile, requires help from others. The process of writing a book such as this is aided and abetted by numerous people. Some of who only subtly assist, and others, who profoundly do so. My thanks go to anyone who however small, has contributed to this novel. My main appreciation, however, is to the people who purchased and read my books: The Hanging Tree and The Romanov Relic. Your support is greatly appreciated. Many thanks go to my writing friends – The Monday Horsemen - for their invaluable support and help in making this book possible. A huge thank you to Vicky, for helping greatly with my editing. Finally, to anyone who is reading this book. I hope you find it enjoyable, and any feedback is always appreciated.

February 2018.

# DISCLAIMER

Many of the places mentioned in this book exist. However, the author has used poetic license throughout, to maintain an engaging narrative. Therefore, no guarantee of accuracy in some respects should be expected. The characters depicted, however, are wholly fictional. Any similarity to persons living or dead is accidental.

# PERSISTENCE OF VISION

## VISION

### Seeing is not believing

## JOHN REGAN

# THE STORYTELLER

Consider what reality is. If we can see, touch, smell or taste it, does that make it real? What about fantasy? The dreams and reflections floating through our mind. The two are distinct. As different as chalk and cheese, one might say. But what about the area in between? Where the outskirts of reality and fantasy merge. Where the boundaries between the two become less apparent. Where the lines become blurred. This is the area of interest. The region often hidden from view; out of sight. Let's move beyond reality towards fantasy. Loitering in the hinterland nestling between them. You may want to keep your wits about you, though. What is real may, in fact, be fantasy and what appears fantasy, real. I'll let you decide.

Does time exist? We can't see it or hold it in the palm of our hands. We can invent devices to show the passing of time but are even these an illusion. Our brains speed up or slow down time at will, or that's what appears to happen. Suppose it is thirty years between two events. Let's say two people's lives. If only time separates them, all we need is something to bridge the gap. A something to make a person's reality coincide with another's. Could such a something be invented? A device so ingenious, it would defy belief. Or maybe there's already something out there. An entity existing. A something that has always been here. Something outside of time itself, or should I say, the time we believe exists. Well then. We would have something to behold.

**Amorphous**. The cyber-organic computer invented in 2045 by Dr Phillips and his team. Born from the DNA making all life on our planet possible. Crudely put, a living brain. Connected and incorporated into the most sophisticated electronics ever devised. Its primary function: To assist in the unravelling of impenetrable crimes. The ability to interface with suspects and witnesses; to shed light where there was none. Humankind needs to be careful, though. For once the genie is freed from its constraints, there's no way of going back. Or maybe there is. That's the point. Even Einstein, one of history's greatest scientists, recognised the intrinsic link between space and time. Maybe Amorphous' arrival, was inevitable.

**Lindsey Armstrong**. A troubled soul. Released from prison after serving the full fifteen years of her sentence. The last decade and a half spent mostly in the confines of her cell. Forced to say goodbye to Maggie, her one true friend and sometimes surrogate mother. She's heading home, or what once was her home. Her mother and father now dead. A lifetime of childhood memories encased within bricks and mortar. Forced to confront her past, and maybe an opportunity to change her future. Remember though. Redemption is never an easy road to travel. Filled with potholes and wrong turns along the journey.

**Beth Pearson**, A temporal lobe epileptic. Recruited by **The Morpheus Foundation,** to work on the **Amorphous Program.** Her ability to link with Amorphous, outstripping any of her peers. Separated from Lindsey by thirty years, or so it seems. Maybe it's her epilepsy giving us the opportunity to see how tenuous a gap it is. To view the face and hear the voice of something higher, something way beyond the wit of man; you need the right key. It is possible Beth, is such a key.

# AMORPHOUS - CHAPTER ONE

**2015 -** She sat alone. Staring out of the window of the train as the cinema-graphic countryside sped by. Clutching to her body a backpack. All her possessions in the world encased within. Her attention is drawn away from the window. The last passenger rose from his seat and retrieved his bag as the train pulled into the station. Lindsey studied the table he vacated, the remnants of his breakfast scattered across it. She spotted the food he'd left as the emptiness in her stomach pushed for her attention. Hours had passed since she'd last eaten. The money she had earned for performing a sexual favour on a businessman in Durham, long gone. Looking around at the empty compartment she made her way over to his vacated table, sat down, and devoured what he'd left.

*'Look at the state of you,' the voice within her head* said. *'Why don't you go and eat from a rubbish bin?'*

'I'm starving. I have to eat.' The thought remaining locked inside her mind.

*'What are you doing going back, Lindsey? No one will welcome you,'* said another, softer voice.

*'That's right. Who the fuck wants a murderer hanging around.'*

She stared out of the window. 'I have to go back. The house needs selling. I've things there I want … things I need,' she thought.

*'Look at what you've become. You're a mess, and you haven't even reached Middlesbrough. Not so hard now, are we? What happened to little miss angry from 'C' wing?'*

'No. I've decided. I'll go there to collect some of my belongings and arrange to sell the house.'

*'You could've asked an estate agent to sell it for you, Lindsey. Why torment yourself?'*

'I can't explain. I just need to come home.'

*'Home! Don't make me laugh. Home is a rectangular room, with bars on the windows and a big steel door. Look at you. You're as weak as piss.'*

She wiped her chin with the sleeve of her coat and stood as the train pulled into Middlesbrough station. Throwing the backpack over her shoulder, she headed for the doors. As she reached the end of her carriage, she noticed a man in the next one along looking out of the window. A smart, new phone sat on the edge of his table in front of him. In one quick motion, she moved towards the table, gathered it up and deposited it into her jacket pocket. She glanced around, and sure nobody had seen her jumped from the train.

*'You fucking little thief,'* the voice goaded her. *'You'll be back inside before you know it.'*

*'This is an opportunity, Lindsey. A chance to go straight. Get your life back on track. Why steal the man's phone? It must've cost him a lot of money?'*

'If he can afford an expensive phone like that, he can afford another,' she said. Within her head, as she raced along the platform.

*'She can justify anything this one. Lindsey Armstrong. Thief and murderer,'* the voice taunted her.

'There's plenty of time for change, I need to get my head straight. Sell the house and buy another somewhere nice. Wait for Maggie.'

*'Maggie's got years to do. Who'll look after you until she gets out?'* asked the softer voice.

'I can look after myself. I'll be ok. I need to gather my thoughts. I …'

*'This town will eat you up and spit you out, Armstrong. You're nothing but a murdering scumbag that everybody hates. A thief and a liar. Giving blowjobs to strangers for money. You're a fucking little whore!'*

*'Shut up! Shut up!'* she screamed out loud.

The other people on the platform stopped to look at her, shocked by the outburst. Lindsey put her head down and raced past them. Reaching inside her coat pocket, she took out her iPod. Inserted the earplugs and turned the volume up high. Pulling the hood of her jacket up, so it covered her face, she sped off as the voices in her head receded into the background.

The town throbbed with people. Lindsey marched through the throng, unwilling to make eye contact with anyone. Spotting a pub on the corner, she stepped through the first set of doors. Pausing, she gathered her thoughts while trying to suppress the voices. Heading into the bar, she found herself in a sparsely populated room which suited Lindsey. Large crowds, she discovered, unnerved her. She viewed the occupants and noticed two scruffy-looking men standing at the end of the bar.

Lindsey stopped close by and smiled. 'Nice phone.' She nodded towards one of the men.

The man with the phone looked up from the mobile, his friend eyeing Lindsey up and down. 'It's ok.' Glancing sideways at her.

'Not as smart as this.' She pulled the mobile she'd stolen from her pocket.

He nodded. 'Mmm.' Looking at the top-of-the-range model in her hand.

'I don't suppose either of you boys wants to buy it?'

He sneered and winked at his friend. 'Stolen is it?'

'£40,' she replied. '£40's a bargain.'

The man with the mobile popped his phone into his pocket. He edged closer to Lindsey, too close for comfort. Lindsey resisted the strong urge to back away. She now regretted talking to them, and as he pushed his face nearer to hers, his beer-filled-breath filled her nostrils.

'I don't want a new mobile. If you're in need of money, maybe you have something else to sell,' he said. He leant back against the bar looking her up and down, and winked at his mate, again. His companion grinned back.

'What were you thinking of?' Lindsey caught her reflection in the mirror behind the bar, realising exactly what he meant.

He pulled £20 from his pocket and held it out towards her, waving it under her nose.

'She's a slapper,' his friend said. 'I wouldn't touch her with yours.' He shook his head and slurped his pint.

'Ten minutes.' He grinned as his friend shook his head again.

Lindsey nodded and put the mobile way. 'Ok.'

She followed him towards the toilet. Stopping outside and checking no one was watching, they entered. Lindsey put her rucksack on the floor, trying not to show the revulsion she felt for him.

'Well.' Holding out her hand. '£20 you said.'

The man put his hand in his pocket and pulled out the note. Lindsey grabbed it from him and secreted it in her jeans.

'Drop them then,' she said. Her false bravado sounded convincing. The man enthusiastically undid his belt, dropping his trousers and boxers to the floor. Lindsey edged towards him and as he stood expectantly, she pushed him in the chest. Unable to maintain his balance, he toppled backwards. His jeans around his ankles acting like denim manacles, thwarting his effort to stand. Lindsey gathered up her backpack and in one swift motion threw it over her shoulder, opened the door, and fled.

'You fucking bitch!' she heard him scream, as she darted for the exit.

His friend, who had been keeping a close watch on the toilet door, realised what had happened and bolted after her. She approached the door and pulled a table full of drinks behind herself, barring his exit. Lindsey burst into the street and heard the crash of her pursuer as he collided with the upturned table. Turning right, she sprinted along an alley, putting distance between herself and anyone following. Finally slowing to a jog, she continued along North Ormesby Road, and stopped to catch her breath on reaching the junction with Borough Road. She glanced back but saw no one. Smiling to herself and convinced nobody had followed her, Lindsey headed to the place she once called home.

Lindsey closed the door behind herself and slumped back against it, breathing in the stale air of the house. She glanced around at the familiar hallway, as the time between the present and the past dissolved before her. Almost unaltered from the last time Lindsey had been there. The colour on the walls a darker shade of cream than she remembered, but not much else had changed. The carpet on the floor, the same. The pictures hanging on the walls, familiar to her. One of them caught her attention. A painting of a landscape, listing at an awkward angle as if someone had knocked it as they'd brushed past. Lindsey pushed up one corner, attempting to straighten it. Satisfied she had, she closed her eyes as memories from her past swept over her in a temporal tsunami.

'Is that you, Lindsey?' the voice said.

'Yeah.' The corners of her mouth lifting into a smile.

'I've made your favourite. It's in the oven.'

'Thanks, Mam,' she whispered to herself. Opening her eyes, she gazed across at the telephone table. Situated - as it always had been - in the corner, with a lifeless, cordless phone on it. A thick layer of dust, from months of neglect, covered both the table and the phone. She ambled across, and pulled her fingers across the top, revealing a dark line of glossy wood beneath. Removing her headphones, she wrapped them around the iPod and slipped it into the pocket of her jeans. The silence of the house, somehow both comforting and daunting. Her emotional dichotomy, confusing. She climbed the stairs to the next floor, trying to suppress the increasing chatter of voices rising in her head. Reaching the top, she paused outside one of the bedroom doors. Her name stencilled on the front of it, captured in vivid pink. The door, repainted at some time, but whoever had done this - her dad she supposed - had painted a square around her name. Allowing it to remain uncovered, almost but not entirely expunged from their lives, she mused. Lindsey traced the paintwork with her index and middle finger, following the lettering. Reaching for the handle, she paused, as her heart rate raised its tempo.

*'Look at her. She's shit scared,'* the voice said. Leaping forward from the maelstrom of noise in her head.

'*Lindsey, don't go in. It'll make you sad,*' said another, gentler voice.

She ignored them. Pushing open the door, she stepped inside. The door banged against the wall, coming to a squeaky rest against it.

She closed her eyes again. 'Are you ready, Linny?' his voice said.

'Yeah, just about,' she replied. 'I hope we win today.' The mental conversation in her head as fresh as ever, as the time between the present and the past evaporated.

'We will. And after we do, we'll go for a slap-up meal and a few drinks.'

'And what if we lose?' she said.

He chuckled. 'We'll go for a slap-up meal and a few drinks.'

'I love you, Dad.' Hugging him, her arms enveloping her father's imaginary form.

'I love you too. You're my favourite daughter.'

'Hmm. I'm your only daughter.'

'Well, there you go. No competition.'

'Are you two ready?' Her Mother's voice drifted across time and up the stairs towards them.

'Yeah, just coming!' The two of them shouted in unison.

Lindsey opened her eyes and glanced around the bedroom, as long suppressed-memories bubbled to the surface. The bedroom just as she remembered it. Her mother having retained it shrine-like for her return. Except, it appeared to have aged along with herself. The posters of long departed Middlesbrough football players adorned the walls. The edges of them curling. The colour bleached from them by years of sunlight. On the dressing table sat a now deflated signed football, which her dad had bid for at a charity auction. She smiled. The day he gave it to her, still shining brightly in her memory. Wandering across to it she picked it up and viewed the still visible signatures. Lindsey replaced it as if it was a delicate piece of porcelain. Taking hold of one of the curtains, she stroked the material between her index finger and thumb. The matching duvet on the bed, with its large Middlesbrough F.C. crest emblazoned across it, caught her attention. She smoothed out the wrinkles on it. Satisfied, she scanned the rest of the room. The furniture unaltered as if the previous fifteen years had never passed.

Her eyes fell on the wardrobe on the other side of the room. She walked across to it and stopped to peer inside. Lindsey pushed aside the sweaters on one of the shelves until she found what she was looking for, and pulled it free of the other clothing. She held up the blue jumper, Craig's jumper, and smiled. Pulling it close to her body, she sniffed at it. Disappointed it appeared almost odourless, except for a musty smell.

'*I see you kept it?*' his voice said.

Lindsey smiled. 'Of course I kept it,' she murmured. 'I kept everything.'

Dropping onto her knees, she searched beneath the pile of jeans. Pulling out a white shoe box she removed the lid, allowing it to fall to the floor, and viewed its contents.

'Everything's in here. Every bus and train ticket. Every cinema ticket stub. The cards you sent me, the paper you used to wrap the presents. Everything. Our whole relationship. Our life and existence encased within this cardboard box.'

*'Why don't you look at me?'* he said.

She closed her eyes again. The action pushing out tears which descended her cheeks and dropped onto the floor. 'I want to, Craig, but it's the blood. I can't look at the blood.' Lindsey roused from her reverie by a knock on the front door, replaced the lid, and then the box. Closing the wardrobe, she turned and headed downstairs.

Stopping at the front door, she pushed her face against the glass to decipher who was knocking. 'Who is it?' she asked.

'Lindsey? I don't know if you remember me. It's Jimmy. Jimmy Jefferson.'

'JJ?' she said.

'Yeah.'

'What do you want?'

'I was in the shop earlier when the shopkeeper wouldn't serve you. I've brought your things.'

She opened the door a little, looking Jimmy up and down. He was only a boy when she last saw him. Now a man stood before her, holding two plastic carriers. 'What did you do that for?' she said.

Jimmy lowered his head. 'I felt ...' He paused.

'I'm not a frigging charity case, you know.'

'I know,' he said. 'I'm sorry. I wanted to help you. That's all.'

Lindsey opened the door wide and glanced across the road, noticing a woman looking across at the two of them. 'Have you had a good fucking look?' she shouted. The woman scurried out of sight. 'Come in, then,' she said to him. 'How much do I owe you?'

'It's ok.'

Lindsey pulled the £20 from her jeans and tucked it into his shirt pocket. 'Have you got the beers?' she said. Looking into the carriers.

'Yeah. They're a little warm though.'

'Who cares? It's been years since I tasted one.'

She hurried into the kitchen and opened a drawer. Pulling out a bottle opener with a picture of Benidorm on the side of it, she paused as the memory of buying it on holiday for her mother arrived. With it pressed between her fingers she tried to create a link to the past, but unable to she sighed, opened two of the bottles, and walked back to the hall.

Jimmy shuffled his feet. 'I got most of the stuff you wanted.' He paused. 'I didn't buy the women's things. I was embarrassed.'

'That's ok. I'll manage for now.' Lindsey smiled, handing Jimmy a beer. 'Well JJ. You've changed. I remember a little spotty kid. Where did all these come from then?' She gave his muscular arm a squeeze.

Jimmy blushed, the pair of them turned towards the door as scmeone knocked.

Lindsey handed Jimmy her bottle and marched towards it. Pulling it open. 'What!' A police officer stood there.

'Lindsey Armstrong?' he asked.

'What if I am?' she said.

'We've had a complaint from a Mr Jones, who owns the mini-mart on Hope Street. He claims you threatened him.'

Jimmy pushed past Lindsey. 'She didn't threaten him. I was there. I saw it. He wouldn't serve her, and she told him what she thought of him. That's all.'

'What are you doing here, Jimmy?' the officer said.

'She's a friend.'

The officer put his notepad away. 'Well. We'll leave it at that. But he doesn't want you in his shop anymore.'

Lindsey sneered. 'Suits me. He's a tosser.' She turned, retrieved her beer from Jimmy, and marched towards the living room.

As Jimmy turned too, the officer tugged at his arm. 'What the hell are you doing, Jimmy? You do know she's a convicted murderer.'

'Of course I know. She's a friend. That's all.'

He frowned. 'People are judged by the friends they keep. What would your dad say?'

'He wouldn't care. Oh, let's see.' Consulting his watch. 'He'll be arse-holed at this time.'

The officer dropped his head a little. 'He took it badly when your mum died. He's a good bloke. It's not easy losing a wife.'

'She didn't die,' Jimmy said. 'She was murdered.'

'I know, but it can't have been easy for your dad. With him being in the police, and us never catching who did it.'

'And I suppose losing a mother is easy, is it?'

The officer frowned. 'I didn't mean it like that.'

'Have we finished here?' Jimmy said.

'You watch your step with that one.' He pointed at the house. 'Being inside changes people. The Lindsey you knew doesn't exist anymore.'

'Well the kid, Jimmy, who had a mother doesn't either.' He stepped into the hall and slammed the door. Leaning back against it Jimmy closed his eyes and blew out hard.

Lindsey came out of the lounge. 'You ok?'

He glanced at her. His eyes glistening. 'Yeah.'

She edged towards him and placed a hand on his cheek. 'I'd forgotten … about your mam.' She smiled. 'What about another beer?'

Jimmy smiled back at her. 'Yeah. Sounds like a plan.'

Lindsey and Jimmy finished the beers and ate the snacks which Jimmy had brought. They talked about the old times. Tip-toeing around Lindsey's prison sentence, and the murder of Jimmy's mother.

As the clock ticked beyond midnight, Jimmy got up to leave. 'I'd better go.' Moving towards the door, he picked up his jacket.

Lindsey stood, too. 'You can stay if you like? You could sleep in the spare room.' She forced a smile at him at him.

'I'm not sure—'

'Please,' she said. 'I haven't been alone for a long time.'

He smiled. 'Yeah. Ok.'

They made the bed up in the spare room, and Jimmy stripped to his boxers and got in. The long day and beers having a soporific effect on him. His eyelids briefly laboured with gravity before he allowed them to close, sleepily. Lindsey, unable to withstand the noises inside her head, along with the nightmarish visions, made her way to Jimmy's room. She slipped underneath the covers and hugged his body. He woke with her trembling body clutching onto him. Jimmy lifted his left hand and gently squeezed hers. Lindsey sighed, the two of them quickly locating and embracing sleep.

Lindsey woke early. The voices in her head, and their constant chatter making further sleep impossible. She glanced across at Jimmy, asleep in bed. Cocking her head to one side trying to decipher his features. He seemed so peaceful and content. She thought about waking him, but decided not to and headed downstairs. Searching through the drawers and finding a pen, Lindsey took out a piece of paper and wrote a note.

**2045 – THE MORPHEUS FOUNDATION –** Beth, roused from her fugue by Dr Phillips' voice, opened her eyes.

'Beth. It's Dr Phillips. Can you hear me?'

She tried to speak, the words stalling in her dry mouth.

'If you can hear me, move your hand.'

Beth complied. The effort monumental, as if someone held her arms down by her side. She persisted and managed to lift her left hand a little.

'Is this normal?' Willoughby said.

Phillips nodded. 'Perfectly. The brain shuts down the motor skills when people sleep. Retrogression is similar to that. There's always a slight delay. She'll recover shortly.' Phillips placed a hand on Beth's arm. 'We're going to give you a sedative. When you wake, you'll be back on the ward.' Beth moved her hand again in acknowledgement.

Willoughby marched towards the door, stopping at the threshold he turned to face Phillips. 'I need to know what she saw as soon as possible. The directors are hassling me over this. Richardson has sunk millions into this project, and they're pushing for results.'

'I understand, sir, but we're only at the boundaries of this technology. We can't rush it.'

He opened the door and fixed Phillips with a glare. 'This afternoon, Phillips. I want something by today.'

Beth woke in bed. Opening her eyes, she squinted against the harsh light shining from the ceiling. Sitting, and swinging her legs around, she planted her feet on the floor. Reaching for the help button, Beth pressed. The effort sapped her already depleted energy. She waited a couple of moments before Dr Phillips and Rogers - an orderly - entered the room.

'Beth. How are you feeling?' Phillips said.

'Bit of a headache,' she said. 'I'm exhausted too.'

'Side effects of the procedure I'm afraid. The previous retrogressions only took you so deep. Each one takes you deeper still. You'll get used to them, I'm sure. Can you tell us what you remember?'

Beth picked up the beaker next to the bed and greedily swigged from it. She sat back and propped herself against the headboard. 'I was someone called Lindsey. From what I gather, she'd recently been released from prison. For murder.'

Phillips frowned. 'Lindsey? Are you sure?'

'Definitely. It was weird. Not at all like the other retro's.' Beth furrowed her brow, the effort causing her head to ache more. 'It was in the past.'

Phillips glanced at the orderly. 'Past? What about Catherine Richardson?'

'She wasn't there. Only a Lindsey and a man. I think his name was Jimmy. He could've been her boyfriend. There's something else Doctor.' She furrowed her brow. Phillips peered up from his pad where he'd busily been jotting down notes. 'I think she's schizoid,' Beth said. 'She hears voices and sees people.'

Phillip's rubbed his chin. 'When you say it was in the past, how far back are we talking?'

'I'm not sure. Not far. 25-30 years ago, maybe. The man called Jimmy appears to know Lindsey from way back. His father was a policeman, and his mother was murdered.'

'Another murder? Interesting,' Phillips said. 'How did it feel? What were the sensations like this time?'

'It felt so real, much more than before. As if I *was* Lindsey. As if I'd somehow been pushed into the background along with the other voices.'

'These other voices,' he said. 'Did you recognise them?'

'Maybe. I can't be sure, but some of them could be from my past retrogressions.' Beth sat back against the wall, the effort of talking, tiring her.

'Have another rest. We'll speak later.'

Phillips and Rogers headed back to Phillips' office. He sat on a chair and stared at Rogers. 'Well. What do you make of that?'

'Bit strange,' Rogers said. 'The engrams from Catherine Richardson's investigation installed correctly. We ran the pre-checks, and everything is A1. The procedure operated as it should.'

'Something is amiss. These memories Beth experienced.' He struggled to find the right words. 'Could they just be a glitch?'

'I'll go and run some diagnostics,' Rogers said. 'Maybe we missed something. This may be just a one-off.'

Phillips nodded, leaning back in the chair deep in thought, as Rogers left.

# CHAPTER TWO

Phillips made his way along the corridor and stopping outside Willoughby's office, knocked.

'Come in,' Willoughby shouted. 'Take a seat.' Pointing to a chair as Phillips entered.

Phillips sat, shuffling in his seat. 'I've spoken with Beth. We may have a problem.'

Willoughby glanced up from his paperwork. 'Problem?'

'There appears to be something amiss with Beth's latest retrogression.'

Willoughby folded his arms. 'What?'

'The retrogression didn't deliver Beth to Catherine Richardson's scenario.'

Willoughby threw his hands open. 'How can it not. You programmed the bloody thing. Didn't you?'

'It appears Amorphous invented a scenario of its own. We're not sure why. My staff are currently running diagnostics to discover what went wrong. Amorphous it appears, is just that. I believe it's inadvisable to allow Beth to retrogress again until we know what's going on.'

'For Christ sake, Phillips,' Willoughby said. 'I can't go to the directors with this. Beth's our best Retrogressor. You said it yourself. The other two come nowhere near to her numbers. You know how important this case is. We need her to find out who killed Catherine Richardson. Can't you get your smart-arse geeks to tweak Amorphous a little?'

Phillips sneered. 'Amorphous can't be tweaked. It's not a mainframe. It's the most sophisticated cyber-organic computer ever built. Any attempt to alter its programming now would be catastrophic.'

Willoughby waved a hand dismissively. 'Yeah, yeah, Phillips.' Standing, he ambled around to the other side of the desk and sat on the corner of it. Too close for Phillips' liking. 'The computer is supposed to do what we want. It's meant to bend to our will. It's not intended to start making up stories. Fix the fucking thing. Pronto.'

'Maybe we could try one of the others to retrogress?' Phillips said. 'Just until we get to the bottom of why Amorphous is putting Beth into this scenario.'

Willoughby shook his head. 'We can't, it would put us back months. The directors wouldn't allow it either. We've told Richardson we can find his daughter's killer. We have to proceed with Beth.'

'It could compromise the Catherine Richardson scenario.'

'Phillips.' Willoughby lowered his face towards him. 'You enjoy living in that smart house of yours? The bank account the company filled for you? Well, I suggest you find a solution, or you may find yourself dissecting rats for a living. Do what you have to do, but I want her retrogressed as soon as possible. Am I clear on this?'

Phillips got up from the seat and without uttering another word, left the office.

Willoughby sat back in his chair and smiled to himself before picking up the phone. 'It's Michael. The little program we introduced into Amorphous appears to be working. It's throwing out random scenarios. I'm confident we can stop them from discovering the truth.'

Phillips raced his way back to the lab. Rogers followed him into his office and stood next to the desk as Phillips slumped into his seat.

'Willoughby's an idiot, Jake,' Phillips said. 'He thinks you can tweak Amorphous as if it's some average mainframe. He's adamant he wants Beth to retrogress again.' Phillips began sifting through the mountain of paperwork in front of him.

'I spoke with Beth,' Rogers said. 'It's more complicated than we thought.'

Phillips looked up. 'Complicated? In what way?'

'The girl in Beth's retrogression.' He shuffled his feet. 'She existed.'

Phillip's dropped the papers. 'What do you mean, *existed?*'

'She was a real person. Her full name is Lindsey Armstrong. She lived in the north east of England.' He glanced at the small, electronic pad in his hand. 'She was sentenced to 15 years in prison for the murder of her boyfriend in 2000. After serving her full sentence, she was released from prison in 2015. Returned home to Middlesbrough and was murdered two days later. They never caught her killer.'

'How can Amorphous know this?' Phillips said. 'I thought it was inventing its own scenarios. My God. Where's Amorphous getting this information from? Is it accessing the internet somehow?'

'I don't believe so. We ran several diagnostics. It doesn't appear that it's linking to anything outside the regular interfaces.'

'Then how can it know about this girl?'

Rogers shrugged. 'Beats me. Beth wants to go back in though. She said, and I quote, *"feels she has to do something."* Find who killed Lindsey.'

'Find who killed her? This happened 30 years ago. The killer may not be alive and if he or she is, do we want to get involved in an old murder case?'

'Are you saying we shouldn't retrogress her again?' Rogers said.

Phillips sighed, heavily. 'Willoughby's putting pressure on me. He wants to find out who killed Catherine Richardson. Without her father's money, we can't continue with the programme.'

'Amorphous might not return Beth to this *Lindsey scenario.* It may have been an anomaly. We won't know until we retrogress her again.'

Phillips rubbed his chin. 'Get Beth ready. It's all we can do for now.'

Rogers nodded at Phillips and left.

**2015** - Lindsey marched away from the house and the slumbering Jimmy. Searching in the front pocket of her backpack she pulled out a book, its cover crumpled with age. Leafing through the pages, she stopped at the name Karl. Taking out her phone, she rang the number next to the name and waited.

'Hi. Karl Smith,' the voice on the other end said.

'Karl. It's Lindsey.'

For a moment there was silence, but finally he spoke. 'Lindsey, long time no hear.'

'I need money,' she said.

'Money? How much?'

'Couple of grand. Enough, until I sell my mam and dads' house.'

'I'm not sure I can give you that much.'

'Listen, Karl. You owe me. I kept my mouth shut and did my time. Now I want what's due. I'm not asking you for a lot,' she said. 'Just a bit of cash to help me out.'

'Yeah, ok, Linds. Don't get out of your pram. I'll get it. Do you want to meet?'

'Where were you thinking?'

'The old place?' he said.

'No. I want to meet somewhere public.'

'Christ, being inside has got you paranoid. Ok. What about Costa in the centre?'

'What's Costa? A shop?'

'Of course. You won't know about Costa coffee shops. They're everywhere. It's in the Cleveland Centre. Go in through the entrance on Grange road, and it's 100 yards on your left. Two this afternoon?'

'Two's fine.'

Lindsey reflected for a moment. The voices in her head had all but stopped. One remained, a woman. She knew that. But the voice wasn't saying an awful lot. As if this voice suppressed the others, somehow.

'Beth,' she mouthed to herself. Her name was Beth.

Lindsey jumped in a taxi and headed for Newton-under-Roseberry. The driver stopped in the parking area at the foot of Roseberry Topping. She handed him the £20 note, retrieved from Jimmy's shirt pocket, telling the driver to keep the change as she got out. She paused, unsure how she'd get back to Middlesbrough without any money. She pondered it, before pushing it aside.

'One problem at a time,' she muttered to herself and headed up the hill. Following the well-covered route to the top but diverted from the track two-thirds up. Lindsey wandered around for a while, the land had changed a lot over the past fifteen years. Eventually, locating the large, familiar rock, she pushed the undergrowth aside, finding the entrance to the hole. It was much smaller than she remembered and unsure she would fit inside, paused. Satisfied she would, she removed her backpack and dropped it on the ground. As she prepared to climb inside, she heard footsteps behind her and turned around.

**2045 –** Dr Phillips and Rogers held onto her as she thrashed about. **'**Beth. Beth. It's Dr Phillips,'

Beth sat upright on the bed, sweating profusely, her body shaking violently.

'You ok?' Phillips said.

Beth's eyes focused on him as she calmed. Her breathing returning to normal, the shaking subsiding.

Beth stared wide-eyed. 'I was there, Doc. When she died. I was there.'

'Did you see who killed Catherine?'

'No. Not Catherine. Lindsey.'

'Lindsey?' Phillips glanced across at Rogers.

'I turned around, and he stabbed me. He wore a ski mask, but it was definitely a man.' She rubbed her face. 'There's something else. I felt the knife.'

'That's impossible. The retrogression isn't tactile. You're mistaken.'

'I'm telling the truth,' she said.

'You couldn't have felt the knife, Beth. It's only memory engrams. You can't—'

'Christ! I don't know how it happened, but I felt the knife. I felt the blade as it pierced me. It was like being punched. I felt it as the killer twisted the knife. I'm telling you. I felt the blood.'

'You saw a memory of Lindsey. She's not you. You're not Lindsey.'

Beth got up from the bed and, tottered across to the window, staring outside, her eyes glistening. 'I felt it, I felt it.' She turned to face them. 'I felt Lindsey die. But it felt as if it was me. I must go back. I need to save her.'

'Beth.' Phillips put his arm around her shoulder. Rogers stared across at the pair of them. 'Lindsey died in 2015. You can't go back and save her. She's dead.'

'I have to, Doc,' she said. 'Amorphous wants me to.'

'Amorphous is a computer. What it's doing is just some anomaly. We don't know what's happening yet, but we will.' He guided her back to the bed. 'Have a rest, and we'll speak later.'

Beth lay down as tiredness overwhelmed her. She closed her eyes, and sleep gathered her up in its arms.

Rogers sat in Phillips' office. The silence deafening as Phillips chewed his bottom lip. 'What's going on, Jake?'

Rogers shook his head. 'She told me that Amorphous wants her to go back and save Lindsey. She talks about Amorphous as if it's a person.'

Phillips shook his head. 'Beth's a Temporal Lobe Epileptic. Lots of famous people throughout history have claimed they've had visions, religious experiences, etc. It's well documented. That's all it is.'

'You think she's mistaken?' Rogers said.

'I think what Beth's saying, about Amorphous, can be taken with a large grain of salt.'

'But you did say her epilepsy may be the reason she retrogresses so well.'

'It's just conjecture. Let's stick to the hard facts.'

Rogers frowned. 'I suppose.'

'Jake,' Phillips said. 'Don't let your faith cloud your judgement.'

'I'm sorry,' Rogers said.

'Let's suppose for a moment, that what Beth believes is real. Or rather she believes it to be real. How can she go back and save Lindsey if she's dead?' he said. And shook his head.

'No idea.' Rogers said. 'But I think we'll have to let Beth retrogress again. If only to convince her that Lindsey is dead. What do you make of her saying she felt the knife?'

'She didn't. She's got that wrong. Things can appear real. We put so much faith in our senses, anything contradicting them we ignore. We'll have to allow her to rest.' Phillips sighed. 'I'll speak with Willoughby again.'

'Do you want the team to keep investigating? Run more tests on Amorphous?'

'Yeah,' Phillips said. 'You do that.'

Phillips visited Willoughby, telling him the outcome of the latest retrogression. Willoughby insisted they must continue. He told Phillips he intended speaking with the directors, and Richardson later in the day. Impressing on Phillips the need to come up with headway in the Catherine Richardson murder. Phillips left exhausted and trudged back to his office.

Willoughby headed out of town, travelling along a country lane for a couple of miles before turning down a farm track. He could see the massive house ahead and in front of it, Karl Jenkins' vintage Aston Martin. Willoughby pulled his car alongside it. The door to the property opened, and Jenkins stood on the threshold smiling. He turned as Willoughby followed him inside and closed the door behind him.

'Drink?' Jenkins said. Opening a cabinet full to overflowing with bottles of every size and colour.

'Small scotch,' Willoughby said.

Jenkins poured two drinks and handed one to his guest. 'So,' he said. Taking a seat in an armchair, he took a sip. 'What's new?' Pointing to a chair for Willoughby to sit opposite.

'Nothing much. The Jericho program we installed in Amorphous appears to be working fine. I need to speak to Rogers later to discover how the latest retrogression went, though.'

'Are you sure they won't detect it?' Jenkins said.

'Rogers assured me they won't. He's included a cloaking program to mask it. None of the checks will pick it up. It's invisible. It's impossible to look for something when you don't even know it exists.'

'Catherine's scenario?' Jenkins said.

'It can't run it. Amorphous is coming up with some random shit.'

'Great. Richardson's already becoming impatient. I've been whispering in his ear as well. Trying to undermine the whole project.'

'What about the money we took?' Willoughby said.

'I've covered our tracks well. It's pure luck Catherine found out. The nosy cow thought I was having an affair and stumbled across it.'

Willoughby laughed. '*You are* having an affair.'

'With a woman, I meant. Don't worry about the money. It's invisible like your Jericho program.'

'Good.' Willoughby held out his glass for a refill.

'What about Rogers?' Jenkins said. 'We'll need to deal with him in due course.' Taking Willoughby's glass from him, he topped it up.

'Not yet though. We need him to keep an eye on Beth. Just to be sure. But this Lindsey Armstrong scenario will keep him busy for a while yet.'

Jenkins turned. 'Lindsey Armstrong?' Handing Willoughby his drink, he sat back down.

'Yeah. Amorphous is making up this scenario involving a woman murdered back in 2015.' Willoughby laughed. 'Beth thinks she can save her, or something. I suspect the girl's going to end up in the nut-house.'

Jenkins sipped his whisky, digesting what Willoughby had said. 'Say that again.'

'Amorphous has created this story about a woman called—'

'Lindsey Armstrong,' Jenkins said.

'She was supposedly murdered in 2015. Somewhere in the north-east. Near Middlesbrough.'

'Newton-under-Roseberry,' Jenkins said.

Willoughby narrowed his eyes. 'Yeah. That's it. Someone stabbed this woman. They didn't find the killer. Well, in the story Amorphous is making up. How do you know about this?'

'Is this a fucking joke, Michael?'

Willoughby widened his eyes. 'Sorry?'

'I knew a Lindsey Armstrong from Middlesbrough. She went to prison for murdering her boyfriend in 2000. Served a full life term and was stabbed to death two days after being released.'

Willoughby frowned. 'I don't understand …'

'How can Amorphous know this?' Jenkins stood. 'Who the hell's inputting this information?' He stared at Willoughby.

'Karl. I haven't a clue about this. I thought it was just a random story.'

Jenkins sat back in his armchair, glaring across at Willoughby, a deep frown appearing on his face. 'Speak to Rogers. I want to know everything about Lindsey Armstrong. I want to know every minute detail of what Beth discovers.'

'It could be a coincidence.'

'Coincidence!' Jenkins screeched. He stood and started to pace. 'Don't make me laugh. There's something not right here. Someone's taking the piss.' He replenished his glass and downed it in one.

'Ok,' Willoughby said. 'I'll have a word with Rogers.'

'Yeah. You do that.'


Willoughby tapped on the office door and entered, the talking in the room subsiding. A huge table in the centre where three men sat on one side of it, and two men and one woman sat on the other.

Oliver Richardson sat at the head of the table. He glanced up at Willoughby and pointed for him to sit. 'I hope this is good news, Willoughby?' he said. And took a sip of water.

'I'm sorry Mr Richardson. The Morpheus Foundation is experiencing problems.' He shifted uncomfortably in his seat.

'What sort of problems? They're not asking for more money, are they?' Folding his arms across his chest, he looked directly at Willoughby.

'No. Nothing like that, sir. Amorphous isn't delivering Beth – the Retrogressor – back to Catherine's scenario.'

Richardson unfolded his arms, took another swig from the glass and banged it on the table. 'When I agreed to finance this venture, I was assured by your people you could find who killed my daughter. The killer is out there somewhere enjoying life while Catherine is cold in her grave.'

'I realise that, sir, but—'

'Willoughby, I'm not interested in excuses. I want you to find a solution.'

'We're working hard on it, sir. Amorphous keeps taking Beth back to a historical murder case.'

'Murder,' he said. 'Whose?'

'A woman called Lindsey Armstrong. She was stabbed to death in the north-east in 2015. At first, we thought it was a story Amorphous was creating. When we checked, she existed.'

'What if it keeps running this scenario?' Richardson said.

'We're not certain, sir. Phillips is unsure what to do. He's aware retrogressions cost a lot of money.'

Richardson waved a hand. 'The money is unimportant. Finding my daughter's murderer - that's paramount. If we keep running this scenario to the end, will it complete Catherine's?'

'Possibly. There's no guarantee, though. It may run another for all we know.'

'Keep going with this Lindsey ...'

'Lindsey Armstrong,' Willoughby said.

'Lindsey Armstrong scenario,' Richardson continued. 'She must've had a family too. Maybe we can solve two murders for the price of one.' He half-smiled. The other people around the table nodded enthusiastically.

'Yes, sir.' Willoughby said.

'I'll foot the bill for the retrogressions. Then, hopefully, we'll catch Catherine's killer. But there is a caveat to this, Willoughby. My patience and money aren't endless. Are we clear on this?'

'Crystal, sir.'


Willoughby waited until he was back in his car, and taking out his mobile he called Karl Jenkins. 'I've been in a meeting with Richardson. I was surprised you weren't there?'

Jenkins sneered. 'I'm playing the grieving boyfriend. What did Richardson have to say?'

'He wants us to continue with the Lindsey Armstrong scenario. The hope is, when it's finished, Amorphous will run Catherine's.'

'And will it?'

'Rogers doesn't believe so.'

'Have you any more news on Lindsey Armstrong?'

'They're planning another retrogression tomorrow,' Willoughby said. 'I know you said you knew the woman, but why the big interest?'

'Let's just say, Lindsey Armstrong, needs to stay buried, and leave it at that.'

'They may find out who killed her.'

'We may need to end this scenario sooner rather than later,' Jenkins said. 'This girl, the Retro? If she gets too close …'

'Accidents do happen, Karl.'

'They do indeed.'

Lindsey headed downstairs leaving the sleeping Jimmy snoring. She searched through a drawer, wrote a note and paused. The woman's voice in her head was back, suppressing the others. This voice was different, though. Not demanding or hectoring, like some of them. She whispered, and Lindsey listened to her.

'Lindsey. It's Beth.'

Lindsey, unsure how to respond, opened her mouth to speak but stopped, as Beth spoke again

'Don't go to the hill. You're in danger if you do.'

'I have to go. There's something I need,' Lindsey said. The thought remained locked inside her head.

'Someone will follow you. Someone wants you dead.'

'How do you know?' Lindsey whispered. 'Who are you?'

'A friend.'

'No, I must go. There's something there I need.'

'Please, Lindsey.'

Lindsey shook her head and tried to ignore Beth's voice. She closed the drawer and headed into the hall.

'Please. Please don't go. You're going to die. Someone will follow you up the hill and stab you.'

'Be quiet,' Lindsey said. 'You're not real. You're just a voice in my head. You're trying to trick me.'

'I'm not. I want to save you. Listen to me, please.'

'Shut up. Shut up,' Lindsey shouted.

Jimmy woke. Lindsey's voice from downstairs rousing him from his sleep. Jumping out of bed and pulling on his jeans, he heard the front door close. He finished dressing. Bounding downstairs, he searched the house. Lindsey had been talking to someone, he was sure. Spotting the note, Jimmy read it aloud to himself. 'GONE FOR A WALK. I'LL BE BACK LATER XX.' He grabbed his coat and headed after her.

Lindsey jumped in a taxi and made for Newton-under-Roseberry. Jimmy, intrigued by where she was going, followed her in his car. The cab dropped her off in the car park and as he watched she set off up. Jimmy, surprised by how quick Lindsey climbed the hill, almost lost sight of her on a couple of occasions, but somehow managed to keep her in view. Lindsey veered off the track two-thirds up, heading into the undergrowth. He waited and watched her as she wandered about looking for something. A figure emerged from near to where she stood. Sensing all wasn't well, Jimmy paused then rushed towards them.

'Lindsey!' he shouted.

The figure stopped five metres from her and spun around. Jimmy could see he wore a ski mask and carried something in his hand. The realisation dawned on him. The man held a knife. Jimmy searched for a weapon himself and grabbed a large piece of tree branch nearby. Lindsey, who'd turned around on hearing Jimmy shout, stared at the figure. The man looked first at Lindsey, and then at the advancing Jimmy before he turned and fled. Jimmy raced across to Lindsey, and the two of them watched as the man disappeared from their view.

'He had a knife,' Jimmy said. On reaching her.

'She was right. Beth was right.'

'Who's Beth?' Jimmy said.

'I can't explain.' Throwing her arms around Jimmy, she hugged him.

# CHAPTER THREE

**2045 -** Beth woke, tired and weak, but not as bad as the previous retrogression. Opening her eyes, she studied the faces of Phillips and Rogers.

'We saved her,' she said.

'Who?' Phillips said.

'Lindsey. I warned her, and Jimmy followed us up the hill. He shouted to her, and the attacker fled.'

Phillips frowned. 'Lindsey Armstrong died 30 years ago. The victim of a hit and run.'

'She can't have. We saved her on the 28th. On top of the hill.'

He glanced across at Rogers who shrugged. 'I'm sorry, Beth. Lindsey Armstrong died on October the 30th. She was knocked down,' Phillips said.

Tears formed in Beth's eyes. 'Why did Amorphous send me back if I couldn't save her?'

Phillips glanced at Rogers again who was busy making notes. He glanced up from his pad and shrugged again.

'Have a rest, and we'll talk later,' Phillips said. He and Rogers left.

'She sounds confused,' Rogers said.

'Yeah. Why would Beth think Lindsey Armstrong died on the 28th? The retrogression may be affecting her. Run some scans. We don't want anything to happen to our star pupil.'

Rogers phoned Willoughby to discuss the outcome of the latest retrogression. He made a lot of notes during the procedure and was able to give him extensive information.

Willoughby rang off and phoned Karl Jenkins. 'Can we meet, Karl?' I've got some news for you.'

'Yeah,' Jenkins said. 'Come around about one. Be discreet, though'.

Willoughby sat on the leather chair, and Jenkins handed him a glass, sitting opposite on a sofa.

'Well,' Jenkins said. 'How did it go?'

'Beth thinks she saved Lindsey in the past. She believes Lindsey died on October 28th. But—'

'She died on the 30th,' Jenkins said.

Willoughby sipped from his glass. 'Yeah. It sounds as if Beth's getting confused.' Willoughby leant forward. 'What's your connection with this girl? I think it's time you filled me in.'

'Like I said. I knew her.'

'It's more than that though. Isn't it?'

Jenkins got up to replenish his glass. Pouring himself a large scotch, he turned to face Willoughby. 'Lindsey's boyfriend, Craig, and I were mates. Along with another guy called Sean Grant. We knocked around together. Sean was a bit of a …' He paused for a moment and took another swig of his drink. 'Sean was mental. He had this thing with an older woman. A coppers wife. She grew tired of him. Once the novelty of having an illicit toy-boy wore off.'

'This Sean and Craig,' Willoughby said. 'Are they alive?'

'Sean's dead. His body is down a hole on Roseberry Topping. A hill near Middlesbrough.'

'And Craig?'

Jenkins slumped onto the settee. 'Sean had this idea to get back at this woman after she jilted him. He obtained a key to her house, and persuaded Craig and me to go along with him to burgle the place. She had some nice things - stuff we could sell. Her old man was working nights, and Sean said she'd be out. At the last minute, Craig backed out. Craig wasn't interested in stuff like that, after meeting Lindsey. She was from a decent family. Unlike us three.'

Willoughby narrowed his eyes. 'What happened to this woman?'

'What you've got to understand is …' He briefly looked upwards and took another swig. 'I was shit scared of Sean. He was psychotic. When we got there, this woman was home. He grabbed her and tied her up. Told me to ransack the house, while I left him with her. When I came downstairs, he'd raped and strangled her. He threatened me. Said he'd tell the police it was my idea if I didn't help him dump the body. We put her in a car and drove out to some woods. Dug a hole and set fire to the body before burying it. We didn't do a great job of that, though.'

'Jesus, Karl.' Willoughby shook his head and took a large gulp of his drink. 'Did they find her body?'

Jenkins brought his hands up to his face. 'Yeah. Some walkers discovered it a couple of days later.'

Willoughby strolled across to Jenkins and sat next to him. Putting his arm around his shoulder, he kissed him on the cheek.

'What happened to Sean?'

'Sean had an argument with Craig. They fought, and he stabbed Craig. Lindsey found out and killed Sean. I helped her dump the body.'

'And Lindsey?'

'The police charged her with her boyfriend's murder. The way she figured it, she was going inside either way. She knew about the woman. Said, if I helped her when she was released, she'd take the rap for killing Sean. But she was asking me for lots of money. Money I didn't have. She was different from the Lindsey who went inside. Prison changed her. Made her harder. I paid someone to kill her.'

'We can't have this coming out,' Willoughby said. 'It'll spoil our future together.'

'What are we going to do?' Jenkins said.

'We've come this far,' he said. 'We can't let a little scrubber from thirty years ago spoil what we have. We have to make sure the truth about Lindsey Armstrong, stays buried.'

'What are you planning?'

Willoughby smiled. 'I got rid of Catherine. I can get rid of Beth. Then Amorphous' link to the past will be severed.'

'It could be messy.'

'Rogers could be our patsy,' he said. 'With the money we've embezzled off Richardson, we can start afresh somewhere.'

'Yes,' Jenkins said, smiling. 'Love that plan.' The two of them embraced and kissed.

**2015 -** Jimmy sat on the settee in the lounge of Lindsey's parents' house. Lindsey came into the room with a cup of tea for them both and sat in an armchair opposite, stirring the tea deep in thought.

'Who do you suppose it was?' Jimmy said.

'Don't know.' She avoided looking at him. 'Could've been a mugger.'

'Halfway up Roseberry Topping?'

She turned to face him. 'What made you follow me?'

'I heard you moving around before you left, and wondered where you were heading. So, I went after you. I know I shouldn't have, but—'

'I'm glad you did.' She smiled at him.

Jimmy smiled back. 'I'm keeping an eye on you from now on. This man may come back.'

'I don't think he will,' she said. 'It was probably a local nutter.'

'We'd better ring the police,' Jimmy said.

'I'd rather we didn't. I don't have a lot of time for coppers.'

'I know, but—'

'Please, Jimmy.'

'Ok.' Realising he was fighting a losing battle, he changed the subject. 'Who's Beth?'

Lindsey's eyes widened. 'Beth?'

'Yeah. You mentioned her name on Roseberry Topping.'

'I'll tell you later. It's a long story.'

Jimmy surveyed Lindsey's face. 'What were you doing up there?'

'I went there to get something. Something from the past.'

'What?'

She sighed. 'Long story.'

'The same long story?'

'Yeah.' She smiled. Lindsey put her cup down and moved across to Jimmy. Sitting next to him, she kissed him. 'Thanks.'

He touched her cheek with his hand. 'What's it like inside?'

The smile on Lindsey's face fell away. 'Not too bad. The first couple of years were the hardest. Getting to know the routine and that. Finding out who you could trust.'

'Did you have many friends there?' he said.

'Two years into my sentence, I ended up in a cell with a woman called Maggie.' She smiled, remembering her. 'Maggie's like my mam. She looked after me.'

'What was she in for?'

'She was in an abusive relationship and snapped one day. Took an axe to her old man.'

'Bloody hell! You keep good company.'

'Maggie was, is, wonderful. She's the kindest person I've ever met. Her husband was a monster. The things he did to her were awful. She told me everything. But nobody knew what she'd gone through, and the prosecution pulled her to bits in the courtroom.'

'That's terrible.' Jimmy squeezed her hand.

'When she gets out, she's going to move in with me.'

'When will that be?' he said.

'A couple more years.' Stroking his hand with her thumb.

'Let's see if I can't keep you alive until then.'

He looked at her face, and Lindsey gazed back at him. His dark-blue eyes drawing her in. Time slowed to nothingness as they continued to stare at each other. Their lips met in a passionate union. The tension, finally broken.

Lindsey and Jimmy lay in bed. Conjoined in a post-coital embrace.

'I have to go into town later,' Lindsey said.

'What for?'

'I'm meeting an old friend.'

Jimmy brushed the hair from her face. 'Do you want me to come along?'

She kissed him on the cheek. 'No. I'll be ok.'

'I'll drop you off then,' he said.

'Thanks.' Lindsey smiled. Tumbling headlong into his irresistible, dark-blue eyes again.'

Jimmy pulled his car up outside the entrance to The Cleveland Centre. Lindsey kissed him on the cheek, and he watched as she headed inside. Jimmy was smitten. He'd fallen for her all those years ago when he was a boy. Time hadn't dulled his feelings either. There was a certain something about her, he found captivating. What once was a childhood crush had grown over time into something more profound. He was sure of that. He felt guilty regarding the events fifteen years ago. He should have spoken out at the time, but hadn't. The remorse about the past was almost overwhelming. He'd thought it through umpteen times over the years, as the shame grew within him. He'd have to discuss it with Lindsey at some point, he realised that. He worried how she'd react. How it would affect their blossoming relationship. The wait for her to return from prison seemed like a lifetime, and he couldn't bear it if he lost her now. Putting his head on the steering wheel, he blew out hard. His confession would have to wait. Closing his eyes, Jimmy gave his head a shake, parking the memory in the furthermost corner of his mind. He drove away and left his vehicle in a nearby car park. Interested in who Lindsey was meeting, a mixture of jealousy and concern about her safety vying for supremacy. Putting on his coat and a beanie hat, to disguise himself, he set off into the mall. Trying to blend into the crowd he wandered around, entering a shop here and there, but couldn't find her. It dawned on him what a fruitless exercise it was. She could be anywhere after all. He couldn't even be sure she was still in the shopping centre. He passed by the Costa coffee shop and stopped. She was there inside. Her bright blue coat acting like a beacon. She sat on her own waiting for someone, but who. He melted into the doorway of the HMV shop. His perfect vantage point allowing an unrestricted view of her. He watched and waited.

Lindsey sat inside. She bought herself a white coffee and was sipping it as she waited for Karl. Deep in thought, staring out of the window when he arrived.

'Well then,' he said. 'You look good.'

Lindsey forced a smile. 'For a dead woman, you mean.'

'Sorry?' He placed his coffee on the table.

'Why did you send someone to kill me?'

'What the hell are you on about?'

'This morning, when I was up Roseberry Topping. You sent someone to kill me.'

'Are you mad?' he said. 'Why the hell would I do that?'

'I know too much,' she said.

'Lindsey.' Moving his face closer to hers, he lowered his voice to a whisper. 'You're paranoid. Look, I've brought the money you asked for. Would I have done that if I'd sent someone to kill you?'

'Come off it, Karl. You knew he failed. You had to turn up to front it out.'

'How do you know it wasn't someone from Craig's family?' he said. 'They were pretty mad at you after the trial. I wouldn't have you killed. What happened, happened. It's in the past. A chance for you to start afresh. Look, I haven't a lot of money, but I'll give you what I can. I owe you a great deal.'

Lindsey thought for a moment. She sipped her coffee and snatched the envelope Karl placed in front of her, depositing it into her backpack.

'What the hell were you doing up Roseberry Topping?' he said.

Her eyes darted left and right. 'I needed to recover some things,' she whispered. 'From Sean's body.'

'What for? He's been there for over fifteen years.'

'He had stuff from the robbery. Stuff you two took. He also has some items of mine. Things I gave him, so he'd leave Craig alone. If the police find them, they'll make the link between me, Sean, and the copper's wife's murder. It's only a matter of time before they come calling.'

'These things. How can they link them to you?'

'A gold bracelet, with my name and date of birth engraved on it.'

He sat back in his chair and sighed. 'They may never find the body. It's managed to stay hidden for this long, and if the police do discover it, you could say Sean stole them from you.'

'The police won't believe that. Listen, I've done fifteen years for something I didn't do. I don't intend to spend another fifteen for something I did. The way I see it, I've done my time. I'm going to retrieve the things and leave Middlesbrough to start a new life.'

'Yeah. Ok. I understand,' he said.

'I'll keep our secret, and I won't bother you again,' she said. 'If I believe I'm in danger, though, I'll spill the beans. Have you got that, Jake?'

'Of course.' He looked into her eyes. 'I didn't send anyone to kill you. You've got to believe that?'

Lindsey threw her backpack across her shoulder and stood. She stared one last time at Karl. A deep penetrating stare burrowing deep into his psyche. It told her everything she needed to know.

Jimmy watched from across the mall as Lindsey bounded out. She turned right and headed towards Linthorpe Road. Jimmy waited as the man with Lindsey, stood and left too. He headed for the opposite door to the one she used and emerged into the throng of people. Jimmy gulped. He had aged over the past fifteen years, but he still recognised him. Karl Smith. What was Lindsey doing talking to Karl Smith?

His phone sounded and retrieving it from his pocket, he composed himself before answering. 'Hi,' he said. In a false, becalmed voice.

'Thought you might fancy a bite to eat,' she said. 'On me.'

'That'll be good. Where were you thinking?'

'The Italian we passed,' she said. 'On the corner of Southfield Road and Linthorpe Road.'

'I'll be ten minutes.'

Karl Smith headed away from the Cleveland Centre and onto Newport road. He pulled out his mobile and phoned. 'I've seen Lindsey, and she knows it was me who sent you.'

'What do you want to do?' the other man said.

'She's going to go to Roseberry Topping again. I can't allow that. She'll find out about Sean.'

'What do you want me to do?' he repeated.

'I imagine we both know the answer to that.'

**2045** - Beth sat reading a magazine. Interrupting this now and then to fork a mouthful of food into her mouth. Although not hungry – the growing worry she felt in the pit of her stomach, taking precedence over anything else – Dr Phillips had told her to eat. The retrogressions were physically and mentally demanding. He reminded her of the importance of keeping her nutritional levels high. She raised her head from the magazine, sensing someone next to her.

'Hi. It's Beth, isn't it?'

'Yes,' Beth said. Taken by surprise. Firstly, by being interrupted by someone she didn't know, but who knew her, and secondly by how handsome he was. His dark, wavy, shoulder-length hair, brushed back casually, and his flawless complexion. He was tall. Perhaps six-feet-three, wearing the ubiquitous white lab coat. His muscular form beneath it, evident. Smiling he held out his hand, the dimples appearing in his cheeks only adding to his features. But above all this, one attribute stood out. His dark-blue eyes. She sat open-mouthed. Enthralled by her first glimpse of them but also a feeling she'd seen them before. A sort of déjà vu, but more than that. It started as a vague recollection and then gathered pace, arriving like a long-forgotten friend.

'I'm Matthew Blake. Matt.'

'How do you know me?' Her rabbit-caught-in-the-headlight features returning to normal.

He smiled again. 'You're famous. Well, within the foundation. The best Retrogressor in town.'

'Have a seat.' She said. Trying to suppress her inner schoolgirl.

'I'm joining Dr Phillips' team.' He sat across from her. 'I'm looking forward to it. I worked on the Oracle project. They're doing something similar to the Morpheus Foundation. Dr Phillips' team are light years ahead though.'

'You're not from around here?'

'No. From up north.'

'You can't have been here long?' she said. 'At the foundation, I mean.'

'A while.' He thought a little. 'Two years, three months.'

'Really?' she said. 'I'm sure I'd have seen you before now.'

'We've probably passed on the staircase.'

Beth wasn't convinced. If he had been working at the facility for two years, she'd have seen him. Even allowing for the fact he was working in a different department. There's no way she'd have missed him. If she had, and she doubted it, she would be getting her eyesight checked.

'Yeah. Probably.' Her features breaking into an involuntary smile.

Beth's wristwatch buzzed. She read the message. "Beth Pearson, please go to Dr Phillips' lab.'

'Ah, that's me,' she said. 'Duty calls.'

'Nice to meet you, Beth. Maybe I'll see you later.' Getting to his feet, along with her.

'I'm sure you will.' She shook his hand and headed off. Resisting the temptation to turn around and look back on reaching the door, as overwhelming as it was to do so.

Matt headed outside into the car park. Jumped into his car and took out his mobile phone.

'Hello,' said a man's voice on the other end.

Matt closed the door. 'I've managed to make contact with her.'

'What's she like?'

'Pretty.' He paused. 'More than pretty, actually. Stunning.'

'Remember why you're there, Matt.'

'What do you want me to do?'

'Keep a close eye on her for now,' he said. 'We'll talk later.'

Phillips popped his head out of his office. Two lab assistants, a young man, and a middle-aged woman were busy clearing up.

'Has anyone seen Jake?' he said.

The woman shook her head and returned to what she'd been doing. The man thought for a moment. 'I think he popped downstairs, Doc.'

'Beth's due to be retrogressed, and I need his help,' Phillips said.

'Do you want me to go and look for him?' he asked.

'No. Ask Matt to assist me. It'll be a good experience for him.'

Rogers climbed the stairs leading to Willoughby's office, tapped on the door and entered. Willoughby, talking to someone on the phone, motioned for Rogers to sit. Which he did.

'He's here now,' Willoughby said. 'I'll ring later.' Willoughby hung up and sat back in his chair, fixing Rogers with a stare. 'Beth?'

'She's due to be retrogressed today,' Rogers said.

'We've a problem, Jake. I've been speaking with Karl. Whatever happens, this needs to be Beth's final retrogression.'

'Why? What Beth's coming up with is no help to the Catherine Richardson scenario.'

'Lindsey Armstrong. A name from Karl's past. *She's* the prob em.'

'In what way?'

'All you need to know is this retrogression needs to be her last.'

Rogers frowned. 'Richardson's sanctioned further retrogressions. He wants it running to its conclusion. He's hopeful Amorphous will run Catherine's scenario. But my programme will—'

'I know about that, Jake. You're not listening. Whatever happens today, we want it to be her last.' He smiled at Rogers.

'What are you suggesting, Willoughby?'

'We were hoping you could help with that.'

Rogers' eyes widened. 'Kill her?'

Willoughby smirked. 'Retrogressions are dangerous, unpredictable. Something could go wrong. Beth might not wake up. Things like that happen when you're at the cutting edge of science.'

Rogers stood. 'Now wait a minute.'

Willoughby glared at him. 'Sit down.'

Rogers moved towards the door. 'I won't be a party to this. This wasn't what I agreed.'

'Sit down!' Willoughby said. Rogers sheepishly returned to his seat. 'You're right in this up to your neck. If this goes pear-shaped, you'll be implicated in the Catherine Richardson murder too. There's a paper trail and more importantly, a money trail. Guess where that's leading.'

'But I can't just ...' He paused. The words sticking in his throat '... Murder her.'

'It's up to you.' He smiled. 'If Beth doesn't wake up, great. If she does, and her heads scrambled, so be it. We're not bothered how you do it. Just do it.'

'I'll try. But I can't promise.'

Willoughby stood and moved around to Rogers' side of the desk. Sitting on the edge, he leant forward. His face inches from Rogers' own. 'You wouldn't want your wife knowing what you get up to in your spare time, either. Would you? Just fucking do it!' He spat at him.

Rogers dropped his head. Stood, and without saying another word, left the office.

Rogers made his way back to the labs, entering and heading for the retrogression chamber. He waited outside. Watching through the inspection window as Phillips and Matt readied Beth.

He pressed the intercom on the wall. 'Sorry I'm late, Doc,' he said. 'I had to make an urgent call. Family stuff.'

Phillips turned to face him. 'Nothing serious, I hope?'

'No. I can be ready in a couple of minutes. I just need to go and change.'

'It's fine, Jake. Matt's assisting me today. It'll be a good experience for him.'

'Are you sure?' Rogers said. 'It's complicated. If anything went wrong.'

'We'll be ok. I'll give you a shout if we need a hand. Go and get yourself a coffee.' Turning away from him and back to Beth.

Rogers paused, before admitting defeat. He exited the lab and headed to his office, slumping on a chair. Rogers considered his options. He took out his mobile and searched through his contacts, stopping at Willoughby, pausing with his finger above the call button. He put the phone back in his pocket, headed downstairs and out of the building. Lifting the boot of his car he removed a small case containing phials with a clear liquid within. Removing two, he placed them in the pocket of his white lab coat, closed the boot and raced back inside.

Beth, connected to Amorphous, slipped into a fugue. Her shallow breathing, and the occasional beep of the monitoring equipment, the only sounds.

**2015** - Lindsey and Jimmy sat in a restaurant. Jimmy hadn't the courage to broach the subject of Lindsey's meeting with Karl Smith. Deep in thought, he pushed his food around his plate. Picking up a little now and again, before popping it into his mouth.

Lindsey stared across at him. 'Everything ok?'

'Yeah. Why shouldn't it be?'

She took hold of one of his hands in hers. 'What's wrong, Jimmy? You were in a good mood earlier. Now …'

'Why did you meet Karl Smith?' he said.

'You followed me?'

'I'm sorry about that. I was worried. After Roseberry Topping.'

Lindsey sat back in her chair and sighed. It was hardly the time or place, she thought. In all honesty though, when was? She summoned her courage and began. 'I didn't kill Craig.'

Jimmy lowered his head. 'I know.'

Lindsey's jaw dropped. Her mind whirred, trying to figure out how he knew. She felt uneasy, and not in control. 'You knew? How?'

Jimmy dropped his head further. He felt embarrassed and ashamed. He'd kept the secret to himself all these years. 'I followed you and Craig to his flat. I was …' He paused, searching for the right words '… In love with you.'

Lindsey grabbed hold of his hand again and smiled. She'd known that. He followed her around like a lap-dog. She had found it endearing and didn't have the heart to chase him. 'I know,' she said.

Jimmy felt his cheeks redden. His childhood memories causing him to blush. 'I saw you leave Craig's,' he said. 'I waited a few moments after you left, and was about to leave myself when Sean and Karl turned up. I don't know why, but I was curious and made my way across to the window. They talked for a while. I couldn't make out what they were saying, but it got quite heated. Craig punched Sean … They fought—'

'I know,' She said. 'Sean stabbed Craig.'

'No,' Jimmy said. 'Karl killed Craig.'

Lindsey reeled back in shock. The words reverberated in her head. She stared at Jimmy, hardly able to fathom what he said. A waiter appeared at Jimmy's side.

'Is everything ok with the food,' he asked.

'Yeah,' Jimmy said. 'Can we have the bill, please?' Sensing the time for eating had passed.

Lindsey didn't know what to say. Neither did Jimmy. The pair stood in silence as she paid the bill, and the two of them left. They strolled for a while saying nothing.

Finally, Jimmy spoke. 'I should have said something at the time.'

'But you didn't.'

'I'm sorry. I was a kid, I …' Tears filled his eyes. 'When Karl and Sean left, I made a run for it. They must've seen me, or guessed it was me.'

Lindsey put her hands over her eyes, slowly pulling them down her face. She composed herself and gazed at Jimmy, his face full of remorse. Lindsey stepped forwards and hugged him. 'It wasn't your fault. You weren't to blame.' Jimmy sobbed. The memory stripping away the time, and presenting him with his sixteen-year-old self.

'When they found Mam, I lost it. I forgot about you, Linds. That's unforgivable.'

'Oh, Jimmy.' Tears rolled down her cheeks. 'None of this was your fault. I knew Sean and Karl were going to rob your mam's house. They wanted Craig to go along with them, but I persuaded him not to. I never thought they'd do what they did. I should've gone to the police. If I had, your mam would be alive. You see, nobody is immune from guilt.'

Jimmy stepped back. The revelation taking him by surprise. 'But if Sean and Karl killed Mam. Why didn't you say?'

'Karl told me they intended to burgle the house. He said it was the only reason he went along. When they were there, your mam came home. While Karl was upstairs, Sean murdered her. Sean threatened Karl, and … well, you know the rest.'

'Where's Sean?' he said.

'Sean's dead. I killed him. Karl dumped his body in a hole on Roseberry Topping. The things they took from your house … they're there too. That's why I went back. I remembered reading about it in the paper. Your dad said he found it heart-breaking they'd taken precious items of your mam's.'

'You killed him?' Jimmy said.

'I thought he killed Craig. Karl phoned me and said Sean was going to recover the things he'd stolen from Roseberry Topping, and do a runner. I followed him up there and hit him on the head with a branch.'

'But why admit to Craig's murder?'

'The whole thing was a mess. Everything would've come out. It didn't matter which death I went to prison for. I thought Karl was an innocent party in all this. Had I known …'

'Just before the court case started,' Jimmy said. 'I had a visit from a couple of thugs. Karl must've sent them, but I assumed it was Sean. They told me to keep my mouth shut regarding Craig, or my old man would end up the same as him. I nearly came forward on the day of the trial, but then I found out you'd pleaded guilty.'

'Well now you know why,' she said. The two of them moved closer.

'The man up Roseberry Topping?' he said.

'Karl,' she said. 'Or someone he sent.'

'You're in danger, Lindsey. He may try again.'

'I've told him I intend to move away. I'm hoping he'll leave me alone.'

'If he's seen us together, he'll know I've told you about Craig.'

Lindsey shook her head. 'We can't go to the police. They'll charge me with Sean's murder.'

The two of them sat on a wall outside the Dickens Inn pub, wondering what to do.

Jimmy's mobile rang. 'Hello.'

'Jimmy Jefferson?' a male voice on the other end asked.

'Yeah.'

'It's the Landlord of The Yellow Rose. Your dad's a bit worse for wear. He told me to ring you.'

'I'll be right there,' he said.

'What's up?' Lindsey asked.

'Dad's pissed. I have to go to the Yellow Rose and get him.'

# CHAPTER FOUR

They flagged a passing taxi and jumped in, travelling the short distance to the pub. Jimmy paid the driver and paused outside, waiting for Lindsey.

'I'd better wait here,' she said. 'I don't think your dad would be happy to see me.'

'I'll be two minutes.' He disappeared into the pub.

Lindsey ambled around to the car park and sat on one of the benches outside. The voices in her head bubbled to the surface and started their usual chatter. Reaching into her pocket, she pulled out her iPod. The voices receded, and Beth's appeared. Lindsey, who felt Beth's presence before she spoke, stood, and raced to the edge of the car park waiting for Beth to speak.

'Lindsey. It's Beth.' In a calm and measured tone.

'Hi, Beth.' The words locked in her head.

'You're in danger.'

She scanned about. There was hardly anybody around. A man walking a dog disappeared from her view. A couple exited the front door of the pub and headed off to her right.

'Jimmy?' Lindsey said. 'Is he ok?'

'Jimmy's fine. It's you who's in danger.'

Lindsey felt vulnerable and nervously inspected left and right again. A car revved up in the car park and headed off, and as it approached her, it quickened its speed. Hearing it accelerate behind her, she turned. Lindsey, who desperately tried to move out of the way, was taken off her feet and thrown across the tarmac. Coming to a grinding halt, as gravel sprayed up around her. She groaned and tried getting to her feet, but stared on in dismay. The bone of her right leg protruding through her jeans. The car slammed into reverse. Lindsey, realising what the driver intended doing, rolled across behind a wheelie bin. The car smashed into it, as its driver attempted to hit her again. She was lucky, the plastic container flying off in the opposite direction to her. She heard voices. The pub's customers and staff, on hearing the commotion, poured outside. The driver put the car back in gear and with a screech and a grinding of gravel, raced off. Careering clear of the car park, and out of sight. Beth felt Lindsey's pain as it struck her like a hammer blow.

'He's gone,' Beth said.

Lindsey struggled to stay conscious. 'It was Karl. It was Karl Smith who sent him.'

Beth ripped from Lindsey, was catapulted back to the future. Through space and time, she sped. The blinding pain in her leg replaced with an even more painful one in her chest. The sensation, unlike anything she had experienced before in her retrogressions. Her consciousness slammed into her body, as thoughts of Lindsey dissolved away.

**2045** - Beth convulsed on her bed. Phillips and Matt attempted to hold her thrashing body down, her eyes now white in her head. She continued to shake from side to side as blood trickled from her nostrils, and then from her ears.

'What's happening?' Phillips said.

Matt grabbed Phillips arm. 'It's Oxytectricide poisoning.'

'That's impossible. We don't use Oxytectricide to bring her round. She's allergic to it.'

'I've seen it before,' Matt said. 'At the Oracle.'

Phillips stared at him. 'Are you sure?'

'It's the same, Doc. We're going to lose her.'

Phillips pressed the alarm on the wall, starting a loud siren, and within seconds a team burst through the door. They connected a drip and airline to the now still Beth as the team, Phillips and Matt tried desperately to save her. Beth's lips now tinged blue, her heart stopped, her body giving up the fight.

The pain in her chest and arms dissipated. She drifted into a sea of tranquillity and felt at peace. The peace she felt once before. Time stopped or appeared not to exist for her. She wanted to stay here. She felt so at home, so comfortable. She could now hear a heartbeat, but not her own, and this too was somehow comforting. She drifted through eddies and currents. Through clouds and gentle breezes, through colours of every shade and hue. Beth felt her consciousness float along endlessly, and time became an abstract thing. No longer constrained within seconds and minutes. She had no beginning and no end. The boundaries of her body, no longer existing. Her being, her essence, blown along like a leaf amongst warm, summer zephyrs. Then she heard it. Not a voice as such, for there were no words. A seed was planted and grew. Slowly at first, but it quickly gathered pace. Her knowledge stretched on endlessly as her lucidness accelerated towards eternity. And every atom, every molecule ever existing, compressed into a point so small, it defied all understanding. Beth understood though. She recognised what is, what was, and what always had been. Amorphous bathed Beth within infinity. It anointed her with the knowledge of a countless number of lifetimes. She saw the birth of the universe and its inevitable death. She saw stars spring into life, live and die, all within a time span so small it was beyond measurement. She saw worlds come and go and felt the energy and presence of everything that ever lived. Beth didn't feel love, for love she realised now, was an evolutionary construct. What she felt, transcended love. It dwarfed love. The way a planet dwarfs an atom. In an instant she understood everything. And as amorphous subsumed Beth's essence and absorbed her soul, it added her entity to what is, what was, and what would ever be.

Phillips and Matt stared at the inert body of Beth as the members of the crash team stood at the foot of the bed. The blood which had escaped from her body dropped sickeningly onto the floor. Matt stared at Beth, her beauty undiminished by death. He had read a book once when the writer was recounting a sad event. The words: *If you have tears, prepare to shed them now,* came to mind. He couldn't cry though. They stubbornly refused to appear, and this somehow amplified his sadness. He reached across and gently closed her eyelids.

Phillips turned towards the door. 'I want to know what happened here today,' he said. 'I want to know how Beth died.' He stopped at the threshold for one final look at her. Matt followed him, as Rogers stared through the observation window at Beth's inert form. He bowed his head as they passed, only now understanding the enormity of what he'd done. Trudging along to his office, Rogers picked up his mobile and texted. *'She's dead.'* And pressed send. The *'Message sent'* flashed up on the screen. He took out his notepad and scribbled a brief note. Reaching inside one of the drawers, he pulled out a syringe and pushed the needle in. Injecting oblivion into his vein.

Fifteen minutes had passed, when a nurse tapped on Phillips' door. 'I'm sorry to disturb you, sir,' she said. 'Should I go and clean Beth up?'

'If you don't mind, Anne.' He forced a smile. 'There'll have to be a post-mortem,' he muttered to himself rather than the nurse. She nodded and left. Phillips stared out of the window. The blue sky fringed by the green countryside below. He closed his eyes as tear after tear chased one another the length of his face, dropping unabated onto his lap.

Beth's body lay on the table still connected to Amorphous. Within her, the veins which had refused to hang on to the precious red liquid began to repair themselves. Fissures and ruptures, starting at a molecular level, spontaneously began to mend. Nerve-endings fired once more as neurons and synapses jumped into life. The heart engorged with blood received a jolt and started beating, as oxygen deficient blood moved around the body. The lungs which had lain deflated, filled with air and Beth gasped. The oxygen greedily gathered up by the haemoglobin, and pushed to her outer extremities.

Anne entered and stood transfixed at the fall and rise of Beth's chest. She stared, her mouth open, stunned for what seemed like an eternity before pressing the alarm. She waited, mesmerised by what she was watching. Beth's cheeks and lips getting redder and healthier-looking with every second. Phillips and Matt entered and stared across at Beth.

'How?' Phillips said. 'How is she breathing?'

Matt focussed on him. 'She was still connected to Amorphous. It somehow kept her alive.' He moved across to Beth.

'But how?' Phillips said. 'How could it repair the damage? She wasn't breathing for more than fifteen minutes. She'll have brain damage. She must have?'

'We should get her to ICU,' Matt said.

'Yes. Straight away,' Phillips said. 'I want a full body and brain scan.'

Anne nodded and left the room. Matt turned to Phillips and smiled. Phillips shook his head and shrugged, at a total loss for words.

Beth felt her consciousness reach somewhere different, somewhere new. A thought entered her head. She didn't know from where, it just arrived. She was in Karl Smiths body, or Karl Jenkins body, for they were the same person, Beth understood this now. She peered down the hill and could see the disappearing Lindsey heading away, unlike her previous links, when merely an observer. She heard a groan from the floor and stared down at the face of Sean, his name appearing as if she'd always known it. He sat up, blood running down the side of his face. 'What the fuck happened?' he said.

Karl helped him to his feet. 'Lindsey hit you. We have to get you away from here. She's going to the police.'

Beth watched through Karl's eyes as he helped his friend down the hill and into the car. In a blink, she found herself looking across at the body of Sean. A knife protruding from his chest. Lifeless eyes fixed on something beyond the living. She watched as Karl got out of the car and released the handbrake. The vehicle, with Sean inside, rolled down a bank and into the dark, still, water of the lake. Karl picked up the bag, the contents clinking within, and threw it over his shoulder. He turned and marched off.

She blinked once more. She was in an apartment, looking across at Michael Willoughby seated opposite.

'She knows about the money,' Karl said. 'She's going to tell her old man if I don't.'

'Jesus,' Willoughby said. 'Does she know about my involvement?'

'No.'

Willoughby stood. 'Right. Leave Catherine to me.'

'What are you going to do?' Karl said.

'I'll get rid of Catherine. You make sure you have a good alibi.'

'I've got a speech to do at the University. I told Catherine I'd speak to her dad after that. She promised she wouldn't say anything until then. The stupid bitch still loves me.'

'Ok,' Willoughby said. 'You go, and I'll ring you later.'

Beth was wrenched from Karl. Her essence picked up and transported back. Returning her to somewhere familiar, somewhere called home.


Matt entered Phillips' office. Phillips stared up from his desk, expecting him to speak.

Matt didn't disappoint. 'Beth's scans are complete. They've come back perfect.' He smiled.

'Wow.' Phillips said. 'I can't believe she suffered no ill effects. Maybe we should wake her?'

'My thoughts exactly.' Matt said. 'I've primed the team. Not sure where Jake's got too though.'

'Yeah, Jake. I haven't seen him either. I think he was pissed off I used you on Beth's retrogression. I'll see him later and smooth things over. Right,' he said, rising from his chair. 'Let's see what she has to say.'

The two of them raced their way along the corridors and entered the high dependency unit. Beth lay in bed asleep. She appeared as if she was taking a nap, and any effects from her ordeal weren't evident. A nurse stood at the end of the bed holding a tray with a syringe on it. She handed it to Phillips. He paused to look at Matt, before injecting the fluid into the plastic insert attached to her wrist. The three of them waited in silence as the drug took effect. Beth's eyes fluttered and slowly opened.

Matt wandered across to her. 'How are you?'

She smiled. 'Fine. I feel fine.'

Phillips edged closer. 'What do you remember?'

Beth laughed. Matt and Phillips looked at each other, not seeing the joke, as she sat up in bed. 'We've invented God,' she said. Matt and Phillips stared at her. 'Amorphous,' she continued. 'Is God.'

The two men and the lady orderly began to laugh as well. Beth grinning from ear to ear. 'I died. I saw everything. I know everything.

Amorphous saved me, and I was reborn.' She laughed again at the absurdity of it. 'It's the only way I can explain it.' She frowned. 'Catherine Richardson's in danger. Michael Willoughby and Karl Jenkins have been embezzling from Oliver Richardson's company. Willoughby plans to murder her.'

'Are you sure about this?' Phillips said.

'Yes. I'm certain. Amorphous showed me.'

'Phone the police,' Phillips said to the nurse. 'I'll speak with Mr Richardson regarding your allegations. Tell us what the retrogression was like.'

Beth went on to explain what she had experienced. As she talked, though, the memories faded. It was as if they were being expunged from her mind. That the recounting of them was eradicating any trace. Matt and Phillips jotted down notes until she could remember no more. The memories nothing more than the vaguest recollections, until these faded as well. She looked exhausted and allowing her some more rest, Phillips and Matt left her.

Willoughby stood in the underground car park of Catherine Richardson's apartment. He watched from the shadows and waited, her Vintage Jaguar car in full view. After several false alarms, he watched as she entered from one of the stairwells. His eyes following her towards the car. As Willoughby stepped from the darkness, three police officers with their guns trained on him leapt out from behind parked cars. He followed their instructions, as he was told first to drop his weapon and then lay on the floor. The gravity of his situation slowly dawning on him.

Phillips phoned Oliver Richardson, who organised an investigation of his accounts. The following day the police swooped on Karl Jenkins' apartment and arrested him. Jenkins had been only too willing to implicate both his partner in crime and lover. Jake Rogers' body had been discovered late in the evening. A note accompanied it, apologising for what he had done to Beth. When the contents of his hard drive were deciphered, it became apparent what Willoughby and Karl Jenkins had on Rogers. Fortunately for the police, Rogers had also left damning evidence on the other two.

**Two Months Later -** Matt and Beth, who had been seeing each other for a while, had managed to keep their relationship a secret. Fearing Phillip's disapproval. When he found out, however, he gave them his blessing. Matt invited Beth to his parents' home, making the drive north. Stopping at a large Victorian house in the Nunthorpe area of Middlesbrough.

'You ok?' Matt asked.

'I'm nervous. What if your family doesn't like me?'

Matt leant across and kissed her on the lips. 'They'll love you.'

He took her by the hand and led her into the house, depositing their coats in the hall, and entering the living room.

'The three people inside the room, who were sitting, stood as they entered. An elderly couple and a middle-aged man.

'Beth, I'd like you to meet my grandparents and my dad.'

'I'm Maggie,' the woman said. Embracing Beth. Usually, she would have found the familiarity unnerving, but for some reason, she didn't. The elderly man did likewise. She turned her attention to Matt's cad and looked at him. A brief recognition appeared and vanished as quickly as it arrived.

'I'm Jimmy,' he said. And embraced her too.

'Have we met?' Tilting her head. 'You seem familiar.'

Jimmy glanced at the other three. 'I don't believe so.'

'It's the eyes,' she said. 'Matt has yours.'

'Everyone says that,' Jimmy said.

The four of them turned as the door to the kitchen opened. A middle-aged woman limped in, her walking assisted by a brightly-coloured cane.

She tottered towards Beth and stopped in front of her. 'You were right, Matt,' she said. 'She is beautiful.' She turned towards Beth and offered her hand. 'Hi. I'm Lindsey.'

Beth, for some strange reason, was overcome with emotion. She put her hand up to her cheek as tears fell. 'I'm sorry,' she said. 'I don't know what's come over me.'

Lindsey took hold of her hand. 'Don't worry, it's nothing to be embarrassed about.'

'You must think I'm a lunatic. Bursting into tears like this.' Accepting the tissue Maggie handed her. Lindsey pulled Beth towards her and hugged her close. For the briefest of moments, Beth knew and squeezed Lindsey back. A moment, a connection, passed between them and then was lost.

'Thank you, Beth,' Lindsey said. kissing her on the cheek. 'Thank you for everything.'

## THE STORYTELLER

You can't cheat death, so the saying goes. Maybe, though, we can make him wait a little longer. Of all the possible outcomes in life. All the infinite scenarios, there's only one that matters. Time, with all its shades and moods, can be a severe taskmaster. As the celestial dice are thrown time and again, we can but wonder what might have been. Maybe, though, the outcome of everything is already a foregone conclusion. Perhaps the game has already been played.

# LEGERDEMAIN – CHAPTER ONE

Charlotte sat back, pulled the helmet from her head and screamed. 'I've done it! Sophie. I've done it!'

Sophie came running into Charlotte's bedroom. 'What the hell are you shouting at?' she said.

'I've done it. I've reached the end of Amorphous.'

Sophie's mouth fell open. 'You're kidding.'

Charlotte nodded at the screen. 'Look.'

Sophie hurried across to it and dropping to her knees, read the flashing message.

**'CONGRATULATIONS! YOU HAVE SUCCESSFULLY COMPLETED AMORPHOUS'**

'Oh my god, Charlie. How the hell did you manage that? What was the final clue?'

'The football. The autographs on the football. One of them was wrong.' Charlotte squealed.

Sophie pointed at the screen. 'Look,' A new message appeared. The two women gawped at each other.

**'RING THE FOLLOWING NUMBER TO CLAIM YOUR PRIZE'**

It said. Below this, a phone number. And under this, an eleven-digit numeric code.

'I've won a prize?' Charlotte said.

Sophie thrust the phone at her friend. 'What the hell are you waiting for?'

Charlotte grabbed the phone and called the number. The phone rang out for a few times before it connected. They listened as an automated voice spoke. *'Welcome to the Gainford Corporation. Please enter your eleven-digit code, now.'* Charlotte typed in the number and waited a couple of seconds before a human voice spoke.

'Hi. Is that Charlotte Richmond?' a female voice said.

'Yes,' Charlotte said.

'Congratulations, Charlotte. You've completed Amorphous. Because you're one of the quickest to finish the game, you've won a cash prize of £10,000.'

Charlotte stared at her friend, who was as speechless as her.

'Are you still there, Charlotte?' asked the voice.

'Yes,' she spluttered.

'I know it's a surprise, but there's more. In addition to the cash prize, Mr Gainford is awarding ten winners of the game a unique opportunity. More of that later. First I need to take some details.'

Charlotte answered the questions. Giving her personal data, her address, bank account number, and sort code. She hung-up after being informed that they would be in touch in due course.

'Oh, my God!' Sophie said.

Charlotte stood. 'I think this calls for a drink.'

'Vodka?' Sophie said.

Charlotte grinned. 'What else.'

Charlotte was collected by a posh taxi at 10.30 am the following Monday, and conveyed to Darlington railway station. Following the advice on the emailed itinerary, she had received, Charlotte made her way to the ticket office. She was finding it difficult to believe this was real, and not some dream. She had seldom won anything in her life, well, nothing of note. Here she was with a £10,000 cash prize, and more to come.

She and Sophie had booked a couple of weeks away in the sun, later in the year, out of her winnings. The money had been transferred into her bank account on the same day as the phone call, much to her surprise. She had never had anything approaching this amount of money before. A few pounds had already been spent on new clothes, a top of the range mobile, and quite a bit of it on alcohol.

Charlotte collected her first-class ticket to Kings Cross, another surprise. She had never travelled first class in her life. It was turning into some adventure. Finding her seat, she put her new designer suitcase in the luggage rack and settled down to the two and a half-hour journey. The train stopped at York and passengers got on, but only a couple in first-class. A businessman she guessed, by his attire and financial times tucked under his arm. And a second man in his early twenties. About the same age as her. She studied him. Surprised by the likeness to Jacob, her ex. She had been dumped by Jacob after two years together. Something she could have handled, if it wasn't for the fact he was now going out with Victoria. Her one-time friend. Apparently, they'd been seeing each other behind her back for some time. The shock and embarrassment she felt about this, months later, still made her seethe. Victoria had been ostracised by Charlotte's other friends and consigned to the, *If I ever see your face again, I'll claw your eyes out, you bitch,* ex-friend category.

Jacob hadn't got off lightly either. Charlotte had taken a pair of scissors to anything cut-able, and a hammer to anything not. Great delight had been felt in pouring a pint over his head in a nightclub, as well. Something she'd been thrown out for, but a price worth paying she reasoned. The idea of running into Barbie and Ken in there again, made her blood boil.

The guy smiled across at her. Charlotte looked away. He possessed the same smile as Jacob. The, *look at me I'm gorgeous,* smile. Well, she wasn't about to let her defences down. As far as she was concerned, all men were wankers. Literally and metaphorically. She plugged in her iPod and stared out of the window, as the countryside sped by, absorbed in the latest Ed Sheeran album.

The train pulled into Kings Cross station. Charlotte reached for her suitcase, now wedged between two large and heavy-looking bags. She yanked to free it, but lost her grip and fell into the lap of the businessman. 'I'm so sorry,' she said, extracting herself from him.

The businessman muttered something as he got up himself, pushed past Charlotte and the young man, and headed for the exit door. Charlotte pulled a face at him as he left, which caused the young man to smile. He moved towards Charlotte's case. 'Can I help you with that?'

'I'm capable of getting it myself,' she said. 'I'm not a bimbo who can't do anything for herself you know.'

'Sorry,' he said. 'I didn't mean to offend you.'

'You didn't.' She gave him a false smile. Her next pull freed the intransigent luggage. She followed the same route the businessman had taken and found herself on the platform. Charlotte peered both ways and spotting the exit sign, bounded off pulling her suitcase behind her. She reached the exit door, and headed for a well-dressed woman holding two cards aloft. One with her name on it - the other - JACK WOLVERSTON. Charlotte marched up to her, stopping in front and fished in her pocket for the itinerary.

'Charlotte Richmond?' asked the woman.

'Yes,' Charlotte said. Giving up the search.

'Hi. I'm Vanessa Clifton-Welbury. Your chaperone. We're just waiting for one more person, and then we can go. Have you come far?'

'Darlington.'

Vanessa looked past Charlotte and smiled. 'Jack Wolverston?' she said, holding out a hand. Charlotte turned around and looked into the face of the young man from the train.

'Yes.' He smiled at Vanessa, shaking hands with her. Charlotte forced a smile, not wanting to appear ignorant in front of Vanessa.

Vanessa clapped her hands together. 'Right then you two lucky people. Follow me.'

Charlotte and Jack followed Vanessa as she made her way out. Finding themselves in a large car park, they headed for a waiting limousine. The three of them climbed in. Charlotte and Jack gazed around at the opulent interior.

Vanessa handed Charlotte and Jack envelopes. 'Right. I have some things for you to read and sign. Mostly legal stuff.'

'Legal Stuff?' Charlotte said.

'Yes. Mr Gainford is offering the ten winners an opportunity to visit his development laboratories, and if you are willing, a chance to try out his latest game. We're insisting on strict confidentiality. So, we're asking the winners to sign a non-disclosure agreement. Should they wish to take up this offer, of course?'

Charlotte peered across at Jack and smiled. Jack smiled back. The first time Miss Frosty Knickers had dropped her guard, he thought. Charlotte resumed her previous demeanour as Jack grinned back.

Jack flicked through the paperwork, giving it nothing more than a cursory glance. He signed the final sheet, handing it back to Vanessa. Charlotte who would have liked to have read it through more thoroughly – she was usually fastidious on such matters, having once signed an insurance agreement costing her a lot of money – but not wanting to make a fuss, reluctantly did likewise. Vanessa took out her mobile and photographed Charlotte and Jack. The pair of them glanced at each other.

'Why the photos?' Charlotte said.

'Just for our records.' Vanessa said. Jack shrugged at Charlotte, who shrugged back. 'Ok. William, the driver, will take you to your hotel. Someone will meet you there and give you further details. There's plenty of drinks in the cabinet. Feel free. Think of this as a start of an adventure. The greatest adventure you're ever likely to have.' She smiled and then she was gone. The driver started the engine, and the car smoothly pulled away as Jack and Charlotte leant back against the luxurious leather seats.

'Well,' Jack said. 'How about some Champagne? Vanessa did say to help ourselves.'

Charlotte glanced at her watch. 'It's a bit early, isn't it?' Feigning disapproval.

'Chill a little,' he said. 'It's ten o'clock at night somewhere in the world.' Handing her a glass of bubbly. Charlotte snatched it from him and downed it in one, holding the glass out in front of her for him to refill it. The pair sat in silence sipping Champagne. Occasionally glancing at each other, the couple sitting on different sides of the car, as the London streets, with its people, flashed by.

Jack leant forward. 'So, you managed to reach the end of Amorphous?'

'I wouldn't be here if I hadn't,' she said.

Jack sat back in his seat. 'You need to work on that. You've mastered sarcasm. You should work on other aspects of your personality.'

'Sorry,' she said. 'Yes. I finished it last week. I struggled for ages with the last clue. The football.'

'I got that one early. I'm a Boro fan you see. I knew straight away. John Hickton's autograph shouldn't be in the F.A. Cup final squad. The one stumping me was the beer. I never noticed the spelling mistake. Spelling is not my strong suit.'

'Loved the story, though,' Charlotte said. 'Gainford's best to date.'

'Really? I thought it was nowhere near as good as The Hanging Tree.'

Charlotte bristled a little. She was a massive fan of Gainford and disliked anyone who criticised him. It was as if they were talking badly about a friend or a member of her family.

'What was wrong with Amorphous?'

'Well, all the different timelines. They didn't make sense. I mean, when Beth went back and changed time, it didn't alter the future as it should have. I reckon Gainford was lax on quite a few issues if I'm honest.'

'Lax! Let me tell you about Christian Gainford,' she began. 'He's a genius. He's taken gaming to a whole new level. Way beyond any of his competitors. Not only that, he's one of the most generous people alive. His foundation has helped millions. Saved millions,' she said. Warming-up her routine, honed over many years of practice. 'When he dies, he's going to leave his wealth to the right causes—'

'I don't deny he's generous, Charlotte. I'm just saying his last game had flaws.'

'Flaws.' She snorted. 'The problem with you is, you've watched too many Star Trek episodes. Amorphous is about the infinite number of possibilities, and countless scenarios that can be thrown up. The final ending is one of the millions – billions - that could happen. The storyteller at the end hinted at that. It's not some lame, *Back to the Future* plot-line.'

'I liked *Back to the future*.' He smiled.

Charlotte got angrier. Jacob used to do the same thing. She glared across at Jack and considered smashing the Champagne bottle across his head. 'Well, you would.' Grabbing the bottle from him, she filled her glass again.

'It appears we've got off on the wrong foot. Can we start again?'

'You only get one chance to make a first impression, and you blew yours, mate.' She huffed.

'Bloody hell, Miss Frosty Knickers. Turn the thermostat up.'

She glared at him. 'What did you call me?'

'Well, you could do with warming up, Love. Frigid doesn't begin to describe you.'

'Now we get to the truth. What's the problem Jaaaack?' She intoned. 'Don't you like confident women? Prefer a more submissive, supine female, do we? You frigging Neanderthal.'

'Neanderthals have had a bad press, Chaaaalotte! They're nowhere near as primitive as everyone believed. Haven't you watched National Geographic? What's the matter? Does it clash with EastEnders, darling?'

The driver increased the speed of the car a little as he glanced into his rear-view mirror.

'Don't you *darling* me,' she said. 'You patronising twat.'

'It doesn't take much, does it? With your smart luggage and designer clothes. The cracks soon appear, and we see the guttersnipe beneath.'

Charlotte was fulminating. She couldn't bear being in the car a minute longer with him. She leant towards the driver to ask him to stop, just as the car pulled up outside The Grand Viscount Hotel. Charlotte jumped out and grabbed the luggage from the driver, turned and stormed inside. Jack apologised to him, having now calmed, and headed inside too.

The pair of them were spotted when they entered reception. A well-dressed man wandered towards them. 'Charlotte Richmond?' Offering his hand. 'And you must be Jack Wolverston? I'm Oliver Scorton, Mr Gainford's personal assistant. If you follow me, I'll get you booked in.'

The pair shook hands and followed him across to reception, where the lady behind the desk gave Scorton her full attention.

'This is Miss Richmond and Mr Wolverston,' he said to her.

The receptionist organised their rooms, presenting them both with an itinerary. A pair of men in hotel uniform collected their suitcases and escorted them upstairs.

The porter opened the door, and Charlotte stepped through. It was huge. Delighted to discover it was a suite and not a room, she reached into her handbag and pulled out a £10 note. Unsure as to the size of tip she should give.

'That's ok, madam,' he said. 'The Gainford Corporation has dealt with it.' At that, he wished her a pleasant stay and left.

Charlotte examined the room. It had two colossal sofas in the middle. A table to the right of each settee and against one of the walls, a large cabinet. She sauntered across and opened it. Inside an array of bottles. Every spirit you could imagine, along with liqueurs, bottled beers, and lagers. On one of the tables stood a large bouquet, and on the other a bottle of Champagne in an ice bucket. She wandered through into the bathroom and gasped at the enormity of it. Almost every surface covered with marble. The taps on the basin and bath were gold-plated. She'd seen pictures of bathrooms resembling this, in celebrity houses, inside the magazines she read.

Charlotte re-entered the sitting room and kicked off her shoes. The thickness of the carpet, devouring her feet. Ambling through into the bedroom, she stared on in disbelief at the biggest bed she'd ever seen. Diving into it she laughed like a small child. At the foot of the bed sat an immense plasma TV. Next to the bed a large bowl of fresh fruit. Some of the items in it she didn't even recognise. Charlotte took out her mobile and photographed the suite. After finishing, she sent them to Sophie and lay on the bed awaiting the inevitable call. She wasn't disappointed as it rang within minutes.

# CHAPTER TWO

After speaking with Sophie, showering and changing, Charlotte headed downstairs. She paused at reception for directions to The Queen Elizabeth II Suite. Escorted by a porter along a couple of corridors, they stopped outside a door. He nodded politely and left Charlotte to enter the large room. She looked around at the chairs set out in two rows facing forward, and a huge screen positioned in front of the seats. To show a presentation, Charlotte assumed. To her right, a few groups of people, the majority around her age, chatted pleasantly. Milling around were waiters carrying canapes and other assorted delicacies, other staff handed out glasses of wine. She stopped inside the room as one of the waiters came across to her. 'Drink, madam?' he said.

Charlotte took a glass from him. Another waiter appeared, offering his tray of food to Charlotte who plucked a snack from it, thanking him.

'Well, you made it down, Miss Frosty Knickers,' Jack said. He grinned at her.

Charlotte spun around to face the smiling Jack. She felt good and wasn't about to allow him to annoy her, so she ignored the jibe. 'I did.' She smiled broadly back at him.

'So, these are the winners then?' Pointing around the room.

'Yeah,' she said. And took a bite of her snack.

'Have you noticed something?' he said.

Charlotte surveyed the room. She counted ten people, including herself and Jack. 'No,' she said.

'There are five men and five women.'

'So? Random chance throws up things like that.'

'And their ages?'

'About our age,' she replied.

'I'd say the youngest is twenty, and the oldest mid-twenties.'

'Is there a point to this?' she said. 'I'm about to climb aboard the Boredom Express.'

'Ah, there it is.' He moved away from her. 'Your beautiful sarcasm.' He stopped a waiter and took a glass from him. Returning to face Charlotte. 'I overheard the guy who met us at the reception—'

'Scorton,' she said.

'Yeah, Scorton and Miss double barrel. Vanessa thingy-me-jig.'

'The boredom train is leaving.' Collecting another glass for herself.

'I heard them say something about pairing us up.'

She screwed up her face. 'What, me and you?'

'No. The couples. Five men. Five women. Five couples.' He smiled, walking away from her.

'Yeah? Well, if I draw you, I'm going home.'

'Of course, you would,' he said, and winked at her.

Charlotte turned away, not wanting him to know he'd annoyed her. She searched out the waiters and grabbed more snacks and another glass of wine, promising herself it'd be her last. The combined effects of the two downed previously, the Champagne imbibed earlier, not to mention the vodka consumed in her room while taking a bath, was making her merry. She meandered around the room and chatted with the others, avoiding Jack and glaring any time their eyes happened to meet. The others appeared to be from various places around the British Isles. Two Scots, a woman, and a man. Two Welsh women, and a man from Northern Ireland. The Irish man seemed nice, she mused. If Jack was right, and they were getting paired off, she hoped it was him and not Jack. Anyone but Mr Arrogance, she thought, scowling at Jack. Her ruminations interrupted by Scorton and Vanessa entering the room. They made their way to the front as the winners looked on.

'If everyone can take a seat,' Vanessa said. 'We'll begin.'

The ten people complied, filling the two rows. Jack at one end of the front row, and Charlotte at the other. She could see out of her peripheral vision, Jack waving at her, but she ignored him. He was trying to rile her, and she was having none of it.

'Good afternoon, everyone,' Scorton said. 'Welcome to the Grand Viscount Hotel. I'm not going to bore you and ramble on. I'm going straight ahead with the presentation. Enjoy.'

The presentation began. Christian Gainford appeared on the screen. Charlotte reached into her handbag and removed her glasses. She didn't want to miss a minute of this. He was gorgeous, she thought, for an older man. He wore a pair of jeans and a t-shirt. She loved that. Worth billions, yet he dressed so cool, her eyes fixed on his every move.

'Hi.' He waved. 'I'm Christian Gainford, owner of the Gainford Corporation.' His soft Scottish lilt captivating Charlotte even more. 'You people are the winners of the competition we ran this year. We decided to do this secretly, to avoid mass panic.' He laughed loudly. The room laughed too. 'We're offering you a unique opportunity today. Amorphous, my last story, was from our Mark 1 version of the game. The story was just that. A story. You got an opportunity to enjoy it in a 3D format and a chance, by collecting clues, to make your way through to the end. This of course, while entertaining, lacked something. Something only now we can offer the public.'

The people in the room, hanging on his every breath, the silence of the winners, palpable. So quiet, the chirps of birds some distance away could be heard outside. Charlotte couldn't take her eyes off Gainford, hanging on every word he uttered.

Gainford continued. 'What I'm offering you today is the chance to try out our Mark 2 prototype. This version gives you the opportunity to not only play the game but interact as well. You adopt the persona of one of the characters and play the game as if you're them.'

A loud gasp erupted from the audience.

'Yes, you heard me right. You're the characters.'

The lights in the room came back on, and the presentation stopped. Noise from one side of the room as a door creaked open and in strutted Christian Gainford. Charlotte's hand shot to her mouth. She took off her glasses and put them away. Gainford glided his way along the rows, greeting everyone in turn. As he reached Charlotte, he smiled at her, before shaking her hand and moving on.

When he finished, he stood in front of the ten winners. 'Any questions?' he said.

A hand shot up from the second row. An Asian man, acknowledged by Gainford.

'When you say we can interact, Mr Gainford. What exactly does that mean?'

'You decide how the characters develop within the story,' he said. 'There are thousands of possible scenarios to every choice you make. But *you* make the decisions,' he heavily emphasised. 'You decide how it unfolds.'

A blonde woman sitting next to Charlotte put up her hand, along with Charlotte. Gainford acknowledged the blonde.

'What happens if a character dies?' she said.

'Game over,' he said. 'You have to restart. Don't worry. I don't expect anyone here to get to the end. It'll take thousands of hours of play, or a large degree of luck, to complete it.'

'What's the game called,' Charlotte said.

Gainford turned to face her, his piercing blue eyes homing in. 'The game is called *broken.*' He smiled, and Charlotte blushed.

More hands shot up in the air, but Gainford held his hands up, palms outstretched.

'I think the best thing to do is to play. We could go on all day with these questions, but to understand it, you need to play. Tomorrow the people who decide to take up my offer will be flown to my country home in Scotland. I have a specially designed gaming room fitted up there, and that's where you'll play the game. First things first,' he said, picking up a piece of paper. 'Everyone needs to undergo a thorough physical examination before they are allowed to play. The game's quite stressful, and we don't want anyone keeling over on us.' The audience laughed with Gainford. 'In addition to this. You'll be asked to sign a consent form, for legal purposes only. In case the game fries your brain.' He laughed, waving his hands around manically. The laughter more muted, this time.

'Don't worry,' he said. 'We've done hundreds of hours of test time, and no one's suffered any ill effects. You know how particular the legal people are. Finally.' He paused, moving across the front of the audience. 'The game involves two main characters, Steve and Sandi. There'll be five games running simultaneously. With two players, one male, one female per game. To this end, we have decided to match you in pairs. We'd like you to fill in a detailed questionnaire, which the lovely Vanessa will give you. This will enable us to come up with the best possible match for you all. And, subsequently, offer you the most rewarding gaming experience.'

'What happens if you don't wish to take part?' asked a Scottish man.

'You can stay in the hotel for the rest of the week before you return home. With the understanding, of course, you mustn't discuss this with anyone. Is this point clear?' Gainford said.

The assembled audience nodded in unison. Vanessa gave out the questionnaires. Gainford shook hands with the winners, again.

'Meals and drinks are free for you for the duration of your stay. Charge everything to your room. Get a good night's sleep, people. You'll need it.' At that, Gainford left, to loud applause from the audience. Charlotte couldn't believe it. She'd met Christian Gainford. As handsome and charismatic as she'd imagined. A smile stretched the entirety of her face.

Back in her room, Charlotte filled in the questionnaire quickly. The list, although lengthy, was easy to answer. After getting ready, she decided to go downstairs for dinner. A couple of the other women had asked if she'd like to join them, she'd readily agreed. Putting on one of her new outfits - a fetching designer black dress - and satisfied with how she looked, she marched towards the door. Collecting her bag and the questionnaire - to drop-off at reception - she headed downstairs.

Charlotte sat in the corner of the bar in the company of two of the female winners, Louise and Paige. They chatted excitedly during the evening. The main topic, the new game Gainford mentioned. Jack arrived a little later than Charlotte, deep in conversation with two other men and the remaining two women. The final two men sat at the bar talking. Charlotte tried to avoid looking across at where Jack sat, but felt his eyes boring into her. She stole a glance at him, and Jack waved at her, which annoyed her more.

Paige, noticing Charlotte's recent glance across at his table, nudged her playfully. 'What's the deal with you and pretty-boy?' she said.

'Jack isn't it?' Louise said.

'Yeah,' Charlotte said. Taken by surprise at the change of subject. 'Nothing. We were on the same train, that's all.'

Paige nudged her. 'Are you sure, Charlie?'

'Absolutely.' Taking the ribbing in good spirit.

'I hope I get to pair up with him,' Louisa said. 'He's gorgeous.'

'Good luck,' Charlotte said. Looking at her mobile as it sounded.

'Wouldn't you like him as your partner?' Paige said.

'No, I wouldn't.' She didn't look up as she read a text from her friend.

'Ooh!' Paige and Louisa said in unison.

Charlotte put her phone away. 'It doesn't matter who you pair with. We'll be playing characters in a story.'

'Oh, yeah.' Paige nodded. Digesting what Charlotte had said.

'What about if we made a play for him tonight,' smiled Louisa. 'Are you sure you wouldn't mind?'

'Quite sure,' she said. 'I've recently come out of a long-term relationship, and I'm not ready for another.'

Paige giggled. 'Who's talking about a relationship.'

'Feel free, girls. Jack is all yours.' She plucked the empty glasses from the table. 'Who wants another?'

The two women nodded, and Charlotte strolled towards the bar. She waited for the barman, as he served another guest, and took the opportunity to send a text to Sophie. Once served, Charlotte turned to see Paige and Louise now sat with Jack's party. She reluctantly joined them, along with the two men from the bar. Jack smiled at Charlotte as Paige and Louise, eased down either side of him.

'So,' Jack said. 'That's the ten of us then.'

Charlotte stopped and considered moving as far away from Jack as she could, but one of the other men got up and offered her his seat. She thought about refusing it. But, not wanting to appear standoffish or rude, she sat opposite Jack. He smiled. His, *I know this is pissing you off big-style,* smile. Charlotte smiled back. She was getting good at this false smiling. Give it a couple more days, she thought, and I'll be an expert.

The drinks continued to flow, Charlotte hitting the vodka like a woman possessed. The others downing drinks as only the knowledge of a free bar can encourage you to do.

# CHAPTER THREE

Charlotte woke in the morning feeling like crap, and peeped at her travel clock on the bedside cabinet to check the time. Unable to remember getting to bed, she gazed around in astonishment at her clothes-strewn room. Surveying a scene of carnage, she sat up in bed and briefly wondered how one person could make such a mess. Still, she had managed to get back to her room, and there weren't any strange men next to her, which was a triumph. She crept from her bed. Her mouth parched, her head, although not aching, had a thick cloudiness within. The usual pre-curser to a hang-over. Still feeling drunk she wobbled across the room. Reaching the mirror on the far wall, she leant on it for support. Charlotte groaned on catching her reflection in the mirror. Apparently, she had been too drunk to remove any of her makeup the night before, judging by the sight which greeted her. Taking out her make-up remover wipes, she began the onerous task of trying to make herself look presentable.

Charlotte felt much better after showering and changing into a pair of jeans and a sweatshirt. She popped a couple of paracetamols into her mouth and downed a pint of water. To help ward off the gathering storm of a hangover that was rapidly approaching. Picking up her jacket and handbag she headed for something to eat. If she could somehow force a breakfast inside her before sobering up, she reasoned, she would be thankful later. Charlotte paused at the bedroom door as a memory from the previous night hove into view. It brutally pushed its way past her unimportant mental musings, and stood defiantly in front of her mind's eye. She put her hands up to her face and groaned loudly, as it displayed itself in all its glory. A vision of her and Jack, kissing outside her room.

'You frigging idiot,' she said to herself. Banging her head on the wall, as a form of penitence, for her indiscretion.

'Ow!' she said out loud. Rubbing her head, realising she had done it a little too hard.

Charlotte sat alone in the dining room as none of the others had surfaced yet. Sleeping off the effects of the previous night, she assumed. Having managed to eat a full-English, along with something approaching two pints of juice, she contently sipped her second cup of tea as Jack entered. He made straight for her table and sat opposite, flashing her a smile.

A waiter immediately walked over to him. 'Would you like something to drink, sir?' he asked.

'Coffee, please.' The head waiter beckoned to another member of staff carrying a coffee pot, who walked across and filled Jack's cup.

'I'll give you a few moments to decide what you'd like,' the first man said.

'A full-English,' Jack said.

'Splendid, sir.' The waiter turned and left.

Jack sipped his coffee and glanced about. 'Bit thin on the ground this morning.'

'They're probably sleeping off their hangovers,' Charlotte said. Trying to push the image of her and Jack kissing, out of sight, under an enormous mental carpet.

'Your head ok?' he said.

'My head's fine, Jackie-Boy.'

'You have a red mark on it.'

'Bumped it in the shower. What about yours?'

'Great. I don't do hangovers.' Jack smiled at Charlotte. 'Last night's a blur, though. The last thing I remember was drinking flaming Drambuie's.'

She frowned at him. 'You and some of the others were playing daft drinking games.'

Jack nodded. 'Didn't the Scottish lad lose some of his eyebrows?'

'Tom. Yeah, dozy get.' The pair of them laughed.

'And the rest of the night is a bit of a mystery,' he said. 'I Can't even remember getting into bed. The waiter arrived at the table with his breakfast.

'Yeah, me too,' Charlotte said.

Jack took a bite of toast. 'Not looking forward to today.'

'Why?'

'I hate planes.'

Charlotte scoffed. 'It's only an hour flight. A big strapping lad like you isn't afraid of flying, surely?'

'I generally go to my doctor for something to keep me calm. I've been like this for years.'

'You'll be all right.' She smiled, secretly enjoying the fact that Mr Perfect did have weaknesses. 'Get Louise or Paige to hold your hand.' She dabbed her mouth with her napkin and raised her eyebrows.

'Maybe I will.' Winked Jack.

Charlotte stood, throwing her handbag over her shoulder and turned to walk away. 'See you in reception at twelve.'

'Charlotte!' he shouted to her.

She stopped and spun around. 'Yeah?'

'Did anyone ever tell you, you're a great kisser?' he said. Lifting his cup to his mouth, he took a deliberately loud slurp.

'All of them,' Charlotte said. 'Bastard,' she muttered under her breath as she turned away.

The party of winners were collected from the hotel at 1 pm and driven by bus to Stanstead airport, and sat waiting for their plane. Jack hated flying, and his mood wasn't improved any when he spotted the aircraft. A small light passenger plane with propellers. On the rare occasions he had flown, it had always been in large passenger jets. The type the holiday operators run. This one looked altogether different. His apprehension mounting by the minute. Charlotte watched him, taking more than a degree of delight at his discomfort as the group got ready to board. Jack trailed at the back of the party, with Charlotte behind him, as the group mounted the steps. He paused at the foot of them, glanced up and took a large breath.

Charlotte nudged him. 'Come on, Jack, you're holding us up.' Patting him on the shoulder which caused him to jump a little. He said nothing as he climbed the steps, found a seat next to Alex, and sat. Charlotte sat next to Sarah, across the aisle from Jack. She viewed him, nervous tension written across his face. He was sweating as well, despite the fact the ambient temperature was cool. The plane taxied towards the runway and Jack's demeanour worsened. He placed his head against the seat in front of him and closed his eyes. Charlotte, for the first time, felt sorry for him. He appeared genuinely scared. Like a little, frightened schoolboy, she thought. Something she found endearing. Jack gripped the arm of his seat as the plane accelerated along the runway. He jumped, emitting a gasp, as the aircraft left the ground. Charlotte reached across the aisle and maternally took hold of his hand. He glanced across at her, fear etched deeply within his face, and forced an unconvincing smile. Charlotte, sensing his anxiety, squeezed his hand and held it firm as the plane, buffeted by a crosswind, continued its ascent. Finally reaching skywards, like a great bird in flight. The plane eventually levelled, and Jack calmed, releasing the breath he'd been holding on to since take-off. He sat back in his chair and puffed out his cheeks. Finally managing to look at Charlotte, he mouthed a thank-you.

Charlotte leant in nearer to him. 'Can I have my hand back now?' She smiled.

'Sorry,' he said. Releasing his vice-like grip.

The rest of the flight went by fast. The ten winners, except for Jack, chatting excitedly with each other. The plane commenced its descent into Glasgow airport, and Charlotte reprised her trick of holding Jack's hand to calm him. The plane put down with a hefty bump. Jack, with his head against the seat in front and his left leg fidgeting, calmed as the aircraft slowed on the runway. It trundled its way across to the terminal and came to a halt outside. He snatched up a sick-bag and deposited his breakfast into it as Charlotte tried to suppress a smile. They made their way off the plane. Jack meekly handing one of the flight attendants his sick-bag. 'Sorry,' he said.

'That's ok, sir,' she said. 'You're not the first.'

Vanessa led the group inside the terminal building, along a couple of corridors and into an elegant lounge. She turned to face the group. 'Right people,' she said. 'Only one more hop and we'll be there. Mr Gainford's house is on the west coast of Scotland, and quite remote. To enable us to reach it, Mr Gainford has booked a helicopter to take us to *Delphic*, his home. Hopefully the weather will hold, but if it doesn't, the final leg will be by bus.'

Charlotte grinned from ear to ear. She'd read loads about him and his house. Although a private person, Christian Gainford gave enough of his life away for Charlotte to keep up her interest. Scouring magazines and the internet for the merest of snippets concerning him. She was sure, and would on occasions brag to anyone who mentioned Gainford, that nobody knew more than her about him. The thought of going to Delphic, the place she had only dreamt of visiting, was the most exciting thing she had ever done or was ever likely to. 'The helicopter will be another hour.' Vanessa continued. 'You've got an opportunity to use the toilets, make a call or have a drink. Make yourself comfortable, people, and I'll be with you shortly.' At that she left, as a hubbub of noise descended across the room.

Charlotte peered across at Jack, who only now seemed to have understood what lay ahead. She studied him. If he was frightened on a plane, what would he be like in a helicopter? She wandered over to him as the others separated into groups of two and three. She put a hand on his arm. 'You all right, Jack?'

'Yeah. Not looking forward to the helicopter, if I'm honest.'

'Have a drink. It'll calm you a little.' Nudging him playfully with her shoulder.

Jack forced a smile. 'No thanks. It'll only end up in a bag.'

She liked this vulnerable Jack. But then admonished herself for having such thoughts. 'Should we join the others?'

'You go ahead,' he said. 'I've got a call to make and the toilet to visit.' He winked at her, turned and headed off.

She ambled across to Paige and Louise, the pair buried in conversation with Alex and Tom. Turning, she gazed at Jack, her eyes following him as he disappeared out of sight.

# CHAPTER FOUR

Vanessa returned forty-five minutes later, holding in her hand an iPad. The noise in the room dissipating as they all turned to face her.

'People,' she said. 'Our transport is here. Before we head across to it, I'm going to give you the results of our couple matching.'

Everyone held their breath, Charlotte glanced across at Jack, who seemed somewhat preoccupied. Worrying about the flight, she assumed. She hoped she wouldn't get Jack. Although beginning to warm to him a little, she didn't want a relationship. The wounds from Jacob, still raw. She wanted to enjoy this experience, rather than getting side-tracked with men.

'Couple number one,' Vanessa said. 'Paige Brompton and Daffydd Evans. Number two. Sarah Jenkins and Shaami Khan. Number three. Deborah Leith and Alexander Mcdee.'

Jack peeped across at Charlotte. Charlotte glanced back.

'Charlotte Richmond and …' Jack held his breath. 'Thomas Watkins. Finally, Louise Barton and Jack Wolverston.' Paige threw a disapproving look at her new friend.

Louise sashayed across to Jack and grabbed hold of his arm. 'Don't worry about the flight, Jack. I'll hold your hand.' Linking his arm, she grinned at Charlotte and Paige.

Jack smiled at Louise. Stealing a glance towards Charlotte, who forced a smile back.

The couples, along with Vanessa, boarded the helicopter. Jack, even more nervous than he'd been on the plane flight, gripped Louise's hand. Louise stroked his arm and whispered in his ear. Charlotte sat two rows back, her eyes fixed on him. She wished she was sitting next to him. For some reason, Charlotte felt sorry it wasn't her holding his hand. She felt sure Jack would have wanted her there too. The helicopter lifted into the air. Jack closed his eyes and thought of Charlotte. Imagining it was her, and not Louise, holding him together.

The helicopter put down on an open area of land outside of Gainford's estate. The worsening weather forcing the pilot's hand. Vanessa telephoned someone, and a minibus arrived shortly after. The ten winners along with Vanessa, transferred into the vehicle and, travelled across the snow-covered landscape towards Christian Gainford's house. Charlotte had marvelled at the remoteness during the flight. Flying over the white landscape, across the genuinely breath-taking terrain. The excitement of the winners palpable, as they continued their journey by land. The minibus turned off the main road and down a track, through two brick columns with a lion rampant on each. Two ornate gates, with *The Gainford Estate* emblazoned across them, squeakily closed behind them. They carried on along the track for a couple more moments before it appeared. Delphic rising gloriously into view. It was stunning. Its architecture Gothic-inspired, the walls a glistening white stone. The building stretched skywards impressively. Charlotte gazed on in awe. It was breath-taking. A thing of beauty made even more so by its barren and isolated surroundings. It captivated her as the minibus drew to a halt outside the front doors. They got out. For a moment she stared up at the edifice. It's crisp white walls, and snow-covered roof giving the building the appearance of a giant, ornate wedding cake, covered in icing. It appeared almost edible. Staff swarmed outside, collecting the luggage, as the winners - escorted by Vanessa into the house - made their way through a door to the right. The room, huge but in keeping with the scale of the building. The biggest open fireplace Charlotte had ever seen took pride of place at one end, an impressive fire-surround framing it. The walls adorned with paintings of different sizes and shapes, from portraits to landscapes. Even the curtains were impressive. A dark, red velvet, falling majestically from above each window to the floor below. In the centre of the room was a massive table, set for fourteen dinner guests.

'Welcome to my home,' he said. The ten winners spun around to face a smiling, Christian Gainford. 'Welcome to Delphic.'

He marched across to them and shook their hands in turn, reaching Charlotte last. His eyes sparkled as she gazed at him.

'Charlotte. Welcome.' Allowing their handshake to linger. 'I'm so pleased you could make it.'

He turned away and positioned himself at the head of the table. The winners looked on, hanging onto his every word.

'I'm sure you're all tired and in need of a shower or bath. My staff will show you to your rooms, and we'll meet back here for dinner tonight at seven. I've decided to make it black-tie. The men will find their outfits in the wardrobe of their rooms. The ladies are a little more demanding.' He laughed. 'You'll find several dresses inside your wardrobes. Feel free to swap with each other if you're the same size. The girls, not the boys.' He laughed again, the winners joining in with him. 'In your rooms, you'll find a bell. Should you need anything just ring, and one of my staff will assist you. I'll see you tonight.'

Vanessa motioned for the group to follow her, and one by one they were escorted to their rooms.

Charlotte lay on the four-poster bed, staring up at the ornate ceiling. Her room was huge, with an equally large en-suite bathroom complete with a mammoth-sized bath. The room, full of what appeared to be – to Charlotte's eyes anyway – antiques of every size and shape. She glanced again at her mobile. Disappointingly she had no signal. She had taken loads of photos and had hoped to send them to Sophie. It would have to wait, she thought. Sitting up and taking a swig of Champagne she found in the room when she arrived. She bathed, opting for a bath rather than a shower, luxuriating in it for an hour. Charlotte stood and took off her bathrobe, catching her naked form in the large mirror to the right of the bed. She looked good. Maybe a pound or two to lose she thought, pulling in her stomach. A knock on her bedroom door shook Charlotte from her thoughts. Grabbing and putting on the dressing gown, she answered.

Jack stood outside in his dinner suit. He looked gorgeous, Charlotte thought. Opening the door wide, allowing him to step inside.

'Wow!' she said. 'You scrub up well.'

'I feel a little overdressed if I'm honest.'

'Not at all.' Charlotte adjusted his dickie-bow. 'How come you're ready so early?'

'Christian's asked the boys down for a drink before dinner.'

'What about the girls? I'd love a drink with our host,' she said. Feigning annoyance.

'Vanessa's taking the women.' Jack wandered around Charlotte's room. 'This room's much bigger than mine.' He popped his head into the bathroom.

'That's the luck of the draw, Jackie-Boy,' she said. 'I'm afraid I'll have to ask you to leave. I have to pick out my lovely frock and get myself ready.'

'I can wait here while you finish.' He exaggeratingly winked.

'Sorry, Jack.' Opening the door. 'Louise would be devastated.'

'Yeah, you're probably right.' He stopped at the threshold. 'See more of you later.' A huge grin filling his face.

'Maybe.' She smiled back and closed the door behind him. Leaning back against it, she giggled. 'Charlotte, Charlotte, Charlotte,' she said under her breath. 'You can cut that out right now, young lady.' She opened the wardrobe. 'Now then.' Standing with hands on hips. 'What can I wear to have the men, and Christian, drooling?'

They enjoyed a sumptuous meal, complete with copious amounts of drink. Gainford regaled the gathering with stories of how he came to create his gaming machine. The ten winners politely asked questions which he enthusiastically answered. However, no one was brave enough to broach the subject of his new game. Although, Charlotte guessed, like her, they were all eager to know about it. Jack spent most of the evening looking across at Gainford, like the others. Every now and again, though, he glanced across at Charlotte. She sat on Gainford's left, and it amused him how she hung on his every word. She did, like Jack, steal a glance occasionally. Jack, unsure if this was because she sensed him looking at her. The innate sixth-sense women seem to have. She looked stunning. She wore a fitted, dark-red gown. Which, with a plunging neckline, was just the right side of decent. The other men in the room noticed too. Most, surreptitiously looking in her direction. She knew it as well. Jack had warmed to her after their rocky start. He hoped, likewise, she had warmed to him. Louise sat next to Jack, too close to him for his liking. Attractive enough, but Jack wasn't interested. His eyes on one woman in the room, and she was resplendent in red.

Gainford stood, raising his glass. 'A toast to new adventures,' he said. The guests raised theirs as well.

'Mr Gainford,' Charlotte said.

Gainford turned to face her. 'Christian. Call me Christian.' He smiled.

Charlotte blushed and smiled back. 'I'm sure I'm not unique in this room, but could you tell us a little about Broken.'

'Ah! I wondered who'd mention it first. I'm not surprised it was you, Charlotte,' he said. Charlotte blushed further.

'Where do I begin?' Sitting back in his chair. 'We developed Broken, more than two years ago. We had this great idea of making a story much more life-like. My programmers have exceeded my expectations though. The possible scenarios are enormous. It would take a player, playing twenty-four hours a day, over a decade to exhaust every possibility.'

'Is there only one winning scenario?' Alex asked.

'No,' Gainford said. 'There are many. What you need to do is get the character Steve home safe. I can't tell you more than this as it would spoil the story. I'm offering a prize for the couple that completes it. I don't expect any of you will though.'

The ten assembled winners stared at each other. Charlotte glanced across at Jack, who raised his eyebrows a little.

Gainford swigged his brandy. 'The winning couple will receive one million pounds each.' The ten gasped.' You heard right. Tax-free.'

The chatter in the room erupted. Gainford sipped his drink again, smiling at the assembled crowd.

'How realistic is the game, Christian?' Shaami asked.

'You wouldn't believe how realistic it is. When you enter the game, you give yourself over completely to it. So much, in fact, you'll forget who you are. You'll become the character. You'll see tomorrow.' Gainford sat back in his chair and studied them all. 'The game tricks you into believing what you're experiencing is real. So, before you enter the game, we put in place a mental prompt. If we feel you are getting too deep into it, we trigger a visual aid which alerts you to the fact what you're seeing isn't real life.'

'Is it dangerous?' Jack said. 'If we don't react to the visual prompt, I mean.'

'In tests, one in twenty of our testers failed to respond to the prompt. We had to bring them out manually. They were no lasting effects. It's similar to a bad hangover. So, as you can imagine, it's better for you if you leave the game voluntarily. All will become clear tomorrow.' Gainford swigged from his glass. He now appeared tired as Charlotte scrutinized him. Maybe the long day had taken its toll, she thought.

'I suggest, people, you get a good night's sleep. Believe me, you'll need it. I'm going to say goodnight, and I'll see you at twelve tomorrow.' With that, he stood, smiled politely and left.

The hubbub of noise started immediately. The winners rose from their seats and headed into the drawing room. The discussions continued amongst them until, one by one, they retired to bed. Charlotte and Jack headed up with Tom and Louise.

'See you in the morning,' Jack said to Charlotte, Louise, and Tom, making for his room and the welcoming sight of his bed. Charlotte climbed into her own and was fast asleep within minutes. The house groaned, the way old houses do, while the winning ten slumbered on.

The two men, carrying the body of a man across the courtyard, entered an outbuilding and dropped it next to the inert form of a woman. They turned and stepping back outside, one of them locked the door. They briefly checked around, paying particular attention to the darkened bedrooms of the great house, before heading into the frigid air once more, and back inside Delphic.

Eight of the winners had eaten a late breakfast. Charlotte's partner, Tom, and Jack's partner, Louise, were curiously missing. The others discussed their absence, but no one had any idea why they weren't there. The weather had closed in during the night, a feeling of isolation permeating the group. After eating, the eight returned to their rooms and waited in readiness for their appointment with the gaming machine. Gainford, Vanessa, and Scorton had been absent from breakfast too, leaving the eight none the wiser as to Tom and Louise's absence.

There was a knock at Charlotte's door. She opened it to a concerned-looking Jack outside, a deep frown etched on his face.

'What's up?' she said.

'I've been talking with Vanessa. I'm concerned about Louise.'

Charlotte shrugged. 'And?'

'Louise received a phone call in the night. A relative of hers has been in an accident, and they've taken her home.'

'How awful,' Charlotte said. 'And Tom?'

'Well, apparently, he got cold feet. Went to see Gainford late last night and decided to leave.'

'Really?' said a surprised Charlotte. 'Tom seemed the keenest.'

'That's what I thought. Bit strange don't you think?'

'Strange? What do you mean?' she said.

Jack frowned. 'I don't know. Just a feeling.'

'Come on, Jack. Things like this happen. How does it leave us though?'

'Without a partner. I asked Vanessa, and she said they would re-evaluate the pairings.'

Charlotte nodded. 'Right. Are you ready?'

Jack shrugged. 'I suppose so.'

Jack and Charlotte were the last to reach the drawing room. Vanessa and Scorton already there, with the other six. The news of Tom and Louise had apparently reached the others by now and seemed to have dampened spirits, somewhat.

'I know it's sad about Tom and Louise,' Vanessa said. 'But life goes on. If there's anyone else unsure, speak up now. I must warn you all, it will be both physically as well as a mentally demanding time for you. It will also be incredibly rewarding, however. Christian has decided, in light of recent events, to award the prize money to the couple who gets the furthest in the game.'

The eight talked excitedly. Charlotte made a money sign with her right hand at Jack, who smiled back.

Vanessa viewed the eight in turn. 'This is your final chance, people. Is there anyone who doesn't wish to take part?' There was silence. 'Ok,' she said. 'Follow me.'

They travelled along a series of corridors, stopping at a large wooden door. Vanessa tapped a four-digit number onto the keypad, and it clicked open. 'Welcome to Christian's game-room.'

They filed through the door one by one. The lights flicking on automatically as they entered. The eight stared on at ten large black chairs arranged in a circle. Each chair tilted back, enabling the occupant to sit comfortably. Near to each chair, a helmet which fitted over the head the way a motorcycle helmet does. A monitor, with leads connected to it, on the left-hand side of each chair. Against one wall a sophisticated-looking control panel.

'How do you like it?' Gainford said. The players turned in unison. 'Charlotte and Jack,' he said. 'As you've lost your original partners, we've decided to pair you two up. If that's ok?' Charlotte and Jack peered at each other, before nodding their approval.

'Ok, then,' he said. 'I'd like you to make your way along the corridor, one at a time. A doctor and nurse are there who'll carry out your medical. You'll be asked to sign a consent form. For legal purposes. The others can wait here. Have a sit on the seat or try on the helmet, while you wait your turn. Vanessa and Oliver will take you through the machine and answer any questions. When all of this is complete, I'll come along and get you started on the computer. It's not too late to drop out.' He laughed. The eight laughed too. 'Right then. I'll see you later.' And then he left.

The medicals took two hours to complete as Vanessa and Scorton explained how the machine operated. They had each chosen a visual image of their choice, to prompt them to leave the game, should the medical staff become worried by the vital signs of any of the players. This was precautionary only, they were informed, as few problems had been encountered in the trials. The medicals went well, with everyone deemed fit. After trying out the chairs and helmets, and when the last person returned from the medical, the eight sat in their seats waiting.

Christian Gainford entered, as the room fell silent. 'Are we ready, people?' The eight nodded. 'Ok,' he said. 'We'll begin.'

The players sat patiently as medical assistants buzzed around them. Meticulously connecting leads to keep a check on their vital signs. The monitoring machines sprang into life, and the console fired up. The players were handed their helmets and put them on, rendering them deaf to any noise in the room. As the last of the eight put their helmet in place, Gainford turned on his machine. In the blink of an eye it created total sensory deprivation as the distance between what's real, and what's unreal, vanished into nothingness.

## THE STORYTELLER

Memories are strange things. These precious gifts that open a doorway to our past. Each time we remember something, the memory is rebuilt from scratch. Over time, though, they change. Subtle errors from the previous remembrance infiltrate them until they barely resemble what happened. This isn't a problem, of course, as the vague outline of the memory remains.

Consider what would happen if a significant fault occurred. Profound damage, rendering the whole remembering process suspect. How can we be sure of anything? The pieces of the jigsaw scattered around and mixed with many other jigsaws. How strange, how perturbing it would become. How could you cope when robbed of the most fundamental capacity? When everything you have ever believed complete, turns out to be broken.

# BROKEN – CHAPTER ONE

Sandra Watson stood in the kitchen cooking a late breakfast of bacon, sausage and eggs. Thirty-eight, attractive and pregnant. Singing along to the radio when her husband of ten years, Steve, entered. He ambled across, and wrapping his arms around her, he kissed her on the cheek.

'How's, Mum, this morning?' Gently patting her large bump.

'Mum's fine. I'm hoping baby Watson makes an appearance sometime soon, though.'

'He'll come along when he's ready.' He sat at the table. 'You know us Watsons. Stubborn little buggers.'

'When's Jamie getting here?' Sandra said. 'I've made enough for the both of you.'

Steve glanced at the kitchen clock. 'He said half-ten. You know he's rarely on time.'

'I can't believe he agreed to go to a Deep Purple concert with you,' she said.

'I had to do some arm-twisting. Emotional blackmail. Jamie's a friend. It's what friends do. Well, that's what I said to him. Having said that, I had to agree to go to a Gary Numan concert.'

'My God, you were desperate not to go on your own. I wish I was going.' She placed a plate in front of him.

'So do I. Jamie's sure to moan. And I can't imagine cuddling up next to him in bed, either.'

There was a knock on the front door. Steve put the bottle of sauce he'd picked up, back on the table. 'Speak of the devil.' He got up to answer the door.

Steve returned, followed by Jamie.

Jamie grinned at Sandra. 'Morning, Sand,' he said. Planting a kiss on her cheek.

Sandra placed another plate on the table. 'I've done you some breakfast. Sit yourself down.'

'How's my godchild,' Jamie said. His mouth already half-full of sausage.

Sandra laughed. 'Who said we're going to ask you to be a godparent?'

'Yeah,' Steve said. 'Godparents are responsible.'

'I can be responsible.' A piece of bacon hung precariously from his fork. 'If anything happens, I'm usually responsible.'

'Mmm,' Sandra said. 'Let's wait and see, shall we.'

The pair finished their breakfasts. Steve, collecting his overnight bag from upstairs deposited it near the front door. He returned to the kitchen where Jamie and Sandra were saying their goodbyes.

Steve hugged and kissed his wife. 'Any movement on the baby front, ring me.'

'I will.' She kissed him back. 'Jamie,' she said. 'Look after him, will you. My baby needs a dad.'

The pair headed towards the door. 'I will, honey!' Jamie shouted back. And then they were gone.

They set off down the road as Steve rummaged in his holdall. 'Crap!' he said. 'I've forgotten my iPod.'

'Oh dear,' Jamie said. A huge grin filling his face. 'We'll have to listen to Radio Two.'

'Ah, wait. Steve triumphantly held a CD aloft. 'Machine Head. Deep Purple's Magnum Opus.'

Jamie sighed. 'Do we have to? You're watching them live tonight.'

'You have to get in the mood.' He smiled, as the opening bars of Highway Star blasted out.

They headed along a country lane, the two of them singing along to Smoke on the water, and rounded a bend. Jamie, engrossed in the music, failed to notice a man on a bike ahead of them. Steve spotting the cyclist, shouted at Jamie, just as the rider lost control and slid to the ground ahead of them.

'Christ!' Jamie said. He swerved to avoid the prostrate rider, narrowly missing him but only succeeding in skidding off the road. They careered through the undergrowth, Jamie trying desperately to wrestle back control as the car came to a sudden stop, crashing into a tree with a huge thud. The front of the vehicle lay crumpled in the now eerie silence, as steam drifted slowly from the mangled wreck.

# CHAPTER TWO

Steve sat up in bed, disorientated for a moment and unsure where he was. Slowly his senses returned him back to reality. Puffing out his cheeks, the realisation it had been a dream dawned on him. He rubbed his face, got out of bed and headed for the toilet when he heard a knock on the front door. Pulling on his jeans and t-shirt, he went to answer it.

Jamie stood outside, pushing past him as he headed inside. 'God, you look rough, mate.'

'Yeah. I feel rough too.'

'Any tea going?' Jamie said.

'Help yourself. I'm going for a shower.' Jamie marched into the kitchen.

Steve headed for the bathroom and blasted himself under the shower. He felt a little better. His thick head lifting somewhat. Taking out his toothbrush from the wall cupboard he applied a small amount of paste. He wiped the steamed-up mirror with his free hand, jumping back as he caught sight of his reflection. Blood ran down from a large gash on his cheek, his right eye, red and swollen. He appeared as if he'd been in some sort of accident. Stepping away from the mirror, he put his hand against the wall for support, allowing the nausea he felt to subside. Composing himself, he gingerly stepped in front of the mirror again. His face now unmarked. He lifted his hand and prodded his cheeks to confirm this. Closing his eyes and re-opening them, just to be sure. His face fine. Steve smiled to himself. Maybe he'd still been dreaming, but how could it have been a dream, though, he thought. He had just opened the door to Jamie. Steve shrugged. Satisfied he had imagined it all, he cleaned his teeth.

Jamie sat in the front room, munching on toast as Steve entered rubbing his chin, deep in thought.

'I made you a cuppa,' Jamie said. Not bothering to look away from the television.

Steve frowned. 'What a weird dream I had last night.'

'Oh, yeah?'

'Yeah. I was married to a woman, and she was pregnant.'

'Christ. Sounds like a nightmare to me. What was she like? This lady.' Feigning interest.

'Attractive. Long brunette hair. Nice figure, apart from the bump. I can't remember much else. It's starting to fade already.'

Jamie stood. 'That's dreams for you. Drink your tea, we have to get going.'

'Going? Where?'

'The Red Lion.' Jamie said. 'I'm meeting Timmo. He's got some gear for me.'

Steve rubbed his chin again. 'Yeah?' Downing his tea in one.

They headed away from the flat. Steve glanced across the road at a man sat opposite on a wall. Small, maybe five-feet-five, slightly built, wearing a tweed suit and matching waistcoat. His clothing, along with the round glasses, looking somewhat dated. In his early-sixties, Steve guessed, and he vaguely reminded him of someone. The man watched the two of them but got up and raced off when Steve met his stare.

'The dream I was telling you about.' Focussing back on Jamie.

'Oh, yeah.' Jamie fiddled with his phone. 'Timmo. I'm on my way. I'll be five minutes,' he said into it.

'It was so real.'

Jamie frowned at his friend. 'What was?'

'The dream. The one I had last night.'

'Steve, it's a dream. I have them all the time. Get over it.'

The two of them entered The Red Lion, Jamie disappeared into the corner to talk to someone as Steve headed for the bar. The man who had been watching them outside the flat entered after the two of them. Steve glanced in his direction as the man made his way into one of the corners, and sat behind a pillar. Steve ordered beer for Jamie and orange juice for himself. The hangover he was still suffering had put him off anything alcoholic for the moment. Jamie wandered across clutching a bag in his hand and sat next to his friend.

Steve sighed. 'What's in the bag?'

'Ralph Lauren polos.'

'Snide ones?' Steve said.

'Good copies, though. Should get £50 each. I can let you have one for forty. Mate's rates.' Jamie raised his eyebrows.

'Yeah, right. £40 for a fake. I haven't forgotten the after-shave you sold me last year. The one where the writing on the bottle rubbed off. I'll pass, mate.' He took a swig of orange.

Jamie took out his phone. 'Please yourself.'

Steve peered across at an attractive woman at the end of the bar. He hadn't noticed her when they came in. She was slim with blonde hair, cropped short. Wearing tight-fitting jeans, a purple T-shirt with – *Shady Lady* – emblazoned on the front. He pondered her face for a couple of seconds, trying to remember where he knew her from.

'J.' Nudging Jamie as it dawned on him. 'See the woman at the bar, the blonde one?'

'Blonde? Yeah, what about her?'

'That's the woman from my dream.'

'Give me a break,' Jamie said. 'You sound like a love-struck teenager. I thought you said the woman in your dream was a brunette.'

'You were listening then?'

'I always am.' Tapping the side of his head. 'Ears like a bat, me.'

'It goes with your head like a ball,' Steve said.

'Hilarious.' Continuing to fiddle with his phone.

'Seriously, though,' Steve said. 'Apart from the hair colour, she's identical.'

'Steve, mate.' Patting his friend on the shoulder. 'You've probably seen her in here before. Then dreamt of her. Psychologists will have a smart-arse theory about it.'

Steve rolled his eyes. 'I'm telling you.' Raising his voice, a little.

'Ok. Keep your hair on.' Jamie smiled.

'She's looking this way. I'm going to talk to her.'

'And say what? You're the girl of my dreams?' Jamie said. 'She's going to think it's the most pathetic chat-up line ever. Or worse, you're a nutter.'

Steve stood. 'Maybe. Maybe not.' He headed across.

'Hi, I'm Steve,' he said, as he reached her.

The woman, who had turned around to face the bar, swivelled back on her stool. 'Steve.' Taking a sip from her glass. 'I'm—'

'Sandra,' Steve said.

She laughed. 'Sandra. Only our mam called me Sandra. It's Sandi. Spelt with i.'

'Shady Lady, from Shady Lane.' Pointing at her T-shirt.

'Lying in my bed again,' Sandi said.

'Purple fan?'

'Maybe.' She swivelled back around to face the bar.

'Have we met before? Your face seems familiar.'

'I don't know. I've met lots of people. It goes with living.'

Steve glanced at Jamie who was shaking his head at him. 'Listen. I don't want you to think I'm a weirdo or something,' Steve said. He glanced again at Jamie, now making curly signs next to his head. 'And this isn't a chat-up line. But … you were in my dream last night.'

'Really. What did we get up to?'

'It's fading now,' he said. 'The only thing I remember is your face.'

'I don't think you're weird. But it does sound as if it's a ridiculous chat-up line. If I'm honest.' Smiling at him. 'It's so lame, it should be claiming incapacity benefit.'

The door to the pub opened, and three men entered. One of them strutted towards Steve and Sandi. Six-feet tall, muscular, with short-cropped hair. His face etched with a *don't fucking mess with me* look.

He grabbed Sandi's arm. 'Come on, we're going.'

Steve caught sight of himself and the man in the bar mirror. They were identical. Like twins. For a moment Steve stood nonplussed, and then looked back at the man.

'Ricky, this is—' Sandi said.

'I couldn't give a shit who he is.' Pulling Sandi from her stool.

'Heh!' Steve said. 'There's no need for any rough stuff. We're only talking.'

Ricky spun around to face him, looking Steve up and down before turning to walk away.

'Move, Sandi.' Pushing her towards the door.

Steve grabbed hold of Ricky's arm, 'Heh! Mr hard man.'

Ricky swung around, punching Steve full on the chin. Steve caught unawares, fell backwards banging his head on the floor.

'What did you do that for?' Sandi said. Pushing Ricky in the chest.

Jamie, along with a few other people, jumped up from his seat. The landlord leapt from behind the bar as the two men Ricky came in with, advanced towards them. As the customers jostled, Sandi bent down and pushed something into Steve's jeans pocket.

'I can help you,' she whispered in his ear, as Steve lost consciousness.

'Right, you three,' the landlord said. 'I'm calling the police if you're not out of here in ten seconds.' Ricky and the other two men left. Sandi dragged along by her boyfriend.

# CHAPTER THREE

Steve sat on the edge of a hospital bed, as a plump, attractive nurse applied a dressing to the back of his head.

'The stitches need to come out in a weeks' time,' she said. 'You may have a headache later.'

'I've got one now.' Gently touching his injury.

The nurse handed Steve a leaflet. 'If you experience any dizziness, nausea or blackouts, seek medical help.'

'Yeah. I know the drill,' Steve said.

Jamie appeared at the door. 'It's not the first bang on the head he's had, nurse. Why'd you think he's so mad?'

The nurse smiled at Jamie. 'I'll go and get you some tablets for your head.'

'Don't worry, nurse,' Jamie said. 'I'll look after him. I'm his guardian angel, me.' He watched her disappear out of sight.

'More of a saint,' Steve said. 'Sorry about the match. I bet we won as well.'

'Yeah.' Jamie sighed. '4-0.'

Steve touched the back of his head again. 'Sounds like we missed a good one there, mate.'

Jamie lowered his eyes. 'In future, Steve. Can you keep your dream girls to yourself? Especially on match days.'

Steve put his hand inside his jeans pocket, pulled out a piece of paper and opened it. It was a ticket for *Fireball*, a nightclub in the town. On the reverse was written, 19.30.

'What's that?' Jamie said.

'It's a ticket for Fireball.'

'That new nightclub in town?'

'Yeah. Shady Lady put it in my pocket.'

'Who?'

'The woman of my dreams.' Winking at his mate. 'Sandi with an i.'

'Not the one from the pub?' Jamie threw his hands up. 'Are you mental?'

'Yeah.' He put the ticket back in his pocket. 'We've already established that.'

'Listen,' Jamie said. 'I made a few enquiries while you were in the ambulance. Her boyfriend? The one who twatted you, remember? His name's Ricky Nelson.'

'Like the sixties singer?' Steve said.

'Who?'

'Ricky Nelson. An American singer in the sixties. Richie Blackmore nicked the riff from his hit, *summertime,* and used it on Deep Purple's Black Night. It reached number two in the charts. Black Night, not summertime.'

'What are you on about?' Jamie said.

'Forget it. What about this Ricky Nelson?'

'He's well known in Redcar.' Jamie said. 'A bit of a bad boy. He's into drugs, protection and God knows what else. He's also done time for GBH. A piece of advice, mate. Give Sandi, with an i, a wide berth.'

'The thing is, J, she slipped this ticket into my pocket for a reason. And before I passed out, she said something to me. She said, "*I can help you." Then it went black.'*

'I can help you?' Jamie said. 'What the hell does that mean?'

'I don't know. Aren't you a little bit intrigued, though? Don't you want to know how this pans out?'

'Steve. I already know how this pans out. Lots of trips to A&E. If you're lucky, that is.'

Steve jumped up from the bed. 'I'll be all right. I've got my guardian angel to look after me.' He patted Jamie on the cheek.

'You were the same as this at school. Wanting to take the bully on. It was always me who bailed you out. Now you're getting in deep with a gangster's moll.'

'Stop exaggerating,' Steve said. 'He's a small-town crook, not Al Capone.'

The nurse returned carrying two paracetamols in a plastic cup. Steve swallowed them down with water, thanked the nurse, and he and Jamie left.

Jamie shrugged. 'It's your funeral.' Jamie flagged down a taxi as they headed onto Marton Road.

'I'll keep it low key,' Steve said. 'I've got to go. You must admit she's a looker?'

Jamie rolled his eyes. 'What was wrong with the Australian bird you were banging?'

'She went home to Oz. And in any case, *she* never starred in any of my dreams.'

Jamie adopted a serious face, 'Look, don't do anything stupid. Be careful. For me.'

'For you.' Steve playfully punched his friend on his arm.

Jamie dropped Steve off at his flat and headed home. Steve fixed himself dinner. After eating, he set the alarm on his phone and went for a lie-down.

He woke from a deep sleep just after six-thirty. Showered, making sure to wash the dried blood from his head. After shaving and spending what seemed like an eternity trying on different outfits, Steve settled on dark jeans and a black shirt. Squirting on a little of his favourite aftershave, he pulled on his leather bomber jacket, and made himself a drink while waiting for the taxi. One drink turned into two, but he resisted the urge to have a third - not wanting to turn up drunk. Finally, the taxi arrived. Collecting his mobile phone and house keys, Steve headed out.

# CHAPTER FOUR

Steve arrived at Fireball just after seven-thirty. Handing his ticket to the doorman, he headed inside and ordered himself a Jack Daniels with coke. After checking around the nightclub, and satisfied Sandi wasn't there, he positioned himself at the end of the bar. With a good view of the door he would spot her as soon as she arrived, he thought. Two drinks later, Steve checked his watch for the umpteenth time. It was now quarter to nine. He was deciding whether to have another or go, as Sandi entered. He waved across to her, and she headed over. She looked gorgeous in a pair of tight-fitting trousers and a purple top. Having put on lots of mascara which beautifully framed her eyes. Her lipstick perfectly matching her top.

'Hi. Sorry, I'm late,' Sandi said.

'I'd about given up.' He turned towards the bar. 'Drink?'

Sandi edged nearer to him, her body pressed against his. She squeezed closer still, allowing people to pass by them.

'Vodka and lemonade,' she replied. The noise from the music making it difficult to hear each other.

Steve nodded and ordered her the drink. After being served, she took the glass from him, turned and moved away from the bar. Steve followed.

'I'm sorry I'm late,' she said, again. 'I had trouble getting away.'

Steve rubbed the back of his head. 'Your boyfriend's not with you, is he?'

'No.' she shouted. 'Sorry about today. Don't know what got into Ricky. He told me to go to The Lion and meet him there.'

'Glad he did,' Steve said.

Sandi smiled at him. 'Is your head ok? It was quite a thud.'

'Not too bad. A little sore.'

Sandi appeared deep in thought for a moment. Steve stared at her, captivated by her good looks.

She took a thoughtful sip of her drink. 'The thing is.' Glancing left and right. 'Ricky told me to wait at the bar, and someone would come and talk to me.' Moving her hand towards Steve's head she tenderly touched it, smiling at him.

'Who?' Emptying his glass.

'You!'

'Me?' Pointing at himself, momentarily thinking he may have misheard her. Sandi nodded.

Steve frowned. 'I've never met him before in my life.'

Sandi drained her glass too. 'At first, I thought he had a deal going down, and maybe you'd got in the way. As we left the pub ...' She paused, her eyes darting left and right, again. 'He said to Robbo, one of the men with him, you were *the one*.'

'The one?'

'They'd been watching us through the window. Ricky said he wanted to flush you out and size you up.' Glancing past Steve's shoulder.

'Really?'

'Should we move on,' she said. 'Too many eyes in this room.'

As she moved towards the door, Steve took hold of her arm and tugged on it. 'When you put the ticket in my pocket,' Steve said. Sandi turned to face him. 'You said,' he continued. *'I can help you.'*

'I imagine you misheard me. You had just cracked your head.'

Steve narrowed his eyes. 'Maybe.'

'Meet me out back in ten minutes,' Sandi said. Moving across the room, Steve watched her vanish and, waited.

He headed outside ten minutes later, making his way around the back of the club and down an alleyway. Slowly he edged away from the street-light and into the dark. He pondered for a moment. Maybe it was a set-up, as his imagination ran amok. He leant against a wall, trying to appear invisible, checking left and right. Spotting someone forty-metres away he backed into the shadows and waited.

'Steve,' Sandi whispered. 'Is that you?'

Steve edged away from the wall, into the light.

Sandi spotted him and strode forward. 'Sorry about that. I noticed one of Ricky's men in there. I don't think he saw me, though.' Reaching Steve, she hugged him while glancing up and down the alley.

'Where is Ricky?' Steve said.

'Out of town on business. Probably drugs. Look, I know this place in Darlington where we won't be disturbed. There's a decent band on tonight. They play lots of seventies rock. Pink Floyd, Led Zep, and they sometimes do Purple stuff. Fancy it?

'How do you know we won't be spotted there?

She laughed. 'You're kidding. 'Ricky's boys would never be seen dead in there. Darlington's off their patch.' She turned to walk away.

Steve clasped hold of her arm. 'Why me? I mean. Why are you interested in me?'

She turned to face him again, moonlight danced across her eyes. 'Ricky fears you. I sense it. I can't explain. Just a feeling I've got. And … you intrigue me.'

'He fears me. I intrigue you. I'm not sure I like that combination, I …'

She stopped him from speaking by placing a finger on his lips, before pressing her lips against his. He responded, as the passion in their kissing intensified. And as it did, the last trace of his protective carapace was shed.

The two of them emerged minutes later looking dishevelled. Buttons and zips were hastily re-fastened. Shirts and tops were hurriedly put back in their rightful place. Sandi grasped Steve's hand. Spotting a passing taxi, she flagged it down and jumped in.

'Episode Six,' Sandi said to the driver.

The driver glanced over his shoulder at them. 'In Darlo?'

'That's the one, mate,' Steve said. The pair sat back against the rear seat and sighed in unison. Steve squeezed Sandi's hand. She peered back at him, smiled, and any doubts Steve had regarding her, disappeared in an instant.

The twenty-minute journey took place in relative silence. Only punctuated by the driver and the passengers asking the usual inane questions. They drew up outside the club. Steve paid the driver and followed Sandi inside.

'How much?' Sandi said.

'For what?'

'The taxi!' shouted Sandi above the music as they entered a packed room.

Steve waived a dismissive hand. 'It's ok.'

Sandi pulled a £10 note from her pocket and offered it to Steve. 'If you don't take it,' she said. 'I'll jump back in another taxi and go home.'

Steve plucked the note from her and followed Sandi, snaking her way through the throng towards the bar. She waved to one of the barmen who acknowledged her. After serving a customer, he ambled along the counter and stopped in front of them.

'Hi, gorgeous,' he said. Eyeing Steve up and down. 'What'll it be?'

'Double JD and coke,' she said. 'And a double vodka and lemonade. Thanks, Dale.'

The barman gathered the drinks together and placed them in front of her. He waved her closer. 'Who's gorgeous?' Nodding at Steve.

Sandi glanced back and smiled. 'A friend. How much?'

Dale glanced along the bar at the other barmen, oblivious to him. 'Fiver.' Winking at her. Sandi handed him a note and blew him a kiss. Turning to face Steve, she gave him his drink.

He took a large swig from it. 'How did you know?' Sandi furrowed her brow. Steve held up his glass. 'The drink. How'd you know I drink JD and coke?'

'Just a good guess.' She slid towards the dance floor. The band playing *Woman from Tokyo.* 'My favourite Purple song,' Sandi said, pointing at the group.

'It's Sandra's ...' Steve stopped mid-sentence.

'What?' Sandi said.

Steve rubbed the back of his neck. 'Nothing.'

He followed Sandi around the room. Occasionally, she would stop to speak with people she knew. Introducing Steve, as her friend, to a seemingly endless number of strangers.

Glancing back at him and sensing his boredom she pulled him close. 'Shall we go?'

'Where?'

She smiled. 'Your place.' Kissing him on the lips, she took hold of his hand and led him out.

The taxi stopped outside Steve's flat. After paying the driver, they headed inside. Sandi grabbed Steve as soon as the door closed, kissing him passionately. They moved towards the bedroom in unison, removing items of clothing along the way. Naked, they fell onto the bed.

Steve came out of the bathroom, glancing at Sandi's still sleeping form. Climbing in beside her, he cuddled up as she responded to his touch. They made love gently. Unlike the night before. Exploring each other. Carefully navigating a maze of sensations, as they slowly and surely discovered what made each other tick sexually.

# CHAPTER FIVE

Steve woke with a jolt, his mobile on the drawer next to the bed blasting out Speed King. He grabbed at it, missing, as it vibrated its way off the edge. Desperately grasping for the phone, he lost his balance and toppled to the floor.

'I need to change that bloody ring tune,' he muttered. And answered it. 'Hello?'

'Morning,' Jamie said. his voice full of mischief.

'Hi, J.' Steve clambered to his feet and realising he was nude, searched for his boxers.

'What did you get up to last night? I wasn't sure whether to ring you or casualty.'

Steve yawned. 'Good one. What time's it?'

'Half-eleven,' Jamie said. 'Listen, I have a couple of errands to make this morning. I'll see you at our mam's house, two-ish. You can tell me about it then.'

'Your mam's?'

'Come on, Steve. Has the knock on the head befuddled you or something? Remember. Our mam invited us for Sunday lunch. Oh! Don't forget the flowers. You know how she loves flowers.'

'The flowers, yeah,' Steve said. 'I'll nip to the shop on the way.'


Steve, Jamie, along with Jamie's mam, dad, and sister, Anne, sat at the table. Having finished eating their lunch.

Steve sat back in his chair. 'Cracking dinner, June.'

'How's your mam?' June said.

'She's fine,' he said. Distracted by Anne playing footsie with him under the table.

'Still liking Spain?'

'Yeah. Loves it.' Steve said. 'Wouldn't come back if you paid her. Couldn't stand the British weather.' Surreptitiously moving Anne's foot from his groin.

June gathered the plates. 'She always liked the sun, your mam.'

Jamie's dad took out his pipe, popping it on the table. 'Is she still with that Spanish fella?'

June glared at her husband. 'George!'

'It's all right.' Steve laughed. 'She's happy with Carlos. It's five years now.'

'Good for her.' She glared at her husband again. 'Sunshine, and someone lovely to enjoy it with.'

Jamie's mother collected the dinner things and headed into the kitchen. Jamie's dad picked up his pipe and wandered into the garden.

'Can I help you with the washing up?' Steve said.

'No,' June said. 'You lads help yourself another drink. I'll do these.'

Anne winked at Steve. 'I'll help, Mam.' Standing, she wandered off, glancing over her shoulder at Steve as she did.

Jamie waited for everyone to leave the room. He peered over his shoulder as the kitchen door closed, turning his attention back to Steve. 'Well. Spill the beans.'

'On what?' Steve said.

'You met her last night, didn't you? Sandi.'

'Jamie, I'm smitten.'

'Steve Watson. The Teesside Don Juan, smitten?'

'There's something about her. I can't explain it. Something …'

'I'll tell you what it is, mate. It's the danger. Christ, Steve, do you know what you're doing here?'

'No. But I can't help how I feel.' He rubbed his face with his hands and blew out his cheeks. 'I haven't felt this way about anyone. I never believed all that bollocks about soul-mates. But I've fallen for her. Massively. I don't know how else to explain it.' He shrugged.

'Yeah, ok, mate. I get the picture,' Jamie said. 'So, what's the attraction with you then?'

'You mean apart from my good looks, washboard stomach, and sparkling wit?'

'And your big head.'

'I intrigue her, apparently.'

Jamie rolled his eyes. 'You intrigue her? What's this, a Jane Austen novel? What about what she said to you at the pub?'

'She said she couldn't remember saying anything. Claimed it was the bang on the head. I wasn't convinced, though.'

'Why? She's probably right.'

Steve leant forward and fixed Jamie with a stare. 'Sometimes, Jamie, you just know.'

Steve and Jamie left the house and strolled along the street. Steve noticed a man across from them. The same man who'd been outside Steve's flat, and in the pub, the day before.

He paused. 'Hold on a second.' And made his way over to the man. The man, strode away when he spotted Steve. Steve quickened his step and caught him up. 'Who the hell are you?' Grabbing hold of the man's arm.

He struggled to break free. 'Leave me alone. I don't know anything.'

Jamie caught them up. 'Steve, what are you doing?'

'He's been following me. Spying. Haven't you?' Shaking the man by the arm.

'Steve,' Jamie said. 'He's frightened. Let him go.'

He released the man, who raced along the street away from them.

Jamie took hold of Steve's arm. 'What was that about?'

He shrugged off Jamie's grip. 'I'm going home.'

'I thought we were going to The Lion?'

'I'm not in the mood.' Brushing past his friend, he marched off in the opposite direction to the one the man took. Jamie threw his hands in the air and watched as Steve disappeared from his view.

# CHAPTER SIX

Steve lay on the couch in his flat. Although the television was on, he was barely watching it. A headache dogged him despite the tablets taken earlier. His mobile rang and glancing at it on the floor, he saw a number he didn't recognise. He picked it up and answered. 'Hello?'

'Hi, Steve,' Sandi said.

'How did you get this number,' he said. Sitting up straight.

'From your mobile this morning.'

'Cute,' he said. 'How are you? You left without saying goodbye.'

'Sorry about that. I had to run. Can I come around?'

'Of course. How long are you going to be?'

'Not long.' She hung up.

Steve was busy storing Sandi's number on his phone as someone knocked on his front door. He opened it to a smiling Sandi. She held a bottle of wine and two glasses in her hands.

Steve beckoned her in. 'Glasses?'

'I always come prepared.' She sat on the sofa. 'I wasn't sure you'd have wine glasses. I didn't fancy drinking from a mug.'

Steve and Sandi lay in bed together, her head resting on his chest, He stroked her hair.

'Ricky returns tomorrow,' she said. 'We'll have to be discreet.'

'You still want to see me, then?'

'Of course,' she said. 'I told you I'm intrigued. That's if you want to see me?'

'For the moment,' he said. 'We'll see how you progress.'

She punched him playfully. He lifted her head with his hand and kissed her.

'What do you see in him?' he asked.

'It's a long story.'

'I love long stories.'

Sandi took a deep breath and began. 'I got into trouble when I was younger. Ricky got me out of it. He hasn't always been as he is now. He used to be a lot like you. Kinder, gentler.'

'From what I've heard, he's bad news.'

Sandi lowered her eyes. 'Yeah, he is now.'

'Leave him. Look, I have this mate who owns holiday cottages in Scotland. He's always bugging me to go up north and do some building work for him. We can stay at one of the cottages. Until we find something more permanent.'

She shifted in her seat. 'It's not that simple.'

Steve put a hand on her arm. 'In my experience, Sandi. Blokes like Ricky will take you down with them.'

'Ricky has stuff of mine.'

'Stuff? What stuff?'

'I sold some jewellery years ago. When I was desperate. Sentimental stuff which means a lot to me. Ricky got them back. He keeps them as insurance.'

'Insurance against what?'

'Let's just say, I know where the bodies are buried. Metaphorically.' Sandi glanced at her watch. 'I'm going to have to go.' She slipped out of bed, and Steve watched her dress. 'Will I see you again?' he said.

She kissed him. 'I'll ring.' And then she was gone.

Steve lay on his bed, his mind running through his encounter with Sandi. He had never felt like this about a woman before. He was besotted. He recognised as much. Excited and apprehensive about their nascent relationship, he closed his eyes and tried to conjure up her image. Someone knocked on his front door. Thinking Sandi had returned, he dressed and went to answer it. 'What did you forget?' He said, as he pulled open the door.

The small man, who Steve accosted earlier, stood there. 'Can I come in?' the man said.

'Yeah.' Pointing him in the direction of the living room.

The man walked in and stopped next to one of the armchairs.

'Sit down …' Steve said.

'Andy,' the man said.

'Sit down, Andy. I'm sorry about earlier—'

Andy sat. 'It's ok. No harm was done.'

'What can I do for you?'

Andy rubbed his chin and pondered for a moment. 'Steve, you're in danger. Ricky knows about you. Not your meetings with Sandi. He knows *about you*.'

'I'm not quite following this,' Steve said.

'You and Ricky.' He paused a moment as if searching for the right words. 'You and Ricky are the same person. Different sides of the same coin.'

'I don't know why you've been following me but ...' Steve put a hand to his temple as a sharp pain shot through his head.

'In the pub the other day, what did you see in the mirror?'

Steve closed his eyes as another lightening-strike of pain introduced itself. He reached out to the wall, the room now spinning.

Andy stood and edged closer. 'He hasn't quite put the pieces together. But he will.'

Steve fell to the floor convulsing. His body gripped by the seizure.

# CHAPTER SEVEN

Steve woke in a hospital bed and surveyed the room. His head ached, and as he put his hand up to it, a spasm of pain burst forth causing him to wince. The door opened and a nurse trod in, the same one who treated him at A&E the previous day.

'Morning, Steve,' she said. 'How are you feeling?'

He grimaced. 'A blinding headache.'

She handed him a beaker with two capsules inside and a cup of water. 'Take these. They'll help with that.'

'How did I get here?'

'The usual way people who bang their head and knock themselves out get to the hospital,' she said. 'In an ambulance. That'll teach you to drink too much.'

Steve glanced around the room. 'Is this A&E?'

'No. Head Trauma,' she said.

'Don't you work in A&E?'

'No. I've worked in this department for years. Never had a job in A&E. Far too hectic for my liking.'

'Well, you've got a doppelganger.'

The nurse opened the curtains and turned to face him. 'Sorry? Didn't catch that.'

'Nothing.' He winced again as another pain spasm introduced itself. Steve ruminated for a moment. He remembered being in his flat with Andy, and he was sure the nurse was the same one from the other day. Maybe the bump on the head had confused him a little. He tried to push the uneasy feeling aside.

The nurse pulled Steve forward, plumped the pillow and lowered him down. 'Breakfast?' she said.

'I'm not hungry.'

'Ok. Let me know if you change your mind.' She left the room. He closed his eyes and fell asleep.

Steve woke. Opening one eye, he saw Jamie sitting in the chair next to the bed reading. He sat up.

'Finally, he's woken up,' Jamie said.

He scanned the room, a deep frown on his face. 'Jamie. What's going on?'

'You'll have to give me a clue, mate.'

'What am I doing here?'

'Don't you remember?'

'I wouldn't be asking if I remembered, would I?' Steve said.

Jamie put aside his magazine. 'Ok, Mr Grumpy. We were in The Lion after the match.'

'The one we won 4 nil?' Steve said.

'4-0! You're having a laugh. One all, mate. I think I'll get a bang on the head if we can win 4 nil.'

'Where's my phone?'

'I don't know,' Jamie said.

Steve rubbed his chin, his eyes darting left and right. 'I need my phone.'

Jamie opened one of the bedside drawers and located it. 'Calm down. Here it is.' Handing it to Steve.

Steve searched through his contacts, and his recent calls. 'Her number's not here.'

'Whose number?' Jamie said.

'Sandi's.'

'Who's Sandi?'

'Jamie, stop pissing about, will you? Sandi from the pub. The woman from my dream.'

Jamie frowned. 'I don't know any Sandi.'

'Sandi! Her boyfriend, Ricky, punched me. Don't you remember? That's how I banged my head.'

Jamie held up his hands, laughing. 'Steve, calm down. You're freaking me out. Don't go on like this when the doctor does his round. He'll commit you. Haven't you seen One Flew over the Cuckoo's Nest? They're charging the batteries as we speak.'

Steve jumped out of bed and paced up and down. 'Something's wrong. I'm mixed up. Sandi … Ricky. And the little guy, Andy.' He stared at Jamie.

'Steve, look at me—' Jamie said.

Steve rubbed his face with his hands. 'The club, *Episode Six*. I've got to speak to her.'

'Who?'

'Sandi! Sandi!!'

Jamie grabbed hold of Steve and putting his head between his hands, looked into Steve's eyes. 'Steve, Steve. Look at me. It was a dream. A nightmare, that's all. We went out last night after the match. You got wasted and fell off the wall at The Lion. When you were messing about. You remember?'

Steve calmed a little, looking at Jamie. 'Just a dream.'

Jamie led him back to his bed. 'Yeah. Just a dream, mate.'

Jamie watched his friend as he fell asleep, before getting up and going outside.

Jamie entered the ward but was stopped by one of the nurses.

'The doctor's in with Steve now,' she said. 'He's assessing him, and shouldn't be too long.'

'Are they going to let him out?' Jamie said.

'Maybe. I did raise your concerns with the doctor, though. It depends on what he decides.'

Jamie nodded. 'Good.' The doctor came out of Steve's room, and Jamie stopped him. 'Is he all right, Doctor?' Steve listened from his bed, through the open door.

'He's ok. Slight concussion. We've done a scan, and there's nothing untoward. So, he can go home,' the doctor said.

Jamie frowned. 'Only, he seemed confused earlier.'

'Your friend was pulling your leg. He told me he'd been winding you up.'

Jamie knocked and entered. Steve, who was dressing, turned around as Jamie marched in.

'You had me worried, you dick-head!' Jamie said.

'You're so gullible.' He smiled, casting a sideways glance at Jamie.

Steve, snoozing on the sofa, opened an eye as his mobile rang. Sleepily scooping it from off the floor he studied the name on the screen. *Sandi's calling.*

'Hi,' Steve said.

'Sorry, I didn't ring earlier.' Sandi said. 'I've been thinking about what you said last night. About getting away from Ricky and, travelling up to Scotland.'

Steve sat up, planting his feet on the floor. 'Can you come over?'

'I'll try. Got to go.'

The phone went dead. Steve opened his contacts up and searched for 'S.' He could see Sandi's name, and below it, puzzlingly, Sandra. He thought for a moment, unsure who Sandra was. He paused with his finger above the call button and pressed. The phone rang several times before it switched to answer-phone.

'Hi. You've reached the mobile of Sandra Watson. Sorry, I can't take your call. Please leave a message after the tone.'

Steve dropped the phone, staring at it for a moment before standing and picking it back up. When he rechecked his contacts, there was only Sandi's number in there. He searched his recent calls and saw the last person he had dialled was Jamie. He sat on the sofa, deep in thought.

# CHAPTER EIGHT

Steve opened the door to Sandi, who entered and carried on through into the living room. She sat in the armchair as Steve followed her inside. He perched on a sofa opposite.

'Sandi,' Steve said. 'Can you remember what happened last night?'

Sandi frowned. 'Of course. I came over. We had wine, sex. Great sex, actually.' Smiling at Steve. 'Talked a while, and then I left. Why?'

Steve took hold of her hand. 'I'm having trouble remembering things. Well, remembering things accurately. I've got gaps. Blanks, you might call them.'

Sandi stood and then sat next to him. 'Could it be the bang on the head?' she said.

'I don't know.'

She stroked his arm. 'Maybe you should go to the hospital.'

He laughed. 'I've been there. Twice.'

'What's funny?'

'Nothing. Let's talk about Scotland.'

'Remember last night. I told you Ricky had things belonging to me?'

Steve nodded. 'Yeah.'

'I know where he keeps them. Inside a safe in one of his lock-ups.'

Steve stroked his chin. 'If we could recover them, would you come to Scotland with me?'

'Absolutely. I couldn't leave them. They belonged to my mam.'

'What's this safe look like?' he said.

'Why?'

'We'd need to get into the lock-up. But I need to know what the safe looks like.'

'It's a huge, old thing,' she said.

'Can you take a picture of it?'

'Maybe? I'll have to make an excuse to go there. But even so, wouldn't you need dynamite or something.'

Steve laughed. 'I think you've watched too many Hollywood movies.'

'But how would you get in? We'd need a key, wouldn't we?'

'I used to work on a building site, years ago, with a bloke called Albert Taylor. Albert was a safe-cracker in the sixties. He once told me, it was a doddle to break into some of the old safes. If this safe is one of those types, he may be able to help me get in.'

Sandi lowered her eyebrows. 'How?'

'He said he used to go in through the back of them. The manufacturers hadn't realised they had this weak-point.'

Sandi scoffed. 'Really?'

'Really. If you can get me into the lock-up, and it's one of those older types, I'll get in it.'

Her eyes widened. 'I'll get the alarm code. If I have an excuse to visit when Jimmy, one of Ricky's boys, is there. I'll distract him long enough to get a look. He has the hots for me, so it shouldn't be hard.'

'You'll have to ring me when you have the information. Give me plenty of notice. I might be washing my hair or something.' Steve laughed.

Sandi hugged him and put her mouth to his ear. 'What should we do now?'

'What we normally do. Have a drink, make love, and then lie in bed until you leave. I'll wake up as Jack Nicholson in the morning.'

'Jack Nicholson, the actor?'

'Yeah. Didn't you know? He's my alter ego.' He laughed again.

Steve ambled into the bar of The Lion, glanced around, and spotting Timmo headed across to him.

Timmo patted the seat next to him. 'Steve. Have a seat. How's the head of yours?'

'Sore, mate. Bloody sore.'

'It was some crack, mind. Some of the lads were sure you'd fractured your skull. We had a bet on it.' He laughed.

'Who won then?'

Timmo raised his eyebrows. 'Who'd you think. Get yourself a pint.' He handed Steve a tenner.

Steve went to the bar and ordered a pint. Indulging in small-talk with a couple of regulars. Returning, he sat next to Timmo.

Steve took a long drink of his pint and looked across at Timmo. 'I'm looking for some info. Do you know a bloke who used to come in here? Sparky Taylor?'

'The safecracker?' Timmo said.

'Yeah, that's him. Is he still around?'

'Don't know,' Timmo said. 'Haven't seen Sparky for years. He has to be dead, though. Hasn't he? I mean, if he's alive, he'd have to be eighty. Why? Have you got a safe you want him to open?' He laughed.

'No. I was thinking back to the old days. Thought I'd pay him a visit if he's still about.'

'Sorry. Can't help, mate,' Timmo said.

'No problem. It was a long shot.' Steve downed his pint and got up. He was heading for the door when one of the regulars shouted over to him.

'Steve!' Waving him over.

'Now then, Bill,' Steve said.

'Did you say you were looking for Sparky?'

Steve nodded. 'Yeah. Do you know where he lives?'

'He's in a home. The one on The Avenue.' Thinking for a moment. 'The Meadows.'

'Cheers,' Steve said. 'Has he still got his marbles?'

'Yeah. I was talking to David, his son, the other month. I asked about Sparky. He said he loves it in there. It's arthritis, I think. Couldn't use his hands much anymore. Found it hard to cope, you see. David said he's still as bright as a button.'

Steve popped a five-pound note on the bar next to him. 'Get yourself a pint. See you later, lads,' he said to the regulars, and headed off.

# CHAPTER NINE

Steve entered The Meadows Care Home carrying a bag and stopped at reception. A middle-aged woman in a blue uniform, talking on the telephone, smiled pleasantly. He waited for her to finish.

She hung up and turned her attention to him. 'Can I help you?'

'I'm looking for Albert Taylor. I believe he's a resident here? I was wondering if it's ok to see him.'

'Albert, yes. Are you family?' Moving from behind the desk.

'No. Just a friend. I used to work with him.'

The woman took hold of a book. 'Can I ask your name?'

'Steven Watson.'

The woman entered details inside a book and handed it to Steve. 'Would you sign here?' He signed the register.

The woman finished entering details. 'If you'd follow me. You say you worked with Albert?'

'Yeah,' Steve said. 'I was an apprentice brickie, and Albert took me under his wing. He taught me everything I know. Well, about bricklaying that is.'

'He's lovely, Albert. One of our most popular residents.'

Steve followed the woman through a series of corridors. Stopping at the door with, *ALBERT TAYLOR,* on a typed piece of card, on the front of it. The care assistant knocked and entered. Steve heard voices inside and waited until the door opened again.

'You can come in, Mr Watson,' the care assistant said.

Albert smiled at Steve as he entered. 'Well, well, well.'

'Now then, Sparky.' Shaking Albert's hand.

'Would you two like a drink?' She asked.

'Not for me, Nancy,' Albert said. 'I've just had one, and if I have another I'll be running to the toilet all night.'

'No thanks,' Steve said.'

'I'll leave you to it,' said the care assistant and left. Steve sat next to Albert.

'How are you, son?' Albert asked.

The two of them chatted through the afternoon, reminiscing about the old times on the building sites. Bringing to mind people from their past. The characters they worked with, and the good times they enjoyed. Albert looked pleased to have Steve visit. A change from the usual faces, and a definite improvement on day-time TV, Steve thought. He was enjoying it too, wondering why he hadn't visited before, Albert being someone he had fond memories of. He made a solemn promise to himself to visit again.

There was a tap on the door, and Nancy popped her head inside. 'Albert, it's tea-time soon.'

'Tea-time. Bloody hell, we've talked for hours. I'll be fifteen minutes,' he said.

She nodded. 'Ok.' And closed the door.

Steve consulted his watch. 'I'll have to go soon. Oh,' continued Steve. 'I almost forgot. I've brought you books and magazines. There are sweets in there too.' Handing him the carrier.

'Thanks, son.'

Steve hadn't mentioned the safe to Albert and didn't know how to broach the subject.

'It's been great seeing you, Steve, but it's not the reason you came. Is it?'

Steve smiled. 'What do you mean?'

'Wisdom comes with age, my boy.'

Steve sat back in his chair. Delving into his pocket, he pulled out a photograph and handed it to Albert.

Albert studied it for a moment or two before handing it back to Steve. 'It's a Wisdom and Stroud safe. Haven't seen one of those for years. Must've been the sixties,' he said.

'Do you remember telling me about your safe-cracking days?'

'I'm a bit long in the tooth for that malarkey now, though.' He laughed.

'I remember you said some were easy to break into.'

Albert folded his hands across his stomach. 'The manufacturers used to have a seam running along the back. The top, bottom, and sides were cast together. The front was put on later of course. But the back was added last, and this was the safe's weak point.'

'You could get in through the back?' Steve said.

'Yeah. People have this idea about safe-crackers. Imagining them sitting there for hours carefully opening the safe. In reality, it's nothing like that.' Albert laughed. 'The manufacturers expected the safe to be placed up against a wall and bolted to the floor. But people are lazy. Most put the safe against the wall and didn't bolt it down. I mean these things are bloody heavy objects.'

'What happened when they were bolted to the floor?' Steve said.

'It depended on the construction of the wall. Idiots put them up against a thin partition wall. We'd knock a hole through it if they had. If the safe was up against a solid wall, though, we'd call it a day. Too much hassle.'

Albert swigged orange juice from a beaker. He appeared to enjoy immensely talking about his safe-cracking days, as much as Steve enjoyed listening to them.

'You see, if it was against a wall, and bolted to the floor, there was only one way of moving it. You had to open the door and remove the screws. If you could open the door, though, you didn't need to go through the back. I call it the Safe Paradox.' Albert chuckled.

'So, if I wanted to get into the back of one of these things,' Steve said. 'How do I do it?'

'Well, I'm not encouraging you to break the law. What you'll need is a crowbar, hammer, chisels and maybe a Stihl saw.'

'A Stihl saw?'

'Yeah. In my days we used brute force to go through the wall. These days, all you need is a great bloody saw. Cut around the safe and get in through the back. The seam needs to be forced out with the chisels. I won't lie to you, it'll take some time.'

'The safe in the picture?' Steve said.

Albert glanced at it again. 'Piece of cake, Son.'

Steve stood. 'Cheers, Sparky.'

'Who is she?' Albert said.

'Who?'

'The femme fatale.'

Steve smiled. 'Femme fatale?'

'There's always a woman where safes are involved.' He winked at Steve. 'Just be careful.'

'I will. I will.' Steve shook his friend's hand and left. Once outside the care home he pulled out his mobile. Searching the contacts and stopping at Jamie's number, he rang. 'J. Where are you?'

'At work,' Jamie said. 'We're not all men of leisure, you know.'

'Non-stop, mate,' Steve said. 'Have you got my Stihl saw handy?'

'Stihl saw. Don't say you've found work?'

Steve laughed. 'No! I've got a safe to break into.'

'Of course you have.' Jamie sighed. 'It'll need a new blade, though. Have you considered dynamite?'

'Right out of dynamite. It'll have to be the saw.'

'It's at our Anne's.'

'Cheers. I'll pop around and get it. I'll give you a ring later.'

'Yeah. Good luck with that. And Steve,' he said, laughing. 'Keep your trousers on.'

'I'll see what I can do.'


Steve headed over to Anne's house in a van he'd borrowed from a mate. He parked outside, knocked at the door and waited.

The hall light came on, and Anne opened the door. 'Steve,' she said. 'Come in.'

Steve kissed her on the cheeks and entered. 'Where are the kids?' he said.

'At their dad's. What can I do for you, then?' Leaning against the wall, she pushed a hand through her hair.

'I've come for my Stihl saw. Jamie said you had it.'

'Under the stairs.' Pointing at the door. 'Jamie laid a patio for me months ago. He left it there and hasn't been back for it.'

'Great.' Steve dived into the under stairs cupboard. He rummaged around until he found what he was looking for. 'Eureka!' he said. Unceremoniously backing his way out of the tight opening. 'Cheers, Anne.' He winked at her and moved towards the door.

She put a hand on his arm. 'You don't have to rush off, do you?'

'I'm a bit pushed,' he said.

She slid closer to him. 'Not even time for a quickie?' And licked her lips.

'You don't do quickies. The last time was the thick end of six hours. I'll have to give you a rain-check.' Patting her on her bum. The smile on her face receding as Steve exited.

# CHAPTER TEN

Enjoying a glass of wine in Steve's flat, Sandi snuggled next to him on the sofa.

'So, you managed to obtain the number for the alarm?' Steve said.

'Piece of cake. I waited outside the lock-up until Jimmy arrived. He was shocked to see me there. I said I'd left my purse in Ricky's office.'

'And he believed you?'

'I think so. Jimmy was too busy looking at my tits. I'd put on a low-cut top to distract him while I memorised the code.' She handed Steve a piece of paper.

'What's the door like?' Steve said.

'Roller-shutter, and a standard door behind it.'

Sandi held two keys on a key-ring aloft. 'Got them cut today. Ricky has a spare set in the house.'

Steve smiled. 'What about the originals?'

'Back where I found them. Look, Steve. Are you sure you want to do this? I mean, it's a massive risk.'

Steve put down his glass and pulled Sandi towards him. 'You need to get away from Ricky. We'll grab your things, and head up to Scotland.'

They kissed, and Sandi straddled Steve who gently nuzzled the side of her neck. There was a knock on the door of his flat.

Steve sighed. 'Won't be a minute.' Heading off to answer it.

He opened the door as Jamie breezed past him. Going straight through into the living room. 'Get the kettle on, mate.' He sat in an armchair.

Steve, close behind him, pointed at the sofa. 'Jamie, this is Sandi.' When he peered at the couch, though, no one was there. He wandered into the kitchen, the bedroom, and the bathroom.

Jamie rolled his eyes. 'Not this Sandi again?'

Steve returned, rubbing his chin. 'She was here a minute ago.'

'You're taking the piss,' Jamie said.

'No, mate. I'm not.'

Jamie shook his head. 'Who are you dating now? An escape artist. No offence. Unless she shinned down the drainpipe or is hiding in the wardrobe, she's disappeared.'

Steve bit his bottom lip. 'I'll put the kettle on.'

'I wish you'd grow up,' Jamie said. 'We're not at school, you know.'

Steve went into the kitchen, returning with two mugs and some biscuits. They chatted for a while.

After finishing his drink, and most of the biscuits, Jamie got up to leave, giving his empty mug to Steve. 'I almost forgot.' Stopping at the threshold of the door. 'I'm away for a couple of days. Some shit training course. I won't be back until Thursday. I'll give you a ring then.'

Steve furrowed his brow and glanced across at where Sandi had sat. 'Yeah. No problem.

Jamie headed out. Steve listened as he left the flat, and slammed the door behind him.

'Who was it then?' Sandi said.

Steve spun around. Sandi was sat on the sofa where he'd left her. She was fiddling with her mobile and appeared as if she'd never moved.

'No one. Just some salesman,' Steve said.

Sandi put her phone into her handbag, stood, and sashayed across to him, throwing her arms around his waist. Steve could hear the opening bars to a Deep Purple song, *Loosen My Strings,* playing. He couldn't decipher if it was just in his head, or not. He took hold of Sandi and pushed all other thoughts aside.

Sandi smiled. 'I've got an hour.' And kissed him passionately. 'Now. Where were we?'

# CHAPTER ELEVEN

Steve pulled the van up 100 metres from Ricky's lock-up and waited until a car pulled up behind him. From his door mirror he saw Sandi get out and make her way towards the van, getting in beside him. Without saying a word, she kissed him on the lips. She smiled. Steve framing her face in his hands, kissed her back.

'Whose van is it?' she asked.

'I borrowed it from a mate of mine,' he said.

She nodded behind them. 'I lent the car from a friend. Jimmy would've recognised mine.'

'Are they still in there?'

She pointed at a black Audi. 'That's Robbo's car. They'll be going soon.'

'Well. We'll just have to wait.' He smiled at her.

A long ten minutes crawled past as Steve and Sandi, who hardly said a word to each other, waited. Hearing a noise from the lock-up, the pair of them ducked down in the van. They heard voices but were unable to decipher what was being said, the vehicle parked too far away. Steve peeked over the dashboard as they heard car doors shut. Watching as the Audi drove away.

He viewed Sandi. 'We'll give it ten minutes,'

Sandi smiled, grasping Steve's hand she squeezed it.

Having waited the ten minutes, Steve opened the driver's door and stepped out. 'What are you waiting for, Butch?' He winked at Sandi.

'I'm coming, Sundance.' Joining in his banter, she got out too.

Collecting the Stihl saw and a bag of tools from the back of the van, he walked off. Sandi followed him as they crept towards the lock-up. Dropping the things onto the floor, he took the keys Sandi held out for him, unlocked the roller shutter, and pushed it up. It noisily made its way to the top, stopping with a loud thud. Steve pushed the key in the lock and turned. Removing the alarm code from his pocket, he pushed open the door. The *beep, beep, beep* of the alarm sounded inside, as he located the keypad and entered the code. The beeping stopped and turning to face Sandi, they both let out the breath they'd been holding. Steve collected his tools. Pulling the roller shutter down, he closed and locked the inner door.

Sandi tapped his arm. 'In here.' Steve followed her into an office. She switched on the light and Steve stared at the safe. Moving towards it and putting his hands on the back, he pulled. The safe moved a little. 'We're in luck. It's not bolted to the floor.'

He sat on the floor with his legs either side of one of the corners to get a much firmer grip, and pulled at the safe. It moved about a foot. Sandi knelt next to him and grabbed the back as well, the two of them pulled again. The safe shifted a little more. Repeating the process several times, they managed to turn the safe around, finally stopping for breath, when the rear of it faced them.

'I think it'll do,' Steve said. 'Keep an eye on the door.'

Sandi nodded. Steve opened his tool bag and got underway. Using a hammer and large chisel, he began work on the seam at the back of the safe. Sandi looked on, her eyes darting between the door and Steve. Eventually, after what seemed like an eternity for Sandi, Steve managed to prise one of the corners away. He put on a pair of heavy-duty gloves and bent it down. Using a club hammer, he banged the corner until he'd managed to bend it down some more. He could now see inside. The hole, although large enough to place a hand in, was still too small to pull anything of any size out. Steve continued to assault the safe with the hammer, the seam moving half an inch or so with every blow. Confident he could get what was inside, out, he sat back, beads of sweat covering his face.

'I'm in,' he said to Sandi. Who quickly raced through to join him in the office.

Steve pulled everything from the safe. He placed a velvet roll, tied neatly in the middle, on the desk near to the safe and opened it. Inside, a pearl necklace gleamed. Next to this a second gold necklace, and a matching brooch.

Sandi ran her fingers across the jewellery. Smiling at Steve, she kissed him. 'I love you.' He returned her kiss.

Steve examined the other items. Several bundles of cash – neatly held together with elastic bands – and lots of paperwork together with two black ledgers.

'We'll take the money and the jewels. That way, Ricky will think it was a burglary.'

Sandi nodded as Steve rolled up the gems and along with the money, put them in his bag. He gathered his tools and put them in the bag too. Replacing the paperwork and ledgers in the safe, he got up and raced towards the door with a screwdriver in his hand. 'I thought I heard a car.' Stopping near to it.

Sandi glanced across at Steve, who was now listening intently. She deftly put her hand inside the safe and located the ledgers. Pulling them free she tossed them into the tool bag. Zipping it up she carried it towards the door and dropped it next to the Stihl saw. 'What's up?' she whispered.

Steve held his finger to his lips, muffled voices sounding from outside.

'You forgot to lock the shutter door,' Jimmy shouted to Robbo.

'Yeah, yeah,' he said.

The roller shutter door opened. Steve and Sandi stood against the wall, trying not to make a sound. They listened as the door was unlocked and Jimmy entered, closing the door behind him. Steve grabbed Jimmy around the throat with his left arm, pressing the screwdriver into his back with his right. 'So much as move, mate, and you're dead,' Steve said.

Jimmy glared at Sandi. 'What the fuck?' Glancing back towards Steve, and spotting he was holding a screwdriver rather than a knife, he shouted. 'Robbo! Get in here.' And lunged for Steve.

They grappled on the floor, Sandi looked on helplessly as they fought. The door flew open, and Robbo burst in carrying a baseball bat. He raised it high, and in one motion brought it crashing down on Steve's head. The thud sickening, as Steve slumped to the floor. Blood billowed out from his wound, creating a large red pool around it.

**GAME OVER! Flashed up on the screen as the chairs powered down.**

They grappled on the floor. Sandi picked up a fire-extinguisher and positioned herself behind the door. Steve managed to gain the upper hand on Jimmy, punching him forcefully as the door, flung open. Robbo entered carrying a baseball bat.

'Hit him!' Jimmy said. As Robbo raised the bat above his head, Sandi stepped from behind the door, bringing the fire-extinguisher crashing down on Robbo's skull with a loud thud. Robbo collapsed to the floor with a louder bang. Steve punched Jimmy again. As Jimmy's head rocked sideways from the blow, Steve caught him smack on the jaw with another. He slumped to the floor, unconscious. Steve stood, panting, a trickle of blood running down from a cut on his eyebrow. Moving swiftly, and rifling through the office drawers he located some duct-tape. He turned Jimmy over and secured his legs and arms with it. Standing, he glanced across at Sandi. She stood transfixed. The prone form of Robbo lying on the floor. A large pool of blood surrounded his head. Steve moved across to him and kneeling down, put two fingers on his neck. He bent closer, putting his ear to Robbo's mouth, looking for any sign of life. There was none. Standing, Steve observed Sandi who continued to stare at the body.

'He's dead,' Steve said.

'He'd have killed you.' She sobbed. 'I didn't mean for him to die.'

Steve held Sandi's face between his hands, forcing her to look directly at him. 'Sandi. Sandi, look at me. You had to do it. It was him or me. We need to get away from here.'

Picking up the tool bag he took Sandi by the arm, led her out, locked the door and pulled down the shutter. Taking her by the arm again, he pulled her towards their vehicles.

'Are you ok, Sandi? I need you to focus.' She stared back at him. 'I want you to drop this car off and jump in a taxi to my flat. Have you got that?' Tugging her arm.

'Yeah. Drop the car off, and meet you at your flat,' she repeated.

Steve hugged her. Sandi responded, hugging him back.

'I love you, Sandi,' he said. And kissed her.

'I love you, too,' she said.

Steve prised himself from her. The pair jumped into their respective vehicles and drove off.

Steve waited anxiously outside his flat. He was beginning to worry about Sandi. She seemed to have been a long time, he thought. Long enough to drop the car off at her friend's and grab a taxi. Maybe Ricky had caught up with her. He took out his mobile and located her name, about to call, when a taxi turned the corner. Ducking into the shadows, he waited for it to pull up. He watched as Sandi got out carrying a holdall.

'Sandi,' he shouted. She looked across and seeing Steve ran to him. They hugged. Steve grabbed her bag and took her by the hand, leading her over the road to the van. He tossed the bag in the back, next to his holdall and the tool bag.

'What have you done with the car?' he said.

'I parked it outside Sarah's, and put the keys through the letterbox.'

'Good girl.' He kissed her before starting the engine and speeding off. They reached the motorway and headed north. Driving quietly into the night.

Sandi finally broke the silence. 'What are we going to do?'

Steve blew out. 'Ricky will be on to us when he finds Jimmy.'

'He won't involve the police,' she said.

'How do you know?'

'He won't want them sticking their nose into his affairs,' she said. 'He's got too much to hide.'

'We'll head for my mate's cottages. I've phoned him, and he said he'd meet me there in the morning. We need to put distance between Ricky and us. Who was the dead guy?'

'One of Ricky's enforcers. A nasty piece of work. I'm not bothered he's dead. He had it coming. It's just …'

Steve put a hand on her arm. 'I know. Forget about it.'

'He won't find us, will he?' she said.

'The only person who knows where we'll be is my mate, Dave. He's the one who owns the cottages. I'll have a word with him tomorrow. In case anyone gets in touch. He's sound, though.'

'I'm sorry for dragging you into this,' she said.

'An out of work brickie? What else am I going to do on a weeknight?'

Ricky entered the kitchen of his house and poured himself a large whisky. Picking it up, he headed for the living room when his mobile rang. 'Yeah, Billy?' He listened to the person on the other end. 'When?' Taking a large gulp of his drink. 'I'll be twenty minutes.' Hanging up, he picked up a chair and launched it across the kitchen. 'Bitch!' he screamed.

Steve turned on the radio as Sandi snoozed. The DJ playing requests. 'The next request is for Steve Watson,' the DJ said. 'It's from his wife, Sandra. She writes, I Love you, Steve, get well soon.'

Steve glanced at the radio, frowning.

'This is Steve's favourite song,' the DJ said. '*When a Blind Man Cries, by Deep Purple.*'

He glanced across at Sandi who was fast asleep. Then back to the radio as the opening bars began, Steve mouthing the lyrics along with it, as they sped on into the night.

# CHAPTER TWELVE

Steve and Sandi travelled through the night, reaching their destination early morning. They drove across to the cottages Steve's mate, Dave, owned. Dave had left a note and a key to one of the properties under a plant pot outside. Making themselves at home, they unpacked and put away their stuff. Steve popped out to the van to collect his tools and deposited them in a cupboard under the stairs. He paused, remembering Sandi's mother's jewellery. Unzipping the bag, he pulled out the velvet roll and noticed the ledgers inside. He grabbed them, bounded up the stairs, and stormed into the bedroom. Sandi swung around as the door was forcibly pushed open.

'Why?' Holding the ledgers aloft. Sandi stared at Steve, speechless. 'He'll come after us. Don't you realise that? He'll never stop looking for us?'

'I'm sorry,' she said. 'It was a spur of the moment thing. I saw the ledgers and just took them. I thought we could give them to the police. Put Ricky behind bars, where he belongs.' Her eyes filled with tears.

Steve rubbed his chin. 'We should dump them. Get rid.'

'Yeah.' She nodded tearfully.

Steve pulled her into his arms. 'Don't worry.' Kissing the top of her head. 'I'm sorry I shouted.'

Steve lay in bed having tried in vain to sleep. Sandi slumbered next to him, her head resting on his chest, her shallow breathing the only noise in the room. Ricky wouldn't let this go, he realised as much. Men like Ricky didn't. He considered the options, his mind swimming with possible scenarios. Maybe he wouldn't find them. They were far enough away, of course, but he'd never be able to go back. Their exile was permanent. No one knew where he was, after all. Not even Jam e. If he contacted Jamie, though, it would put him at risk. He was his best and oldest friend. What would happen if Ricky found out about Jamie? Would he use him to locate where he was? But Jamie didn't know where they were staying. Steve closed his eyes to get to sleep, knowing only too well he was fighting a losing battle.

The days passed, Steve and Sandi settled into their new life. Thoughts of Teesside and Ricky faded from their minds. Steve began work on his friend's holiday cottages. Most only needing minor bits doing. A couple of them, the older ones, requiring much more extensive work. Sandi managed to get a part-time job at a local pub, the money coming in useful. They hadn't spent any of the money they'd stolen from Ricky. The wads of notes tucked out of sight under the stairs along with the ledgers, and their past.

The pair sat down to tea. Sandi placed Steve's favourite meal of steak and chips in front of him. 'Good day?' Sandi said.
'Yeah. Finished the last cottage on the lakeside. Some of the others still need quite a bit doing. I've told Dave we'll probably struggle to finish them for the new season.'
Steve's phone rang. He viewed it and stared at the name on the screen. It said, Anne.
He picked it up and answered. 'Hi.'
'Steve,' Ricky said. 'I believe you have something of mine?'
Steve glanced across at Sandi. 'Go on,' he said. Sandi placed a hand on his arm, and moved her head nearer to the phone.
'I'm not bothered about Sandi. You can keep the stupid bitch. She's tainted goods now. I do want my ledgers back, though.'
'Anne?' Steve said.
'She's fine. For now. If you want her to remain that way, I want the ledgers.'
'Listen, Ricky,' Steve said. 'I couldn't care less about your books. If you harm Anne, I'll come looking for you.'
'Don't you fucking threaten me, you piece of shit,' Ricky spat. 'I know you inside out, pal. Get me those ledgers, and you can have your friend back. Try any clever stuff, and I'll slit her throat myself. You got that, lover boy!' He screamed down the phone at Steve.
Steve, sensing he was dealing with someone unhinged, tried a different tack. 'Ok. Where?'
'Bring them here.'
'No. I want to meet somewhere neutral. Somewhere with lots of people.'
Ricky laughed. 'You're learning quickly. Do you have a place in mind?'

Steve gave Ricky directions for a motorway service station he and Sandi stopped at on the way up. Roughly equidistant from the caravan park and Teesside, and teeming with people when they were there. They arranged to meet at eight o'clock at night. Ricky, satisfied with the agreement, hung up.

Sandi took hold of his hand. 'Steve,' she said. 'I'm so sorry for involving you in this.'

'It was my choice.' Taking hold of her. 'My choice,' he repeated. Taking her face in his hands, he kissed her.'

Steve called Jamie.

'Now then,' Jamie said. 'Where have you been hiding?'

'Working away. A mate of mine has some cottages I'm renovating.'

'Bloody hell. You're earning money?'

'Yeah,' Steve said. Proper folding stuff. How's the family?'

'Fine. Oh, before I forget. A guy was asking after you in The Lion. He looked dodgy by all accounts. Don't worry. None of the lads said anything. It's probably some irate husband.'

'Yeah, probably. Have you seen your Anne?

'Our Anne? No. Why?'

'It's just when I collected the Stihl saw the other week, she said she knows a friend who has some building work for me. That's all.'

'Do you want me to give her a ring?'

'No,' Steve said. 'I'll give her a call myself.'

'When are you home, then?'

'Not sure,' Steve said. 'A couple of weeks, probably.'

'Oh, well. The beers are on you, now you're earning.'

'Absolutely,' Steve said. 'I'll phone next week.'

'Yeah, you do that. I'm missing my drinking buddy.'

Steve and Jamie hung up. Steve put his phone back into his pocket and slipped his jacket on. He headed into the front room where Sandi sat. 'I'm going,' he said.

Sandi stood and moved across to him. 'You'll be all right?' Tears filled her eyes.

'I'll be ok.' Placing his hand on her cheek, he kissed her and left.

Steve arrived at the service station early. Waiting impatiently in a second-hand car he'd bought. He had given a false name to the person he'd purchased it from. Reasoning, Ricky may see the licence number and try to trace him and Sandi. The idea was to dump the car later. It had only cost £500, and he'd used some of the stolen money to pay for it. An irony he'd enjoyed. Sandi told him Ricky drove a Mercedes. But knowing Ricky, he'd come in a vehicle not linked to him. His phone sounded in his pocket, and Steve swiftly retrieved it.

'Lover-boy.' Ricky said. 'It's your date.'

'Where are you?' Steve said.

'If you look to your right, you'll see a blue van. Come over. I'm waiting.'

Steve drove across, stopping fifty metres from the van. Picking up the ledgers he got out. Ricky jumped out of the vehicle along with another thick-set guy, one of his heavies, Steve supposed. The heavy plodded around the back of the van and opened it. He climbed in and exited shortly afterwards with Anne. Ricky grabbed hold of her arm and wandered towards Steve. Steve closing the gap between them as well. They stopped two metres from each other.

Ricky unable to disguise the hatred he felt for Steve, scowled at him. 'The ledgers.' Ricky said. Holding out his free hand, his other still clamped on Anne's arm. Steve held them out to him, and in one motion Ricky grabbed them and pushed Anne towards Steve. 'If you ever set foot on Teesside again,' he spat at Steve. 'You and that whore of yours are dead.'

Steve ignored the remark and backed away a short distance. He turned and strode with Anne to the car, glancing back now and then, his eyes darting about. Opening the passenger door for Anne to get in, he raced around to the driver's side. His eyes hardly leaving Ricky who stood there defiantly glaring at him. Steve jumped in. But as he started the engine up, he felt the cold steel of the gun pressed against his neck.

'Turn the motor off and get out,' the man said to Steve and Anne.

Steve, Sandi and Anne, hands trussed, bounced on the floor of the van as it trundled across the uneven terrain. Steve refused to tell Ricky where Sandi was. But after searching him, he'd discovered a card from his friend's holiday site. They'd headed over there and quickly located Sandi, bundling her into the back of the van, along with Steve and Anne. After travelling for what seemed a long time, the vehicle finally came to a halt. They heard the doors to the front open, and footsteps along the side, before the van rear door opened.

**GAME OVER! Flashed up on the screen as the chairs powered down.**

Steve drove across, stopping fifty metres from the van. He picked up the ledgers and got out. Ricky jumped out of the front of the van along with another thick-set guy, one of his heavies, Steve supposed. The heavy plodded around the back of the vehicle and opened it. He climbed inside and exited shortly afterwards with Anne. Ricky grabbed hold of her arm and wandered towards Steve. Steve closing the gap between them as well. They stopped two metres from each other.

Ricky hardly able to disguise the hatred he felt for Steve, scowled at him. 'The ledgers.' Holding out his free hand, his other still clamped on Anne's arm. Steve held them out to him. In one motion Ricky grabbed them and pushed Anne towards Steve.

'If you ever set foot on Teesside again,' he spat at Steve. 'You and that whore of yours are dead.'

Steve ignored the remark and backed away a short distance. He turned and strode with Anne to the car, glancing back now and then, his eyes darting around. About to get in, when the squeal of car tyres grabbed his attention. His van screeched to a halt next to him and Anne.

The passenger door opened, and Steve spotted Sandi inside. 'It's a trap!' she screamed. 'Get in.'

Steve and Anne squeezed into the passenger side, and Sandi sped off. She'd taken Ricky by surprise. The vehicle accelerated rapidly, and she was out of the car park and onto the motorway slip-road in seconds. Causing vehicles to skid and swerve to avoid them. Pressing the accelerator down hard, they carried on into the night. Ricky and his men trying desperately to manoeuvre around the carnage they'd left.

# CHAPTER THIRTEEN

Steve, Sandi, and Anne continued along the motorway, sure Ricky hadn't followed them. Steve dropped Sandi and Anne at the cottage before heading back to the entrance of the holiday park. He decided to wait there and keep an eye out for anything suspicious. Sandi returned shortly afterwards with a sleeping bag and a flask of soup. Parking his van out of sight, off the road, he settled down for a long night. Ready to call Sandi and alert her and Anne should anything happen. Sandi returned to the cottage while Steve sipped his drink. He put the radio on low and reclined in his seat. As he closed his eyes, a faint song drifted into earshot, one he recognised instantly. The dulcet tones of his favourite singer nudging him gently towards sleep.

Unsure how long he'd slept, he woke to the sound of his phone. It was Anne's number. Reluctantly he answered it.

'You got away tonight, Steve,' Ricky said. 'But we do have some further business.'

'Why don't you get on with the rest of your life, and leave us alone? You've got the ledgers.'

'Do you remember Andy?'

'Who?' Steve said.

'You know who I'm talking about. I have Andy here, on Teesside. He has an interesting theory. He didn't want to tell me, of course, but I managed to persuade him.'

'It's no business of mine,' Steve said.

'I think we both know it is. I'll be waiting when you're ready. You know where I live. Don't wait too long, though. I may become bored with him. See you soon.' Ricky hung up.

Steve, now sure Ricky wasn't in Scotland, trudged back to the cottage.

Steve sat at the table in the kitchen of the house, nursing a cup of tea, deep in thought as Sandi entered.

She ambled across to him and kissed him on the cheek. 'Penny for them?' she said.

'I was thinking about Anne. I'll have to take her to Middlesbrough.' He put down his cup.

Sandi frowned. 'I don't want to stay here on my own.'

'I'd rather you did,' he said. 'Ricky will be waiting for you to show up there. When I spoke to him last night, I got the impression he's never going to stop looking for us.'

Sandi sat. 'What if he turned up here? While you were away? Have you considered that?'

Steve hadn't. Maybe Ricky was waiting for an opportunity of separating him and Sandi. He was reluctant to make it any easier for him to get Sandi. The thought of losing her while he was away, wasn't worth contemplating.

'Why can't we stay here? He doesn't know where we are.' She took hold of his hands and gazed into his eyes.

Steve met her stare. 'He won't let us live in peace. He kidnapped Anne. What's to stop him taking someone else?'

She shook his hands. 'What do you intend to do, Steve?'

Steve's eyes dropped down. 'I'm going to kill him,' he said. So matter-of-factly it took her by surprise.

'Kill him?' she said.

'He's got Andy.'

'Who's Andy?'

'I don't know, but he's the key.'

Sandi frowned again. 'The key to what?'

'I don't know that either.'

'Steve you're freaking me out,' she said.

'I have to make sure Jamie's ok, too. What if Ricky hurts him?'

'Who's Jamie?'

'Jamie's my best mate. I can't let anything happen to him. I'd never forgive myself.' Tears gathered in his eyes. Steve stood and left, slamming the door behind him. Sandi got up to follow him but Anne, who'd been standing outside the kitchen, grabbed her by the arm.

'Let him go, Sandi,' she said.

'But I don't understand. What's Steve going on about?' Turning to face Anne.

'Sit down,' Anne said. 'I can help a little.' Sandi sat at the table.

Anne sat opposite her. 'Jamie was my brother. He and Steve were inseparable since school.'

'Was?' Sandi said.

'Jamie's dead.'

'But Steve was talking as if he's alive.'

'Jamie crashed Steve's motorbike,' Anne said. 'He was travelling to Helmsley and lost control. The inquest said one of the contributing factors of him crashing was the state of the tyres on the bike. In truth, Jamie was going too fast. Steve blamed himself, and it took him ages to recover from his loss.'

'But why is he talking as if he's still alive?'

'He did after the accident. For a while.'

'When did Jamie die?' Sandi said.

Anne lowered her eyes. 'Five years ago.'

'I'm sorry.'

'I heard what he was saying about going back,' Anne said. 'I'm sorry. I didn't mean to eavesdrop.'

'Did you hear what he intends to do to Ricky?'

'Yeah. Steve's exaggerating, though. Steve couldn't murder anyone.'

'The other guy he mentioned.' Sandi said. 'Andy. Who's he?'

Anne shook her head. 'Can't help you there.'

Steve wandered over to the far side of the holiday park and took out his mobile.

'Steve,' Jamie said. 'When are you coming home, mate? I'm missing my drinking buddy.'

'I could have news on that front. I'm home this weekend for a couple of days.'

'Great. What's it like up there? Met any wee Scottish lassies,' he said, in a mock accent.

'Too busy working, mate. I'll give you a ring when I'm back.'

'Great stuff,' Jamie said.

Steve thought for a moment. He couldn't remember telling Jamie he was in Scotland. But he knew, somehow. Steve shrugged and carried on with his work.

Sandi and Steve hadn't seen much of each other throughout the day. Steve, who'd been working on one of the cottages, saw Sandi briefly when she'd brought him a flask and sandwiches for his lunch. She hadn't mentioned the morning conversation or any of what Anne told her. After finishing for the day, Steve headed back to the cottage and found Anne and Sandi preparing a meal for the three of them. After showering and changing, he joined them in the kitchen. The three of them chatted pleasantly about any subject except the events of the previous night. After enjoying the Spaghetti Bolognese, and finishing the second bottle of red wine, the three of them retired to bed.

Sandi snuggled next to Steve. 'I've been giving it some thought,' he said. 'It's best if you come with Anne and me.'

Sandi kissed him. 'When?'

'Tomorrow.' Responding to her kiss. They embraced each other, and as their passion mounted the rest of the world ceased to exist.

The three of them headed to Teesside early. They travelled to Anne's house first, allowing her to collect some clothing. Her kids were away on holiday with their dad, and she had decided to meet up with them. Her ex-husband had invited her along, but Anne had initially declined. The two of them still got on well, despite their split. Anne confided to Steve and Sandi that she felt uncomfortable going on a family holiday, but recent events had forced her hand. She had phoned her ex and belatedly accepted his invitation. Sandi and Steve had avoided talking about Ricky, waiting until Anne was safely on her way. They travelled a little distance up the A1 behind Anne, who was driving Steve's car, primarily to make sure nobody followed Anne. Satisfied no one had, they pulled off the motorway for something to eat and drink. Sandi waited at a table as Steve queued for their meal. After being served he joined Sandi, popping a sandwich and drink in front of her.

'What are you going to do?' Sandi said.

'Ricky's got Andy. I have to free him.'

'Who's this Andy?'

'I don't know,' Steve said. 'Andy came to see me at my flat. He'd been hanging around for a while. He said Ricky and I are the same person.'

'The same person?' she said.

'I know it sounds stupid, but there's something about him that rings true. His face is familiar. I can't place it. It's as if it's inside here.' He tapped his head. 'But it's just out of reach. The more I concentrate on him, the further away it seems.'

Sandi placed a hand on Steve's. 'What if this is a trap Ricky's setting?'

'I don't believe it is. It's hard to explain. I have this feeling Ricky and I are in some way connected, and it's inevitable we'll meet again.'

'What are you planning?' Sandi said.

'I need to go to my flat first.'

'Why?'

'I need some things,' he said. 'That's all.'

She squeezed his hand. 'He could be watching.'

'I know. I'll wait until night and try and sneak in under cover of darkness.' Squeezing her hand back.

'What about me?' she said.

'Is there anywhere you could go? I'll pick you up later.'

'I could stay with a friend,' Sandi said. 'Ricky doesn't know about her. I'll be safe there.'

'Good. We'll finish these and head to Middlesbrough. I'll drop you off first and head to my flat. We'll stay in contact, just in case anything happens.'

'What about Anne?' she said.

'She's going to phone me when she's with her ex.'

Sandi stared into his eyes. 'I love you, Steve.'

'I love you too,' he said.

# CHAPTER FOURTEEN

Steve dropped Sandi off at her friend's flat before travelling to his own. He'd been careful to park the van a short distance from his home, and wearing a parka with the hood up for disguise, he walked along his street on the opposite side of the road to his flat. Surreptitiously he scanned the parked vehicles, looking for any which seemed out of place. After walking the length of the street, he turned at the end of the road and travelled around the block returning to where he had begun. Satisfied there was nothing suspicious, he headed along the road to his flat. Stopping at the door, he glanced around one final time and entered. Steve climbed the stairs, paused outside the door, and checked for damage. Assured there wasn't any, he went inside.

Steve sat at the dining table, hundreds of photos scattered in front of him. He casually flicked through them, pausing now and again to look at one.

'What are you doing?' Jamie said.

Steve glanced up. 'How did you get in?'

'Your spare key. Don't you remember? You gave it to me last year when you were away working.'

'Oh, yeah. I'd forgotten that.'

Jamie sat down. 'So, what's with the snaps?'

'I'm looking for a photo.' Resuming his search.

'Of what?' Jamie said.

'My dad.'

'Your dad? Why are you looking for photos of him? You've not seen him for years.'

'Do you remember Andy?' Jamie shrugged. 'The little fella I had words with outside the flat the other day?'

Jamie shook his head. 'Don't remember any bloke, Steve. Are you sure it was me?'

'Come off it. Can't you remember? The guy spying on me? The one I grabbed?'

'News to me, mate. Listen, I'll make us a cuppa. Life always seems clearer with a mug of tea in front of you.'

'Yeah.' Steve grimaced and put his hand to his forehead.

'You ok?' Jamie said. 'You look tired.'

'Bit of a headache.'

'Have you any tablets?' Jamie said.

Steve nodded over Jamie's shoulder. 'In one of the drawers.' Jamie wandered towards the kitchen. 'I was thinking about Anne the other day,' Steve said.

Jamie stopped at the threshold of the kitchen and turned. 'It was four years last week.'

Steve gazed down. 'I know. I didn't forget. I always visit the cemetery. With me being away, I …'

'It's ok, mate. I went with Mam, Dad, and the kids. We put some flowers on her grave. I'm sure she'd forgive you. She always had a soft spot for Stevie-boy.'

Steve lifted his head, his eyes glistening. 'Do you think it gets any easier… As you grow older? Losing the people you love, I mean?'

Jamie smiled. 'The loss of someone never does. You'd think something inevitable would, but it's like losing an arm or a leg. You've always got this constant reminder. What was once there, isn't anymore. Time offers no barrier either. It only takes a memory to pull the wall down.'

Steve smiled. 'That's quite poetic.'

'I heard it on Radio Four yesterday.' He laughed and went to make the tea. Steve diligently resumed his search.

Steve and Jamie sat at the table searching through the old photos. Steve pushed pictures of himself and Jamie, when they were kids, towards his friend. The two of them laughed at long forgotten dress styles and haircuts. He emptied the last box onto the table and searched through its contents. Stopping, pushing aside a couple of holiday snaps. Picking up a small, faded, slightly crumpled photo, Steve stared at the image of a man dressed in a dated tweed jacket. He frowned studying it carefully.

'Is that him?' Jamie said.

'That's him,' Steve said. 'That's my dad.'

Jamie took the photo from him and stared at Steve, and then the picture. 'I see the resemblance. It's the big nose.'

'I haven't got a big nose.' Wiggling his nose with his fingers.

'I'm only kidding,' laughed Jamie. 'You're gorgeous.'

Steve plucked the snap from Jamie. 'We do look alike. I remember, as a kid, looking at this photo and some of the others. Thinking we looked nothing alike, but now I'm older …'

'You never saw him, did you?'

'No. Dad left when I was two. I used to get birthday cards, and Christmas presents for a few years, but then they stopped.'

'Have you ever thought of looking for him?' Taking the photo from Steve.

'He died. Mam told me. I was eighteen or nineteen at the time. It wasn't that important to me. I remember Mam having tears in her eyes when she told me. How can you get upset about someone who walked out on you nearly twenty years earlier?'

'Maybe she didn't get over him?' Jamie said.

'Maybe. We'll never know, now. The main players in that drama are long dead.' He rose from his seat and gathered the mugs. 'How about something stronger?' he said.

'Now you're talking my language,' Jamie said. 'What was your dad's name?'

Steve headed towards the kitchen, pausing at the door. 'Andrew,' he said.

Steve woke in bed. He couldn't remember how he got there, or even what day it was. There had been someone in bed with him. He knew by the indentation next to him. He put his hand on the sheet, and feeling the mattress realised it was still warm. There was a noise from the bathroom as he heard the toilet flush. A nude Sandi came out and slid under the covers next to him. She snuggled close, wrapping her arms around his shoulders, her bright eyes staring down at Steve.

'Heh, Mr Serious Face,' she said.

'Sorry. I nodded off.'

'Well, before you nod off again, you've got some unfinished business, fella.' She kissed him passionately. Steve responded and returned her kiss.

Unable to sleep after he and Sandi had made love. He stared across at her, the steady rise and fall of her chest indicating she was asleep. He slipped out of bed, pulled on his boxers and jogging bottoms, then headed for the sitting-room. Pouring himself a large Jack Daniels, he sat in an armchair. He put on his headphones and pressed start on his iPod. The music resuming where he'd last left it.

Steve woke from his sleep as his phone vibrated on the table next to him. Although he didn't recognise the number, he sleepily answered it. 'Hello.'

'Steve. How are we?' said Ricky's unwelcome voice.

'Fine,' Steve said.

'Back on Teesside, I see.' He sneered. 'Thought you'd have paid me a visit.'

'Been busy. You know how it is.'

Ricky laughed. 'I've still got our mutual friend with me, although, he's beginning to get on my nerves a bit. I may have some of the boys introduce him to a heavy weight and a deep lake.'

'Is there a point to this, Ricky? You've got your stuff back. Why don't you leave us alone?'

'We both know it isn't about the ledgers and money. It's about *you and me.*'

'Well, I'm not dancing to your tune. You can fuck off.'

'Whoa! Tiger.' Ricky laughed again. 'Let me focus your mind a little. I've got someone else here too.' His voice hardening as he said the words. Steve listened as Ricky passed the phone across to someone.

'Steve. It's Sandi,' she said through tears. Ricky grabbed the mobile from her hand. Steve sprung from his seat and raced to the bedroom. The bed lay empty, and not only that, just one side of it, his side, had been slept in.

'Still there, lover boy?' Ricky said.

'If you harm her—'

'Don't you threaten me, you piece of shit,' Ricky said. 'If you want to see your little slag again, I'd get my arse across here. The clock's ticking. Tick tock.' He sneered and rang off.

# CHAPTER FIFTEEN

Steve dressed and grabbed his coat. Stuffing his car and house keys inside his pocket he galloped from his flat, Jumping into his van. The vehicle screeching as he sped off. He fumbled for the ringing phone sounding in his pocket, but it slipped from his grasp and fell into the foot-well. Skidding to a halt at a bus-stop he retrieved the phone from the floor and glanced at the name on the screen. It was Sandi's. 'Hello?' Expecting to hear Ricky's voice on the other end.

'Where the hell have you been?' Sandi said.

'Sandi. I thought …'

'I've called you loads of times. I was going to come around to your flat. I've been so worried.'

Steve, momentarily nonplussed, raised a hand to his head which had begun to throb. His vision blurred as he struggled to focus on anything. 'Where are you?' he said.

'I'm at my friend, Sam's. Where you dropped me off. Are you all right, Steve?' Her voice thick with concern.

'Yeah. A bit of a headache. I'm on my way now. Don't go anywhere.'

'I won't,' she said. 'How long will you be?'

'Ten minutes.'

Steve's vision gradually came back into focus. He viewed the display of his mobile. There were missed calls and messages. All of them from Sandi. He picked up his voicemail. There were three. The first two, from Sandi, asking where he was. The second one more frantic than the first. He pressed delete after each one, and listened to the third and final message play out.

'Steve it's Sandra,' the voice said. 'Can you hear me? Please don't leave. This baby needs a dad. I love you so much. Please come back to me.'

Steve stared at the mobile, struggling to understand what he'd heard. He pressed a button to replay his messages again. An automated voice informed him there were no more messages. He checked his missed calls once more. Only Sandi had phoned. He thought, deeply. Ricky told him Sandi was with him. Could he have been lying? But he'd heard Sandi's voice on the other end. Steve was sure of it. Sandi had been at the flat, as well. He was sure of that. But when Ricky called, there'd been no trace of her. Where was Jamie, too? He couldn't remember him leaving. It was as if the pieces of his life had smashed and been put back together wrong. Steve rubbed his face with his hands, started the engine, and headed off.

As Steve turned into the street, he could see Sandi standing outside her friend's flat. He pulled up on the opposite side of the road to her and turned off the engine. Sandi headed across to him as a black BMW picked up the pace and sped along the road. Sandi turned as she heard the approaching vehicle, but could do nothing as it piled into her. Catapulting her over the bonnet and roof of the car, her body landed with a sickening thud on the tarmac.

**GAME OVER! Flashed on the screen, as the helmets and seats powered down.**

Steve turned the corner of the street. He pulled up outside the flat on the same side of the road. Sandi stood at the threshold of the door and made her way towards him as he exited the vehicle. They hugged, kissed, and headed inside.

Steve parked up the road from Ricky's house, the massive building encircled by a high brick wall. Steve thought for a moment. He couldn't remember reaching Ricky's, and struggled to remember the last few hours as well. He closed his eyes and tried to recollect where he'd been earlier in the day, but couldn't, the memories remaining stubbornly out of reach. Picking up his mobile, he rang Jamie.

'Now then, buddy,' Jamie said. 'Are you back in town?'

'Yeah.' Not knowing what else to say. 'Jamie, I think I'm going crazy.'

'You're not going crazy, mate,' Jamie said. 'You've always been crazy.'

'I'm serious. I can't remember stuff. I keep forgetting bits and pieces. It's as if my memories have been jumbled up.'

'I'll come over, and we'll have a chat. How's that sound? Help you clear your head.'

'I'm not at my flat. I've got something to do first.'

Jamie laughed. 'What's more important than saving your sanity?'

'I have to rescue Sandi.'

'Who's Sandi?'

'Long story, mate. I have a feeling I've told you before.'

'Listen, Steve. Sometimes in life, you have to disassemble before you can reassemble. You understand?'

'Not really,' Steve said.

Jamie chuckled. 'Give me a ring when you get home. Maybe we can clear some things up.'

'Yeah. I will.'


Steve remained out of sight until dark. He pulled on his jacket and got out of the van. Heading to the rear of Ricky's property, Steve peered around making sure he wasn't watched. Satisfied he wasn't, he climbed the wall and dropped into Ricky's garden. The French doors at the back of the property were slightly open, despite the chill night, the room lit up beyond them. The bright light inside acting like the flame as Steve, moth-like, crept in.

He entered, pushing one of the doors open to reveal an empty room. He ventured further inside, tiptoeing through into the hall. Several doors lay in front of him. One though had a piece of paper attached to it. Steve edged closer and read the writing. There were two words, *THIS WAY*, in bold capital letters. He reached for the handle but paused, his mind whirring with possible scenarios. He'd come this far though, and opening the door he pressed on. He descended the stairs and found himself confronted with another door. He paused once more, his heart banging in his chest.

'Come in, Steve. We've been expecting you,' said Ricky's voice from within. Any hope of using stealth and surprise on Ricky had apparently failed. He wondered why he hadn't thought about bringing a weapon. Feeling incredibly vulnerable, Steve turned the handle and entered the room.  The interior in total darkness except for a dim light placed next to a chair at the far end of the room, and on the chair sat Andy.

'Andy,' he half-called, half-whispered.

'He can't talk,' Ricky said. 'His mouth's taped.'

Steve manoeuvred his head in the direction the voice came from, trying to focus his eyes in the gloom. The light came on, momentarily blinding him. He blinked wildly, allowing his eyes to adjust. Ricky stood in the corner of the room, 4 or 5 metres from Andy. He held a gun, hanging loosely in his right hand.

'What are you going to do, Ricky?' Steve said. 'Shoot me?'

Ricky smiled, slowly circling Andy. 'Take a seat.' Pointing to a chair. Steve sat.

Ricky wandered to the bar on the opposite side of the room. 'Jack Daniels and coke, isn't it?' Pouring a drink, he strolled across to Steve, handed it to him, and resumed his previous position.

'It appears you and I, are close,' Ricky said. 'Closer than even I thought. I'm you, and you're me,' Ricky laughed. 'Andy told me. You know who Andy is?'

Steve nodded, as Ricky edged nearer to Andy.

'Can't see the resemblance myself.' Lowering his face to look at him. 'Looks like you, though.'

'Where's Sandi?' Placing his drink on the floor.

'Whoa,' Ricky said. 'Let's deal with Dad first.'

'Look, Ricky. I came here for Sandi.'

Ricky held the gun. An old type of revolver. He spun the chamber of the weapon around and waited for it to stop. 'He abandoned us.' His voice hardened. 'He left us when we were no more than babies.' Pointing it at Andy, Ricky squeezed the trigger, the hammer falling on an empty chamber.

Steve stood. 'Why are you doing this?'

'He broke Mam's heart. Aren't you bothered?' He fired the gun a second time, the hammer once more finding an empty chamber.

'For fuck's sake, Ricky. It was a long time ago.'

'I haven't forgotten. It's eaten away at me. I remember how Mam would cry over his photos. He left her for another woman, you know? Left his wife and son for a slapper.'

'Listen, Ricky. This won't solve anything.'

Ricky fired again. The noise was tremendous as the sound of the gunshot reverberated off the walls. Andy slumped in the chair, dead, as blood oozed from the hole in his chest. Steve bolted for Ricky, crashing into him as the two of them fell and slid along the floor. Steve picked up the gun and getting to his feet, levelled it at Ricky.

Ricky laughed. 'It's empty. You'll have to reload it. There's plenty of bullets there.' Pointing across to the bar.

Steve crept across to it, hardly taking his eyes off Ricky. He reached the bar and picked up a couple of bullets, his hands shaking. Opening the gun, he saw one chamber with a round in it. Steve glanced up as Ricky crashed into him. The weapon knocked from Steve's hand, skidded across the floor.

'Let's dispense with guns, shall we?' Ricky said. He pulled a knife from his sock and stood between Steve and the gun. Casually holding the weapon, he passed it slowly from hand to hand. 'I intended the other bullet for you, but a knife's better. More personal, don't you think?' Ricky pointed it at Steve.

'You're insane,' Steve said.

'You're probably right. Without your steadying influence, I don't have any limits or boundaries. Just for good measure.' Ricky smiled. 'If you do manage to kill me, you'll never know where Sandi is.'

'I won't fight you.'

'Of course you will. It's inevitable. It's our battle, and the winner takes all.' He moved closer.

Ricky prodded the knife towards Steve. Steve flinched away from it, trying desperately to avoid the blade. They patrolled around in a circle, Ricky pushing the knife at him.

'A fight for supremacy, Steve. Surely that's worth fighting for?'

Steve lunged at Ricky, knocking him tumbling backwards. Ricky was quickly on his feet, as Steve made a grab for the arm with the knife. The two of them wrestled upright. Ricky trying desperately to push the blade towards Steve. Steve maintained his grip, holding him back. Gradually Steve gained the upper hand, and slowly at first, he pushed down Ricky's arm. The manic smile on Ricky's face changed to a grimace, as he sensed he was losing grip. Ricky, in one desperate act, swung his right leg at Steve, catching him unaware. Steve unable to remain upright, fell to the floor. Steve, catching sight of the revolver a couple of metres from him, rolled towards it as Ricky brought the knife crashing down where he'd lain a split-second earlier.

Steve grabbed the gun and levelled it at Ricky. 'I'll fire if I have to.' Steadying the weapon in his right hand with his left.

'You haven't got the balls.' Mocked Ricky. 'I'm the strong one. You're what remains when you take out all the guts.'

'I mean it,' Steve said. His hand now shaking.

Ricky screamed, lunging for Steve. The gun exploded into life as Ricky, hit in the stomach, fell to the floor. Steve jumped to his feet and raced across to him, gently cradling his head.

'Where's Sandi? Please tell me.' Ricky attempted to speak but failed, the words forever lost in his throat. His eyes fixed, as Steve heard his last breath.

Steve lay on the settee in his front room. A half bottle of Jack Daniels hanging precariously in his hand, as music blasted from his music system. He continued to drink from the bottle, the remaining drops spilling from his mouth. Allowing his arm with the bottle to flop by his side, it slipped from his grasp and fell to the floor. Steve closed his eyes, as drunken oblivion welcomed him.

# CHAPTER SIXTEEN

Steve heard the curtains in his front room open. He squinted his eyes, as the shooting pain from his hangover made him wince.

'Look at the state of you,' Jamie said.

Steve swung his legs around and planted them on the floor, as sunlight flooded into the room.

Jamie bent and picked up the empty bottle. 'Good night?' Holding it up, he waved it at Steve.

'I don't remember,' Steve said.

Jamie sauntered towards the kitchen. 'Breakfast?'

'Am I going mad, Jamie?'

'Mad. What makes you think that?'

'Last night I killed Ricky. Shot him.'

'Upset you, did he?' Jamie said.

'He killed Andy.'

Jamie smiled. 'Right. Andy.'

'I've lost Sandi.' Bringing a hand up to his mouth.

Jamie grinned. 'Sandi with an i?'

'Why aren't you taking this seriously?' Steve said.

'How can I take any of this seriously? Who are these people? Sandi, Ricky, Andy. You must know they're not real.'

'Of course they're real,' he said. Steve got to his feet.

'How's your hangover?' Jamie said.

Steve considered this for a moment. He didn't have one. It had somehow vanished.

Jamie nodded towards the empty bottle. 'You drank a full bottle of Jack Daniels, and you haven't a trace of a hangover. Bit strange don't you think?'

'But, I …'

'Have a look out of the window,' Jamie said. 'Day or night?'

Steve realised it had grown dark. It was morning minutes earlier, he thought.

'Wow, these days are drawing in.' Jamie laughed.

Steve held out his hands. 'But how?'

'What do you think, Steve?'

He pondered for a moment, the events of the previous few weeks filling his head. The safecracking. The drive to Scotland. Anne's kidnap. Sandi and his escape from Ricky's men. In a flash, it came to him. 'I'm dreaming.' He grinned

'I reckon he's got it.' Jamie laughed again.

'She's waiting for me. I have to go to her,' Steve said.

'Well. What are you waiting for?'

The two of them bounded out of the flat, but not into the street. Steve found himself in the bar of The Lion. He wandered through, past oblivious regulars, and down the cellar steps. Pushing open the door at the bottom, he found himself inside Perpendicular. The band blasting out Deep Purple's Highway Star. He carried on into the gents, and through the retirement home, past everyday settings. Onwards, through one door after another he walked, ignoring everything he saw. Eventually, he reached two large white doors with Intensive Care Unit above them. The darkness of the room he was now in, slightly illuminated by the light seeping from around them. He could hear the faintest of voices, as it drifted towards him. It was her voice, singing softly.

*'So far away from the garden we loved,*
*She is what moves, in the soul of a dove.*
*Soon I shall see just how black was my night,*
*When I'm alone in her city of light.'*

Steve turned to face Jamie. 'This is it. Isn't it?' Jamie nodded. 'Are you coming?' Steve said.

'I can't. It's as far as I go.'

Steve peered back at the door. 'She's waiting for me.' Tears filled his eyes.

Jamie forced a smile. 'I know she is.'

'You knew all along, didn't you?' Steve said.

'You were broken. We had to fix you.'

Steve crossed to his friend and hugged him. 'I'll never forget you,' he whispered. Jamie disappeared. Steve left clutching a memory. He turned again, and taking a deep breath pushed open the doors.

# CHAPTER-SEVENTEEN

Steve opened his eyes. He was in a bed in a hospital, Sandra on a chair next to him. Her head resting on her chest as she slept. He tried to speak but couldn't form the words, his mouth incredibly dry. Steve coughed, and Sandra stirred.

She sat up straight and slid to the edge of her seat. 'Steve.' Taking hold of his hand as tears cascaded down her face.

He squeezed her hand and forced a smile. Sandra got up, pressed the button for the medical staff, and waited. Her eyes and those of her husband fixed in a loving stare, as Steve tried desperately to push away the urge to fall asleep.

Steve lay in his bed, propped up by several pillows. After he had woken, he vaguely remembered the medical staff fussing around him as Sandra looked on. He must've fallen asleep. Desperately wanting to see Sandra he waited impatiently for her arrival. His iPod lay on the table next to the bed. He picked it up, put in the earplugs, and closed his eyes again as the music washed over him.

He had listened to quite a few songs when he became aware of somebody standing above him. Sandra stood smiling, as he opened an eye. Removing the earplugs, he hugged his wife.

'Hello, sleepyhead.' She kissed him.

'Hello back,' he replied, croakily. His throat still dry and sore. 'How long was I out for?'

'Four weeks, three days and about ten hours.'

'A little exact.'

'You know me,' Sandra said. 'I played your music while you were out.' Nodding at the iPod in his hand. 'I thought it would help.'

'It did,' Steve said. 'Jamie?'

Sandra sat on the edge of his bed and took hold of his hand. Her head dropped a little.

'He's dead. Isn't he?' Steve said. Sandra nodded. Steve closed his eyes. Tears pushed their way out and trickled downwards.

Sandra placed a hand on his cheek. 'He died in the crash. I'm so sorry.'

Steve saw the memory unfold before him. He sat in the passenger seat of the car. A sticky substance Steve presumed was blood, dripped from his head. He glanced across at Jamie. The driver's side had taken the main impact as they'd hit the tree. The front and wing of the car lay crumpled, and although the airbag deployed it now lay deflated. Jamie slumped across the mangled steering wheel, with a large gaping wound on the left-hand side of his head. Steve pushed the memory away, as Jamie's lifeless eyes stared back at him.

'He got me home,' he said.

'Who?'

'Jamie. He got me back to you.'

Sandra hugged him again.

'I have something for you to see.' She got up and headed outside, returning moments later with a baby in her arms. 'Would you like to meet your son?' She smiled.

'What's he called?'

'I thought maybe … Jamie.'

'I'd like that.' Taking the baby from her, he kissed his son's head.

**CONGRATULATIONS! Flashed up on screen, as the helmets and chairs powered down.**

# INSIDIOUS - CHAPTER ONE

Charlotte's and Jack's helmets were pulled from their heads. Disorientated, they scanned the room, their reason returning them to reality. The confusion of playing the game quickly evaporated as two men stood next to them, brandishing pistols. 'On your feet now.' Commanded the one nearest to Charlotte.

'What the hell's going on?' Jack said.

'Listen, fella,' the other man said. 'Do what we say, and I won't have to put a bullet through that head of yours.' Tapping Jack's forehead with the muzzle of his weapon, to emphasise his point.

Charlotte and Jack got to their feet and headed reluctantly out of the room, closely followed by the men. They made their way along corridors and found themselves outside the dining room. The same one where Gainford hosted the dinner party the evening before.

The room fell silent as the four of them entered. Paige and Shaami seated at the dinner table, with Gainford, Scorton and another pistol-carrying man at the far end.

'Welcome. Welcome,' Gainford said. 'Take a seat. Wonderful of you to join us.'

'What the hell's going on?' Jack said.

'Please sit down, or I'll get one of my men to sit you down,' Gainford said. The smile on his lips, replaced with a scowl.

Charlotte and Jack sat at the table opposite the other two. Shaami shook his head as Jack peered across at him.

Gainford smiled. 'You're incredibly good players.' Returning to his more pleasant demeanour. 'I didn't think any of the couples would make it through to the end.'

'Where are the others?' Charlotte said.

Paige sniffed. 'He murdered them.'

'Murdered?' Jack said. 'How? Why?'

'You should read things, Jack,' Gainford said. Taking hold of a piece of paper Scorton held out for him. 'Here. In the small-print. It's in legal jargon, of course. But in a nutshell. If you die in the game, you die in real life. You all signed it!' Raising his voice for effect.

'How could you murder them?' Jack said. 'You're insane.'

'Ah! Jack. Jack, the imposter. Jack, the interloper. What is it you're calling yourself today? Jack Wolverston?' Charlotte glanced across at Jack.

'That's right, Charlotte,' Gainford said. 'His name's not Jack Wolverston. Is it Jack?'

Jack ignored his goading and sat back in his chair.

'It's not Wolverston, is it Jack? It's Buchannon. Jack's a fraud. His friend, Mr Wolverston, got to the end of the game. Unfortunately, he'd already booked himself a holiday of a lifetime. In the Seychelles, I believe. And his friend, Mr Buchannon, here.' Pointing at Jack. 'Came in his place. Isn't that right, Jack?' Jack stared at him. 'I know everything about you, Mr Buchannon.'

'What if it is,' Jack said. 'Nobody got hurt.'

'I detest frauds!' Boomed Gainford, enunciating each word. 'I loathe fucking cheats! Still. You're here, I suppose, and your late friend's missing out on all the fun we're having.' Gainford theatrically waved his hands around the room.

'What do you mean, late?' Jack said.

'Unfortunately, your friend suffered a terrible accident this morning. On one of those Jet-ski boats. Notoriously difficult to handle. Incredibly sad.' Gainford adopted a mocking, sad face.

Jack stood. 'You murdering bastard!' One of the men who'd escorted him and Charlotte to the dining room, pushed him down into his chair.

'Any more outbursts like that, Jack, and I'll get one of my men to take you outside and put a bullet through your head. Is that clear?'

Jack ignored him and felt the muzzle of the gun jab him in the back of the head. 'Perfectly,' Jack sneered.

'Why did you murder them?' Charlotte said.

'Ah, the lovely Charlotte. Because I can. The helmets were designed to emit a severe electric shock to the frontal cortex, to anyone who died in the game. Simple. I mean, you can't expect to win all that money and not risk anything.'

'What did you do with Tom and Louise?' she asked.

'Tom and Louise were frauds too. Just like Jack, there. They were reporters looking for a scoop. They paid the genuine winners for their places. Sadly, for them, it was game over!' He laughed, the gun-carrying men and Scorton joining in with him.

'And the real winners?' she asked.

'Do I need to spell it out.' Smiling at her. 'Now then, people. Let's get down to brass tacks. You four are the survivors. It's a little like the Agatha Christie novel, *And Then There Were None*. Only this time, then there were four.' He laughed again.

'Why are you doing this?' Paige said. 'What have we done to deserve this?'

'What indeed?' Gainford stood. Turning away from them to face a large screen at the end of the room. Jack and Charlotte hadn't noticed it when they'd entered. It was clearly pivotal to what Gainford had to say. The photo of a young girl appeared on it. She appeared fourteen or fifteen, with blonde hair tied in a ponytail. Charlotte, Shaami, and Paige gasped.

'This is Ashleigh Waterstone.' Addressing his remarks to Jack. 'Ashleigh was a bright young girl, who had everything to live for. Except she had one problem. Ashleigh developed suicidal tendencies. One day she ventured onto an internet website. One you probably haven't heard of called, *The Terminus.* You three have though.' Glancing at them in turn. 'Would you like to tell Jack all about it?'

Charlotte stared at Jack. 'It was a chatroom for people who wanted to kill themselves. Individuals who have difficulties and believe their life's worthless. They can speak to like-minded people.'

Gainford snorted. 'You make it sound fantastic.'

'I can't see what this has to do with me,' Jack said.

'I told you. You're a cheat. That's why you're here. Cheats shouldn't prosper.'

'This was a long time ago,' Charlotte said.

'Tell them what happened, Shaami,' Gainford said. Turning his attention to him, and Paige.

'Like Charlotte said,' he said. 'It was a long time ago.'

'These people and the others, including your friend, Jack, encouraged Ashleigh to kill herself. They badgered her relentlessly until she did.'

'It wasn't like that.' Protested Paige.

Gainford circled the table. 'She swallowed a bottle of bleach. Do you know what that does to a person, Jack?' Jack said nothing. 'Imagine how much she suffered?'

'I didn't encourage her to kill herself,' Charlotte said. 'I tried to talk her out of it.'

'Not hard enough!' Gainford boomed. 'Not nearly hard enough.'

'We were just kids ourselves.' Paige was crying. 'We don't deserve to die for it.'

'Really?' Gainford said. 'Well let me tell you something, young lady. I'm the judge, jury, and executioner, and I'll decide who fucking-well dies!' Gainford coughed, Scorton handed him a glass of water. He composed himself and continued. 'At least your friends died quickly. Ashleigh took days.' His voice softened. 'Ashleigh was my daughter. A happy product of a brief relationship I had with her mother years ago. I managed to keep it secret from the media. I wanted to protect her from all the nonsense.'

Charlotte leant forward. 'I'm sorry for your loss, Christian, but there's nothing we can do now. You can't bring her back.'

'It doesn't end there, Charlotte. Ripples and reverberations. Her mother, unable to accept the loss of her only child, took her life too. That's two deaths you three caused. The effect on Ashleigh's family was devastating.' He completed his lap of the table. 'It took my people years to track you all down, and find out every aspect of your lives.'

'You're just going to kill us, are you?' Jack said.

'Not at all. Computer games, no matter how smart and complicated, lack one thing. Realism. I'm offering you four the chance to play a game for real. One with a prize, of course. Who doesn't love to win something?' He sat back down. 'It's a gamble, so I'll expect you to put up something. Let me see. What should that be?'

'Our lives?' Jack said.

Gainford pointed at him. 'Give the man a prize.'

'What if we don't want to play?' Charlotte said.

Gainford pointed at the large screen. It now showed a picture of the other contestants, seemingly dead. Tom and Louise, it appeared, had been shot in the head.

'This is what awaits,' he said. 'My men have already dug your graves. It's up to you. While you decide, I'll have food and beverages brought in. The condemned men and women should eat a hearty meal, as they say.' He stood and left.

The four of them discussed their options, as the armed men watched on. In truth, they accepted they'd little choice but to go along with what Gainford wanted. A sumptuous meal had been provided, complete with wine, but none of them felt hungry. After eating small amounts, they were returned to a sitting room, to await their host's return. The situation becoming surreal, as far as Charlotte was concerned. She and Jack had hardly spoken since Gainford's revelations, and the four of them sat in silence.

Charlotte made her way across to him. 'Penny for them,' she said.

'It'll cost more than that.' He half-smiled.

'What are we going to do?'

'We'll have to see what he's got in store for us. I discussed it with Shaami, and he wants to try and overpower one of the men. Get his gun.'

'That's incredibly dangerous,' she said.

'I know, but it looks as if Gainford won't be happy until we're dead. He's clearly mad.'

'Yeah. I've gone right off Mr Money-bags.' Charlotte smiled, trying to lighten the mood. 'None of the other men I've ever fancied have wanted me dead.'

'None you know of.' Jack winked.

The door opened, and Gainford entered along with two of his men. He stopped in front of the fireplace and began. 'Listen up, people. The nearest town to here, well, it's not really a town. Just a small collection of houses and a pub, is a place called Bannickbrae. It's forty miles away. Reach Bannickbrae, get to the bar in the pub, and you gain your freedom. It's as simple as that.'

'How'd we get there?' Paige said.

'On foot, of course. You'll find suitable clothing and footwear in your rooms. The winter up here's somewhat unforgiving, I'm afraid. I wouldn't want you four freezing to death.'

'And that's it?' Jack said. 'We have to walk forty miles to a pub in a village?'

'Yes,' Gainford said.

'And the catch?' Jack said.

'You'll get one hour start, and then my people will hunt you down. If they catch you.' Gainford smiled. *It's game over.*'

'You won't get away with this,' Jack said. 'People will come looking for us. You can't murder ten people without anyone knowing.'

'No concern of mine. You see, Jack. I have a rare genetic disorder. I won't bore you with the details of it, but let's just say the future looks bleak for me. The drugs I'm taking have managed to hold off the inevitable, until now.' He coughed and took a drink from a glass which one of his men handed to him. 'The disorder will not only become increasingly unpleasant. But it'll render me immobile too. Unfortunately, no amount of money, and I have a lot, will help. When this is over, I'll leave a note to the appropriate authorities explaining everything. And exit this world with a bang and not a whimper.'

'And you're taking us, with you?' Charlotte said.

'I'm sorry,' he said. 'I am. I've grown quite fond of you, my dear.'

Jack sneered. 'Not so fond as to let her off the hook.'

'Quite.' Gainford said. 'Think of this as the ultimate game. Try to enjoy it.' He laughed. 'I know I will. You have thirty-minutes to ready yourself, and then we'll begin.' With that, he left.

The four of them escorted individually to their rooms, got ready before gathering in the hallway. Stepping outside into the freezing Scottish air, as Gainford watched on.

'You have one hour,' Gainford said. Smiling, he shut the door to the house.

# CHAPTER TWO

The four of them headed away from the house, travelling along the driveway. The substantial amount of snow on the ground, slowing them down. At least the clothing they were wearing was managing to keep out the cold and the biting wind, Charlotte thought. They said nothing to each other as Jack led the way, the others followed in his wake. With no idea which direction they needed to travel, he carried on at pace finally reaching the road at the end of the driveway.

Charlotte quickened her step and caught him up, tugging at his arm. 'Jack.' She pulled back the hood of her parka. 'We can't just run in any direction. We don't know where this village is.'

'I know,' Jack said. 'But we need to put distance between us and our pursuers. We only have a one hour start.'

The other two joined them. Charlotte reached into her pocket and pulled out a local guidebook. 'Look, I managed to lift this from the house. I found it the other day. It was in one of the drawers in my bedroom. A guest must've left it there.' She turned it over, allowing the others to view it. On the rear of the book was a map of the area. 'Bannickbrae is on it.' Pointing to it on the map. Someone had put a red dot, marking where Delphic was.

Jack studied it and showed it to the others. 'How do we know Gainford didn't plant it there?' he said. 'It's a little convenient someone left it there for you to find.'

'We don't,' she replied. 'But it's easily the nearest place to us. The other towns and villages look much further away.'

Shaami took the book from Jack. 'Surely Gainford expects us to make for somewhere other than Bannickbrae?' Shaami said. 'He probably thinks we'll look for help.'

'You're saying we should head for this Bannickbrae?' Jack said.

Shaami shrugged. 'Whatever we do, he's going to hunt us down. If we reach the village, we could call the authorities and have him arrested. If we head for any of these other places, we'll give him and his men more time to catch up with us. Walking forty miles, in this terrain, is hard enough. The next nearest place could be fifty or more miles away.'

Paige threw back her hood. 'Couldn't we look for a farmhouse or cottage, and phone from there.'

Jack rubbed at the stubble on his chin. 'Let's head in the general direction of Bannickbrae and hope we come across somewhere with a phone. What we can't afford to do is hang around arguing. Agreed?' He looked at the others for confirmation.

The three nodded in unison, and Jack set off again, followed by Charlotte, Paige and Shaami. They'd kept up their relentless pace along the road. Hoping to spot a passing motorist or a house of some sort. In all honesty, though, the roads were so snowbound they didn't expect to see any cars. Jack stopped and waited for Shaami, who was closest to him, to catch up. The pair paused as Paige and Charlotte joined them.

Jack viewed his watch. 'Our hour is up. We don't know how they're going to follow us. They could be in vehicles, or on foot.'

Charlotte glanced in the direction they had come from. 'If they're in vehicles, it won't take them long to find us.'

'That's what I was thinking,' Jack said. 'I suggest we head across country.'

'Won't we get lost?' Paige said.

'I think Jack's right,' Shaami said. 'We'll have to chance it. They'll expect us to stay on the road.'

Charlotte took hold of Jack's arm as he turned. 'We'll be less likely to run into anyone or come across a house if we do.'

Jack turned to face her. 'It's a chance we'll have to take. Look.' Pointing to the sky. 'It's getting dark already, and it's starting to snow again. The good news is it'll cover our tracks. The bad news is it'll make our journey even harder.'

'It's better travelling at night,' Shaami said. 'It'll make it more difficult for them to track us.'

Jack nodded. 'Yeah. Good idea. Let's find shelter and wait for dark.'

The four of them set off again, Charlotte trying to match strides with Jack. 'How far do you think we've come?' she said.

'Not far.' Jack said. 'A few miles at best. Even if we keep up a pace of two to three miles an hour, it's going to take us a long time to get there.'

'Unless we find help,' she said. Through panting breaths.

Jack surveyed the frigid landscape and looked across at Charlotte. 'Unless we find help,' he said.

The four of them travelled across the most barren terrain they'd ever encountered. Devoid of features, just a seemingly endless blanket of white. Having traipsed for two hours, Paige was struggling to keep up with the other three. Shaami falling back to keep her company. Charlotte still, somehow, managing to keep pace with Jack, much to his amazement. They carried on up an incline, the slope slowing the pair of them down. When the couple reached the top they could see into the valley below, and spotted a derelict cottage. They waited at the upper part for Shaami and Paige to join them. Jack pointed, the wind now whipping the snow up, making talking and hearing harder. The four of them trudged down the slope towards the building. Finally reaching it, they paused to catch their breath. The building appeared deserted. The windows boarded up, and the door nailed shut. Jack put his shoulder against it and pushed, the old door quickly yielding. The roof appeared mostly intact, except for a hole in one of the corners where snow gently fell. They entered and Jack closed the door, forcing the ancient timber back into its frame.

Jack pushed back his hood and tossed his backpack onto the floor. 'We'll rest.'

Paige dropped to the floor. 'Surely they won't find us here?'

'We don't know what equipment he's employing,' Shaami said. 'He could have heat-seeking equipment, night-vision goggles, or anything.'

Charlotte removed her rucksack and paused. 'How can we be sure he hasn't got some tracking device on us.'

Jack and the others glanced at each other, and then rifled through the contents of their bags. Inside there were high-calorie bars and water. Individual packs for making hot drinks, a torch, and in Charlotte's, a compass. She held it up.

Jack took it from her. 'Why give us a compass?'

Charlotte sneered. 'He wants to give us a sporting chance.'

'Yeah,' Jack said. 'He's compassionate, for a psychopath.' Nobody laughed.

The four of them continued to search inside and outside the bags. Taking off their Parka's and thermal leggings as well, checking these too. Satisfied they hadn't a tracking device planted on them, they ate and drank some of the provisions. After their meal, they huddled together for warmth, waiting for the last vestiges of daylight to vanish.

Jack jumped up. Sure, he'd heard a noise outside. The others, roused by his sudden movement, sat up. Jack put his index finger to his mouth, indicating he wanted them to stay silent. He glanced at his watch. They'd slept for two hours, and through the crack of the door he could see it was now night. Slowly, and as quietly as possible, he opened the door. Charlotte stood and joined him.

'Stay here,' he whispered. 'I thought I heard something.' Charlotte nodded.

He stepped outside into the moonlit night. Slowly walking around the building, making sure his back was against the wall at all times. There was no one. But as he completed his lap of the building, he noticed footsteps heading towards, and away from the cottage. It had snowed while they'd slept, yet the tracks were fresh. He raced inside. 'Get your stuff.' Pulling on his backpack.

'Who's out there?' Shaami said.

'I can't see anyone, but tracks are leading away from us. It looks as if someone was here.'

The four gathered their bits together and left, heading in the opposite direction to the tracks. The wind had dropped considerably, and the snow had ceased as well. They trudged on, with the feeling they were sitting ducks waiting to be picked off. They carried on regardless, looking nervously over their shoulders from time to time, but no one was there. Maybe, Jack thought, Gainford was making them wait. He inspected the map again. Even with his basic map reading skills, he realised they needed to travel in a north-west direction. Using the compass, they had found, that's what they did.

They continued their relentless walk for five hours. Jack, Charlotte and Shaami, slowing down to accommodate the sluggish Paige. They hadn't seen any signs of life so far. Maybe, Jack thought, they had managed to get away from Gainford's men somehow. Or, possibly the tracks he'd spotted at the derelict cottage had not been their pursuers. He guessed they'd covered between a third to half of the distance but couldn't be sure of that. They desperately needed to rest. He doubted Paige could travel much further. She looked exhausted.

Charlotte spotted something to her left. She stopped. Was it a glow in the distance? She couldn't be certain. She grabbed Jack by the arm to attract his attention. 'Look.' Pointing in the direction of the light. 'What's that?'

Jack studied it for a couple of moments. 'It looks like a house.'

'Paige needs a rest.' Charlotte said. 'She's struggling.'

Jack indicated to the other two, pointing towards the house. They headed for it. Charlotte, Shaami, and Paige trudging after him. They reached the cottage and knocked on the door. There wasn't an answer. Jack ventured around the rear of the property and knocked on this door too. Again, no one answered so he headed back around to the front.

'There's no one in,' he said to the others.

'Should we break in?' Shaami said. 'It is an emergency.'

'It's someone's house,' Paige said. 'We can't just break in.'

'They may have a phone,' Charlotte said. 'I think breaking in is the least of our worries. Just do it, Jack.'

Jack grabbed hold of the door handle and turned, somewhat optimistically hoping it was unlocked. To his, and the others total surprise it was. He pushed open the door and entered. 'Hello,' Jack shouted. Nobody answered. 'Shaami,' he said. 'You and Paige check the rooms above. We'll check down here.' Shaami nodded, and he and Paige set off upstairs.

Charlotte followed Jack through into the kitchen. It seemed as if the owners of the property had left in a hurry. A half-eaten meal lay on the table. An old-style kettle boiling furiously on the wood-burning stove. Jack took it off and placed it on the metal draining-board. He opened one of the drawers in the dresser on the far side of the room.

'What're you looking for?' Charlotte said.

'A knife. It might be useful to have a weapon.' Charlotte nodded. Paige screamed from upstairs. Jack grabbed a large carving knife from the drawer, and shot off up the stairs. Closely followed by Charlotte, who snatched a brass ornament from the hall as she did. They heard a noise from one of the rooms. Jack, without breaking stride, burst through the door. Shaami was grappling on the floor with a man wearing a ski-mask. Another throttling Paige. He lunged at the man attacking Paige thumping into him, as the man released his grip on her. The attacker thudded into the wall, and Jack sprung to his feet. The man reached into his coat pocket, for what Jack assumed to be a gun. He dived on the assailant plunging the knife deep into his chest. The man grunted and slumped against the wall.

'Look out!' Paige said.

Jack turned, the other man heading for him with a large hunting knife in his hand, Jack threw his arms up in a desperate bid to protect himself. The brass ornament Charlotte carried, smashed into the man's head. The sickening thud resounded around the room as he dropped to the floor, pole-axed. Blood seeped from his head-wound into the carpet. Paige moved across to Shaami, who lay on the ground clutching his stomach.

'Jack,' she said. 'He's badly injured.'

Jack joined her and knelt next to Shaami as Paige cradled him. Charlotte glanced at Jack, who shook his head. Shaami was bleeding massively. The three of them stared on helplessly as the colour drained from him, and he took his final breath. Jack stood, checking the two attackers. Both were dead. Paige gently lowered Shaami's head onto the floor and began to cry.

Charlotte grabbed hold of her arm. 'We can't help him anymore, Paige. We need to think of ourselves.' Paige wiped the tears from her face and nodded.

Jack knelt next to the man he'd stabbed. 'Let's see who these two are.' Pulling the ski-mask from his face, Jack gasped.

'What is it?' Her view obscured by Jack.

'Look.' He pointed at the man.

'It's Willoughby,' she said. 'From Amorphous.'

Jack removed the mask from the second, rolling him onto his back to view his face. 'It's Karl Smith.'

'I don't understand,' Charlotte said.

'Gainford must've used people he knew in real life as the parameters for his characters.'

'He's one sick bastard,' she said.

'We've got to get out of here,' Jack said. 'We'll have to grab what's useful and scarper.'

'What about Shaami?' Paige said.

Jack walked across to her and put his hand on her arm. 'We haven't time to bury him. There may be more men. We need to go.'

He searched both men, disappointed not to find a gun. Only a cosh in the pocket of the man he'd killed. He slipped this inside his parka. The three of them headed out of the room, Paige paused to take one last look at Shaami. Then she, too, made her way down. Charlotte and Paige rifled through drawers in the front room. Jack continued looking in the kitchen. He opened the door to the pantry, staring for a moment, before closing the door and joining the other two.

'Jack,' Charlotte said. 'Look.' Pointing across to a dated-looking telephone on the table. He lifted the receiver and listened. It was dead. He shook his head at the two women and put the phone back, but as he did, it rang. He stared first at the phone, and then at the women. Tentatively, he lifted it back up. 'Hello?'

'Jack?' said the familiar tones of Gainford. 'Somehow I knew you'd be hard to kill. Have we lost anyone?'

'Yeah. Shaami's dead. You sick bastard. But so are your goons.'

He laughed. 'Well done, Jack. Don't worry I've got plenty more.'

'And the owners?'

'Collateral damage, I'm afraid.'

'Why don't you do your own dirty work, Gainford? I'd love two minutes with you.'

'I'm sure you would. Keep going. You've got twenty-six miles to go. Don't bother trying to use this phone, either. I'm disconnecting it now. Goodbye.' The phone went dead. Jack ripped it from the socket and threw it against the wall.

'What did he say?' Charlotte said.

'He's sending more. He killed the couple who lived here. I found them in the pantry. Gather your things. We're heading off. Twenty-six miles to go, according to Gainford.'

'How did they know we'd be here at this cottage?' Charlotte said.

Jack glanced at Paige who dropped her head. 'No idea.'

Jack did a quick search around the property before they left. Satisfied there was no one else about, the three of them set off into the night. Large white flakes falling freely as the temperature dropped another few degrees.

# CHAPTER THREE

The three of them travelled for hours, not daring to stop for any length of time. Exhausted, tired and hungry, Jack, Charlotte, and Paige continued on. Trying to put distance between themselves and their pursuers. None of them noticed as the sun rose in the east. The barren, landscape hardly changing its appearance as they relentlessly carried onwards.

As daylight wrestled control from the dark, Jack stopped and surveyed the countryside. What once appeared beautiful to him, now filled him with a deep loathing. He felt exhausted but realised, as he glanced at the others, they were too. Charlotte and Paige joined him, as they followed his stare.

'What is it?' Charlotte said.

'Over there,' pointed Jack. 'It looks like a shelter, for cattle or sheep maybe. We'll head for that, and rest.'

They set off across the field. Climbing the ancient-looking walls crisscrossing in front of them. As they neared, they could see a stone hut with no windows, a large open entrance at the front. There were no animals, in fact, they hadn't encountered any on their journey. Jack assumed the building was either no longer used, or, the animals usually housed there had been moved somewhere else for the winter. They went inside and were pleased to see some straw bedding still remained.

Jack wearily pulled off his backpack, dropping it to the floor. 'We'll rest here and carry on when it gets dark again.'

'It'll be a long wait,' Charlotte said. 'It's only just got light.'

He sighed. 'I know. We daren't risk travelling through the day, though. They'd spot us easier.' Jack studied Paige. She'd been quiet since the attack at the house. Shaami's death hit her hard, but he had a feeling there was something else on her mind.

'You ok, Paige?' he said. Paige slumped to the floor exhausted, raised her head, as tears ran the length of her face.

Charlotte sat next to her. 'It's all right,' Charlotte said. 'We'll reach the pub.' Putting a comforting arm around her.

'It was you, wasn't it?' Jack said.

Paige nodded. 'I'm sorry.' She spluttered through her tears. 'He promised me no one would be hurt. He said it was just a game.'

Charlotte focussed on Jack. 'What's she on about?'

'She led them to us. Didn't you Paige?'

Paige put her hands up to her face, sobbing. 'He said no one would get hurt. He promised.'

'But you saw the others back at the house.' Charlotte said. 'You saw their bodies on the screen,'

'He told me they weren't dead. He said it was a trick. Special effects.'

Jack sneered. 'And you believed him? You believed a psychopath like Gainford?'

'He told me Ashleigh wasn't his daughter, and he'd invented the story about him being her father. He wanted it to sound authentic. He said he'd delved into our pasts and discovered what happened.'

Jack moved closer to Paige, towering over her. 'How did he find us?'

'He gave me a tracking device.'

Jack pushed out a hand. 'Give it to me.'

'I left it at the cottage. I realised after …' Paige sobbed again. 'After Shaami, I realised he was lying. I'm so sorry.'

Jack turned away from her and booted an old bucket lying on the ground, the bucket clattering into the wall.

'I'm sorry,' she pleaded. 'I wanted to believe Gainford was telling me the truth. I didn't want to die out here.'

'I should leave you here,' he said. 'Leave you to be picked off by Gainford's men.'

Charlotte rose to her feet and followed Jack as he stormed outside. Jack stared at the grey sky as snow dropped onto his face. 'We could be dead. The stupid cow led those bastards to us.' He shook his head. 'What about the couple back at the house?'

'We can't leave her,' Charlotte said.

'She got Shaami killed. She almost got us killed. Why the fuck should I care about her? Why should I risk my life for her?'

'You can't leave her, Jack.' Taking hold of his arm. 'She wouldn't last five minutes.'

'Why not? Why should I care what happens to her? Let Gainford and his men kill her.'

'If you leave Paige, I'm staying with her,' she said. 'I can't leave her.'

'You do what you want,' he said. 'I've got a life outside of this nightmare. People I love. Family. People I'd like to see again.' He pointed back at the building. 'She nearly cost me that. I don't care what happens to her.'

'What about me?' Charlotte said. 'Don't you care what happens to me?'

Jack shrugged. 'Of course. You're different. But I didn't ask for any of this. Why should I feel responsible for other people's lives?'

She moved around, facing him and lifted a gloved-hand to his cheek. 'None of us asked for this.'

Jack lowered his eyes. 'It's not fair I should feel like this. Why should I feel guilty?'

Charlotte lifted his chin, a little. 'I'm so glad I met you. If I die out here, I won't regret it.' Looking into his eyes. Jack met her stare briefly, and turned away from her. Charlotte headed back inside.

'I'd die for you, Charlotte. I'd die for you.' He uttered under his breath. 'Charlotte,' he shouted. 'I'm sorry. I wouldn't leave her. Let's get some rest. We're all tired.'

Charlotte forced a smile, mouthing thanks at him.

The three of them ate the remaining bits of food. After making and drinking the last of the warm drinks, they nestled down together for warmth under the straw. It was surprisingly snug and the three of them, despite their ordeal, found sleep came easily. They slumbered on through the morning and into the afternoon as the sun descended below the horizon.

Charlotte and Paige woke and sat up in the straw. Charlotte viewed Jack as he stared outside into the early evening darkness.

She clambered to her feet. 'Have you been awake long?'

He turned to face her. 'An hour.'

'Why didn't you wake us?'

'We're not in any rush, are we? I thought we'd let Gainford wait.'

'It's dark,' she said.

'Yeah,' he sighed. 'If you two are ready, we'll go.'

'I need a pee,' Paige said.

'Me too,' Charlotte said.

'Right. You two sort yourselves out. I'll wait outside. Leave the backpacks. The food and drink are gone.'

'The compass?' Charlotte said.

'Leave it as well. I had a walk while you two slept, and the road's roughly ten-minutes away.'

'And Bannickbrae?' Paige said.

'It said four miles on the sign-post.'

'Four miles,' she repeated to herself.

'Yeah. I'll wait outside.'

# CHAPTER FOUR

The walk to the road took a little over ten minutes. The dark, winter night offering them additional cover. Jack was confident Gainford's men would be lying in wait somewhere near the village. So, the final bit of their journey would have to involve stealth. The road, with a high stone wall running its length, stretched out in front of them. Jack suggested using it to hide them while walking parallel to the road. The three carried on, trying to remain as quiet as possible. They passed a sign, indicating Bannickbrae was now only a mile from them. Jack stopped and signalled for the women to follow his lead. Crouching behind the wall, he spoke in hushed tones. 'You two stay here. I'm going to make my way into the village, and see what we're up against.'

'What if they spot you?' Charlotte said.

'I'll have to take the risk. There may be more than one way to the village. If I can find another way in, we'll skirt around and use the one they're less likely to expect. If I'm not back in thirty minutes, make your own way in.' Charlotte nodded, understanding what he was implying. The three of them hugged, and Jack disappeared out of sight. While the other two waited nervously.

He steadily made his way behind the wall. Glancing over the top when the opportunity presented itself, only stopping when the wall dipped down towards a river. The noise of the water growing louder as he neared it. He glanced along the road again. A bridge spanned the river, guarded at the end nearest to him by a figure dressed in black. There was no way of crossing the river, he mused. The width and speed of the water making it impossible. The bridge appeared to be their only hope. He saw the pub in the distance, the lights from the windows spilling out into the car park at the front. He'd have to eliminate the man, he thought, but unsure if there were any others, he paused scanning the length of the bridge. Jack felt for the knife in the pocket of his coat and grasped the handle, pulling it out in front of him. A noise from the pub grabbed his attention as another man headed across the bridge to join his friend. Jack melted into the darkness and slipped back along the route he'd taken, towards Charlotte and Paige.

Charlotte, spotting Jack, stood and moved closer to him. 'What's happening?'

'There are at least two men. We'll have to go over a bridge to cross the river to the pub. I couldn't see another way in from this side. We'll have to take Hobson's choice.'

Paige joined them. 'How do we know Gainford will keep his promise? He's already lied once.'

Jack shrugged. 'We don't know he will. What do you think, Charlotte?'

'I think he will. Games are his life. I just have this feeling. I can't explain it. Gut instinct, I suppose.'

'We'll need to get rid of the two men,' Jack said.

Charlotte patted him on the arm. 'Let's go and kill the bastards.'

The three of them laughed. It was the first time in days they'd found anything remotely amusing.

'Got to admire your guts,' Jack said. 'But I believe we need a plan.'

The three of them crouched behind the wall a hundred metres from the bridge. Jack bobbed his head up and could see only the one man there. He crept forward as the women waited for his signal. Jack, now equidistant from Paige, Charlotte and the man, waved towards Charlotte, who sprinted across the road and jumped the wall on the other side. The man, who'd been looking in the other direction, turned as he heard the noise. By then Charlotte was out of sight. He edged forward, a knife in his right-hand glistening in the moonlight. The man reached a position level with where Jack was and stopped. Looking along the road, away from the village, he glanced left and right, before turning around and heading back to the pub. Jack vaulted the wall. In one quick movement, he struck the man forcefully across the head with the cosh. The man slumped to the floor momentarily stunned, he attempted to get to his feet, his progress halted by Jack's right-boot. His head snapped backwards, hitting the tarmac with a loud thud. Jack grabbed the man's arm and pulled him to the side of the road, and through a gap in the wall. He rolled the unconscious man towards the river's edge assisted by Paige and Charlotte, who'd made her way over to his side of the road. The three of them stared at the face of Ricky. Jack paused, a smile appearing on his face, and pushed the dead man into the river. The current picked up his body and carried him out of sight.

'Did you see who that was?' Charlotte said.

'Yeah,' Jack said. 'Ricky, from Broken. It's like meeting old friends.'

'What next?' Paige said.

'One down, Jack said. 'At least another to go.'

They heard a noise behind. The three of them turned in unison as two men came running through the undergrowth. The first crashing into Jack as the pair of them clattered to the ground, rolling dangerously near to the river's edge. Paige screamed as the second man lunged at her. He caught her foot as she tried to escape, causing her to stumble and fall. He loomed over Paige as Charlotte jumped on his back raining blows down on his shoulders and head. The man dislodged her and threw her to the ground. Pulling a knife from a sheath attached to his leg, he bent over Charlotte. Paige jumped to her feet, swinging wildly at the man's head. He turned, stabbing with his knife and caught Paige in her stomach. She slumped onto the floor, injured. Paige had given Charlotte valuable time, though. She picked up a branch striking the man's arm, catapulting his knife towards where Paige now lay.

Jack wrestled with the man, his assailant holding on to Jack's knife-wielding arm firmly. He felt a pain in his thigh and realised he'd been stabbed, the man's knife embedded deeply in his leg. Jack, in desperation, brought his head up forcefully and crashed into the man's face, blood from the attacker splattered over the pair of them. The man briefly stunned, slackened his grip on Jack, allowing him to bring his right knee into his attacker's groin. The man buckled as Jack thrust his knife into his attacker's neck. Copious amounts of blood spurted from the gaping wound. Clutching his throat in a vain effort to stem the flow, he slumped first to his knees and finally to the ground. His body convulsing as the precious red-fluid seeped away.

Paige, although injured, picked up the knife and threw it to Charlotte, who caught it, but watched helplessly as it slipped from her grasp, and fell out of her reach. The man leant forward and grabbed the knife. Paige, summoning her last ounce of strength, crawled towards her friend to help her. He turned and stuck the knife in Paige's shoulder. She screamed in agony as the blade was retracted. Turning his attention away from her, he raised it high. Charlotte vainly threw her hands up in defence. She watched in slow motion, at first not understanding what was happening, as she saw the tip of Jack's knife exit the man's chest. The man stared down at her, trying desperately to speak, but failed, as Jack pulled the dying man clear of Charlotte. She studied her assailant face, only now realising who it was. The lifeless eyes of DS Jones, a character from The Hanging Tree game, stared back. Jack pulled her to her feet as they moved across to the dying Paige. She lay still. Charlotte dropped to her knees and lifted Paige's head.

Paige opened her eyes. 'I'm sorry,' she mouthed.

Charlotte's eyes filled with tears, brushing her friend's hair from her face. 'You've nothing to be sorry for,' she whispered, as Paige quietly slipped away.

Charlotte stood, and Jack took hold of her hand. 'We need to be quick,' he said. 'There may be more.'

'Who attacked you?' she said.

'Dec,' he replied. 'From *The Hanging Tree*.' The two of them realising who would be coming next.

Jack took hold of the handle of the knife and pulled it from his thigh. Grimacing in pain, struggling to resist the urge to scream as blood flowed freely from the wound.

Charlotte, supporting the limping Jack, staggered slowly up to the road and towards the bridge. They stumbled across it, reaching the far side. A noise behind them made them turn. Flint stood at the end of the bridge they'd come from, his massive bulk looming in part-shadow. The spider's web tattoo visible above his neckline. He waited, smirking, appearing to realise how badly Jack was injured, as Jack slumped onto one knee.

Jack glanced at Charlotte. 'Get to the pub,' he said.

'I'm not leaving you.' Gripping his hand tightly.

Jack stood again and turned to face her. Blood from his leg staining his trousers red, pooling around his feet. 'Listen to me, young lady.' Bringing his blood-stained hand up to her face. 'This is about you. It always was. Get to the pub. Now!'

She frowned. 'What do you mean?'

'I'll hold him off. Please, Charlotte. Do it for me.'

'I don't want to lose you.' Tears ran down her face.

'I know you don't,' he said. 'I'll see you further down the road. I won't stop searching. Ever.' The pair kissed.

Charlotte, though puzzled, released her grip and backed away. Jack turned to face Flint. He limped forward. Flint, seemingly realising what Charlotte was planning, ran towards her. Ignoring the injured Jack. Jack, summoning his remaining bit of strength, prepared to intercept him. Timing it to perfection, he smashed into Flint. The force of the impact, sending the two of them crashing over the low side of the bridge, and into the icy waters below.

'Jack!' Charlotte screamed, racing to where they'd fallen from. She searched desperately for him in the gloom. Briefly catching sight of the pair of them, tossed around like rag-dolls in the raging torrent of water. Then they were gone. She slumped against the bridge. Pushing any thoughts of Jack away, she ran towards the pub. Bursting through the door of the bar, and crashing in a heap onto the floor.

# CHAPTER FIVE

Charlotte stared up. A man stood polishing glasses behind the bar turned to face her. A large unerring grin appeared on his face.

'Somehow, I knew you'd make it,' another voice said. Charlotte spun around to see Gainford seated in a motorised wheelchair. He appeared much older now, his body frail, lines of pain etched across his face. 'I'm sorry about Jack. I liked the boy. So brave, sacrificing himself for you. How noble,' he said. Without a trace of sarcasm. 'I watched it all from this window.'

'I suppose you're going to kill me now?' she said.

'Not at all.' Manoeuvring the chair to a table in the middle of the room, he stopped. 'Get the young lady a drink, will you, barman.'

Charlotte eyeballed Gainford, hatred filling her face. She wandered over to his table and sat opposite him.

Gainford smiled. 'I said I would let go whoever reached here, and that's you, my dear. I bet you hate me at this moment.'

'Hate doesn't come close, Gainford.' The barman placed a vodka and lemonade in front of her. 'What now?' She sneered.

He reached into his pocket, removed a revolver and slid it across the table towards her. 'Why don't you do what you'd like to do?'

She picked up the pistol and pointed it at him, the weight surprising. Gainford smiled back.

'Go on, Charlotte. Fire. Put a bullet through my head. Jack would have.' He goaded.

Charlotte studied the now-frail man in front of her. He appeared to be failing by the minute. He was right. Jack would have killed him, but she wasn't Jack. Shooting Gainford wouldn't bring him back. Placing the gun on the table, she pushed it across to him. 'You'll have to do your own dirty work, Gainford.'

The smile fell from his face. 'In that case, you'll need this.' He removed a key from his pocket, and tossed it to her.

Charlotte caught the key and stared at it in her hand. 'What's this?'

'It's a key.'

'What's it for?'

'What are keys usually for?' he said. 'To open something.' Nodding behind her.

Charlotte turned and stared at a door, exit written above it.

She stood, snatched up her glass and drained its contents. Banging it hard on the table. 'For Jack.' Her voice quivering. 'Twice the man you are, *Gainford.*' With that, she turned and strolled towards the door. Charlotte stopped and turned around one last time. Gainford now slumped forward in his chair. His chin touching his chest, his breathing laboured. He looked broken, a shadow of the man she once admired. Opening the door, she headed through.

At the end of a long corridor she could see a light, and made her way along stopping as it opened into a hallway with three doors. She glanced at the first. Two brass numbers on the front. A one and a zero. The door frame was cracked as if the door had been forced open at some time. She stopped at the second, the paint on it yellowing with age. She could make out, below the layers of paint, writing. Tracing it with her fingers, the letters spelling out Lindsey. She smiled to herself, and moved on to the third. The light in the hallway flickered and went out. The glow from around the last door, now the only brightness. Feeling with her fingers, and locating the keyhole, she inserted the key. As Charlotte turned it she felt the levers of the lock as they passed over the key, and finally as the key itself pushed the mechanism drawing back the latch. Charlotte reached for the handle, took a deep breath, and nudged it open.

# CHAPTER SIX

Charlotte woke. She could barely move. Even the effort of lifting her head, beyond her. It looked as if she was in a hospital. Her room possessing the qualities one would associate with such places. The sides of her bed raised, to prevent her falling out she supposed. Archetypal furniture filled the space. Next to her bed, a cabinet with a vase of fresh flowers on top. Feeling thirsty she glanced to her right, the jug and beaker tantalisingly out of her reach. Charlotte tried to move but failed, the sight of her thin arms causing her to gasp. She lay like this for what seemed a long time to her, before someone entered. A nurse. 'Hello, Charlotte.' She opened the curtains.

'Where am I?' she croaked, through her parched throat and mouth.

The nurse picked up the jug, filled a glass of water. Helping Charlotte to sit, she offered her the beaker. 'You're in *The Monroe Medical Facility*, in Durham.'

Charlotte greedily drank the liquid. 'How did I get here?' Her talking a little more comfortable.

'I'll fetch Dr Whitmore. He'll explain everything.'

Charlotte waited a few moments before a middle-aged, grey-haired man entered. He wore a white medical coat and was accompanied by two similarly dressed people. A younger man, and an older woman.

He stood at the end of her bed with the other two. 'Hello. My name is Dr Whitmore. These are my colleagues, Dr Jacobs and Dr Devling.'

'How did I get here?' Charlotte said.

'Do you mind if we sit, Charlotte?' Pointing at the chairs. Charlotte nodded. The three doctors each pulled up a chair to the side of her bed.

Whitmore smiled at her and took a deep breath. 'You're in a hospital, Charlotte. You've been here for the past two weeks.'

'And before that?' she said.

'For two years you've been trapped inside a computer game called *Insidious*.'

'Game? But what about Jack and the others? Gainford and Paige?'

'They were just characters in the game. Look, Charlotte,' he continued. 'I know this is difficult for you to accept right now, but everything you have experienced in that time isn't real. No matter how realistic it appeared. It wasn't.'

Charlotte scoffed. 'Jack was real. I know he was real. You're lying.'

'I'm sorry,' he said. 'I don't mean to be blunt, but there isn't any other way of explaining this.'

'No! You're wrong. I can remember them all.' She shook her head.

'Look at yourself.' He handed her a mirror.

Charlotte accepted it from him and viewed herself. She gasped as she saw her reflection. Her face, pale and gaunt, her healthy-looking features gone. She touched her face, not quite believing her eyes.

Whitmore forced a smile. 'Insidious was a computer game invented six years ago. It took the world by storm. Everyone of a certain age played it. Unfortunately, it had, shall we say, troubling side effects.'

'What sort of side effects?'

'The game learnt as it went along, each player who played the game adding to its memory. It's learning capacity, almost exponential. Much more than the inventors envisaged. Somewhere along the line, someone played the game who had mental issues. Insidious fed on this individual, absorbing and utilising these defects. His whole personality became the game. You've no idea how having an individual as …' He rubbed his chin, struggling to find the appropriate words.

'Evil,' Charlotte said.

Whitmore glanced at his companions. 'Medical people don't believe in evil. We prefer to provide medical explanations. But for the sake of brevity, I suppose we could call this person evil.'

Charlotte rubbed her face. 'Who was he?'

'His name was Devon Wicken. He was shot dead by police three years ago. By then he'd murdered sixty young women. The authorities believe there may have been a lot more. His crimes were some of the worst recorded. He was.' Whitmore paused. 'An incredibly psychotic individual.'

'How did I end up in this game?' Charlotte said.

'Your family aren't sure. After quite a few died while playing the game, the authorities banned it. They seized the majority of the control modules. A couple went missing, and the game went underground. It seems nothing makes something more attractive than banning it. We traced the last module three months ago.'

Charlotte closed her eyes and re-opening them, stared at Whitmore. 'The one I was connected too?'

'You and six others. At first, the authorities had no idea what to do. But after two of the participants died, while playing the game, they decided to act. We attempted to sever the link, but Insidious resented this and two more passed away in the process. Insidious can't survive unless it has someone playing the game. Only three people, you and two others, have successfully escaped it.'

Charlotte frowned. 'The other two?'

'They weren't as lucky as you. Removing the players from the game caused severe mental issues. We've never been able to gather much information from them. Despite intensive psychiatric treatment.'

'Do I know them?'

'Maybe. We can't be sure. Two young women near to your age called Lindsey and Beth.'

'I knew a Lindsey and a Beth in one of the games.' She thought for a moment, her memory of them hazy.

'They may have been incorporated into it by Insidious,' he said.

'Can I meet them?' she asked.

Whitmore glanced across at his colleagues again. The younger man nodded his approval.

'We'll sort that out for you.' Whitmore said. 'Don't build up your hopes, though. The other two didn't fare anywhere near as well as you.'

'Will they be able to talk with me?' Charlotte said.

'Possibly.' Whitmore said. 'You'll see when you meet them. Can you remember anything before you entered the game? Anything at all?'

Charlotte explained to the three of them what she could remember. Telling them about winning the competition and meeting Gainford. The characters, completing Broken, and finally getting out. As she talked, though, her memories faded. As if the act of remembering them was in some way purging her mind.

Whitmore went on to explain how his team had extracted the other two women. Charlotte, though, had come out of it by herself. Insidious had ceased to function afterwards. Whitmore went on to show her pictures of her family, home and herself. She could remember none of her previous life. It was as if the person in the photos was someone else.

Over the next couple of days, she met her mother, father, and younger sister, Megan. They tried to fill in the gaps for her. Although Charlotte had a vague recollection, she couldn't honestly say she remembered them. Dr Whitmore suggested she keep a journal, to help with her rehabilitation.

Towards the end of the week, she visited a mental hospital where Lindsey and Beth were housed. Dr Whitmore and Dr Jacobs accompanied her on her visit. As they led the way, Charlotte followed.

Lindsey sat on the edge of her bed when Charlotte and the others entered her room.

'Lindsey,' Dr Jacobs said. 'This is Charlotte.'

Lindsey turned and viewed the three of them. She stared hard at Charlotte. A vague recollection appeared in her eyes, but then was gone.

'That's not Charlotte,' she said. 'Charlotte died in the game.'

'No, Lindsey,' Jacobs said. 'Charlotte's here. Look.'

Lindsey looked away. 'You're lying. She's dead. Dead, dead, dead.' She rocked back and forth on her bed. Charlotte approached her and sat. Taking hold of her hand, she smiled. Lindsey calmed. 'None of this is real, you know,' Lindsey whispered. 'None of it exists.'

'I know,' Charlotte said. 'Thanks for meeting me.'

'Everyone is dead. All this.' Lindsey glanced around the room. 'None of it's real. It's all fantasy.'

'What about you, Lindsey?' she asked.

'I'm dead too. Dead, dead, dead.'

'Thank you, Lindsey.' She squeezed her hand, realising further conversation would be futile. Charlotte stood and headed for the door with the two medics, stopping at the threshold for one last look.

'Jack sends his love,' Lindsey said. 'He's not dead. He's looking for you.'

Charlotte edged towards her. 'What?'

Lindsey turned away and fixed her stare out of the window.

'She mentioned Jack,' Charlotte said to Whitmore. Her memory of Jack had faded too, but Lindsey saying his name had opened up a window to her past.

Whitmore patted Charlotte's arm. 'It's random. Lindsey mentions a good deal of names. Her experiences in the game will have been completely different to yours. Maybe there was a Jack in hers, too.'

'Lindsey. Do you remember Jack?' Charlotte asked. Lindsey continued to look into space vacantly, fixing her stare somewhere beyond Charlotte and the doctors' vision.

Charlotte followed the two doctors as they led her along the corridor, and entered the second room. Behind a glass window she saw Beth, lying on her bed, staring blankly at the ceiling.

Whitmore frowned. 'Beth didn't do as well as Lindsey. She's been like that since we liberated her from the game. Unresponsive to stimuli, and unable to speak.'

Charlotte peered in, a deep frown filling her features. Beth and Lindsey were so alive in the game. She remembered now. It was as if meeting them had re-established her link. It was upsetting to see them like this. A dark cloud descended on her. Charlotte and Whitmore entered Beth's room, the doctor stopped at the foot of her bed shrugged and forced a smile. Charlotte strolled across and took hold of her hand. Beth didn't move, the bottom jaw of her mouth hung open, her eyes staring vacantly.

'Hello, Beth,' she said. Beth was unresponsive. 'I'm Charlotte.' Squeezing her hand. Whitmore's mobile sounded. Even this didn't affect Beth's demeanour. Her eyes fixed on something way beyond Charlotte's field of view.

'I'll be outside,' Whitmore said.

Charlotte gazed at Beth, gently stroking the hair away from her eyes. Unseeing, vacant, blank eyes. She stood and turned, and headed for the door.

'He's coming for you,' Beth said.

Charlotte turned on her heels. 'What'd you say?' Scarcely believing Beth had spoken. 'What was that, Beth?'

'He's going to hurt you.' Turning her head to face Charlotte, she fixed her with a stare.

'Who?' Charlotte said.

'The evil man.'

'Who?' Charlotte repeated.

Beth moved her head to its previous position. Somehow Charlotte sensed their conversation was at an end, turning she left the room.

'I think I've seen enough,' she said. Not mentioning what had occurred. In truth, Charlotte was unsure if it even happened. Or if she'd imagined it, her mind confused as reality and fantasy briefly merged.

After weeks of tests, both medical and psychological, she had been allowed home. Although she remembered nothing of her former life, she was becoming accustomed to her new one. Her family helped greatly with her reintegration, providing pictures and videos of her past. As days turned into weeks, and weeks into months, her memories of her time in the game faded.

Charlotte sat in her bedroom, writing in her journal. Staring through the window outside. Spotting something out of the corner of her eye, Charlotte put on her glasses to see better. There was nothing there. Sure somebody had looked up at her room, she moved closer to the window. Charlotte scanned left and right, but saw nothing. Maybe it was a trick of the light she reasoned, and returned to her journal. A memory of Jack drifted into her head. It had been ages since she'd thought about him. Smiling to herself, she realised she missed him. His personality. The way he made her laugh, not out loud but inside. Jack wasn't real, though. He'd only been a character in the game, her smile receded and she began to write. *I wish Jack was real. I miss him so much.*

There was a tap on her bedroom door and her sister, Meg, entered. 'I thought you might fancy some retail therapy,' she said.

'Shopping?' Charlotte said. 'Yeah, I'm up for that. I feel a little down.'

'Why? What's wrong.' Meg put an arm around her sister.

'Nothing. Dr Whitmore said it's a side effect of being inside the game for so long.'

'What was it like?' Meg asked. 'Being inside Insidious. You've hardly spoken about it?'

'It felt so real, I remember that. The characters, and what I did in there, have faded somewhat. If I had to explain. I'd say, imagine all this.' Charlotte waved her hands about. 'Imagine all this not being real. It felt surreal. Even now.'

'You've done well. I think I would've gone crazy.'

Charlotte laughed. 'Who says I haven't?'

Meg grinned. 'Well, you get yourself ready. Put on your best strait-jacket, and we'll go.'

'You mean the shiny pink one?' Charlotte said.

# CHAPTER SEVEN

**2021 - The Freedom Foundation -** Jack gasped, his essence lifted from the icy waters of the river and transported back to the lab. The motor on the *Total Sensory Deprivation Machine* powered down, as the cover slowly lifted. Jack stared at the concerned face of his good friend, George Harmby.

'Bollocks!' Jack said.

Harmby helped him out. 'Jesus, Jack. We just got you back in time. A few more seconds and we'd have lost you.'

'I fell into a river. An ice-cold one.' He Clambered free from the machine. Jack groaned, putting his hand on his thigh as pain shot through it. Receding and disappearing altogether.

'What's up?' Harmby said.

'I was stabbed in the leg in the game. I briefly felt pain, that's all.'

'Oh, Christ, this is bad,' Harmby said. Marching out of the room, closely followed by Jack.

'Why?' Jack said.

'You shouldn't have any physical sensations from the game. Insidious must've sensed you.'

'What?' Continuing after Harmby.

Harmby stopped. 'I'll have to discuss this with the team.'

'Why?' Jack said. 'It's gone now.'

'You don't understand. The board wouldn't allow you to go back in.' He walked on again.

Jack grabbed Harmby's arm. 'You're not going to tell them, are you?'

Harmby shrugged Jack off. 'I can't ignore this. It's dangerous. It's your life we're talking about.'

'I know it's dangerous,' lowering his voice as Richard Lewis, one of Harmby's assistants, entered. 'What about Charlotte?'

'Later, Jack. Later.' Entering his office and closing the door. Jack blew out hard, reluctantly heading for the recovery suite.

Jack finished his post-game briefing. The questions were more in-depth than usual. He hated having to go through the rigmarole, and he was finding today's more tiresome than usual. He suspected Harmby ordered the additional questioning. Which Jack found annoying, as he wanted to get back into the game at the earliest opportunity. He'd come close to freeing Charlotte, he was sure. Every day she spent in there made it harder to extract her. Lewis finished his questioning and thanked Jack.

'What are your thoughts?' Jack said.

Lewis frowned. 'I'll have to let Harmby see the data. He'll decide.'

'I know that,' Jack said. 'But what's your gut instinct?'

Lewis tapped his pen on the clipboard he was holding. 'I believe Insidious has recognised you. It's probably aware of the threat you pose. Without Charlotte, it can't continue. Without her mental input, it'll die.'

Jack scoffed. 'Die! You make it sound human.'

'In a way it is. The total sum of dozens of players that have passed through it. But without a consciousness to feed on, it'll cease to be.'

'If Insidious has recognised me, what'll that mean?'

Lewis stood. 'If you go in again, it'll seek to eliminate you.'

'She's my wife, Richard. I can't let her rot in there.'

'I know. But it's not my decision.'

'If it were?'

'I wouldn't let you back in,' Lewis said.

**2016 -** Charlotte and Meg entered the coffee shop, their arms full of shopping bags. Charlotte sat at a table while Meg got the drinks. She took out her journal and scribbled a few notes as she waited. Glancing up from the book, she spotted someone in the corner looking at her. He turned away as she stared across at him.

Meg roused Charlotte from her thoughts popping two cups in front of her. 'He's cute.' Nodding towards the young barista behind the counter.

Charlotte smiled. 'He's all right.' Watching as the man who had been looking at her as he stood, and left the shop.

'You're not looking,' Meg said.

'I am. He is cute. Seems a little young for you.'

'He's twenty-four,' Meg said. 'That's only a year difference.'

'Really. He looks younger.'

'I might get myself a cake.' Meg glanced at him. 'Do you want one?'

Charlotte shook her head. 'No thanks. I've gone right off sweet stuff. Off most things, actually.'

Meg frowned. 'You should eat more. You look a lot better than you did when you first got out. But you could still do with putting on a few more pounds.'

'Ok, mother hen. I'll have a slice of carrot cake.'

'Great,' Meg said. 'It means I don't need to ruin my diet.' Smiling, she got up.

Charlotte watched her sister return to the counter and switched her view outside. She saw the man, who'd been in the shop, now stood across the road. He was looking at her again, she was sure. A bus pulled up in front of him and stopped. She waited for it to leave and when it did, he was gone.

'Paranoia, Charlotte,' she said to herself. 'That's all it is.'

**2021 -** Jack marched along the corridor and stopped at the director's door. He paused and took a breath before knocking and entering. Charles Exelby, The Institute Director, sat behind his desk. Harmby and Lewis opposite him.

'Sit down, Jack,' Exelby said.

Jack forced a smile. 'Bit formal, this.'

Exelby clasped his hands together, allowing them to rest on his ample stomach. 'How are you?'

'No offence, Charles, but you didn't invite me here to ask how I am.'

'Jack, there's no need to be defensive,' Harmby said.

'Let's cut the bull,' Jack said. 'When am I going back in?'

Exelby glanced at the two other men, before turning his attention back to Jack. 'There's no easy way of telling you this, but you're not.'

'What!' Jack said.

'We can't risk it,' Harmby said. 'Insidious knows who you are. It knows you're trying to release Charlotte. If you go back in—'

'It's my wife in there. My life to risk.'

'No, it's not, Jack' Exelby said. 'We have a duty of care.'

'Fuck the duty of care. Charlotte's saved loads of people from the game. You're just going to let her rot,' he said.

Harmby held up his hands. 'Calm down. We've decided on an alternative. Richard is prepared to go in and get her out.'

'No offence, Richard,' Jack said. 'But you won't last five minutes.'

'It's what we've decided,' Exelby said. 'The decision has been made.'

Jack sneered. 'And if he fails? What then?'

Richard stared at Jack. 'Insidious will treat me as another player. It'll give me valuable time to locate and extract Charlotte. Time, you won't have.'

'My wife's going to die in this game, and her blood will be on your hands, gentleman.'

Harmby peered upwards. 'Jack. Let's not—'

'Fuck you, George. I thought we were friends.' He sprung to his feet.

'You're out of order, Jack,' Exelby said.

'Yeah. Well, fuck you, too.' Heading for the door, he stopped and turned. 'Good luck, Richard. You'll need it.' Jack opened the door, glared at the three men and left, slamming it behind him. Making his way along a series of corridors, he entered medical suite one.

A nurse, filling in some paperwork, glanced up as he entered. 'Hi, Jack.' She smiled at him.

'Hi, Jen. I've come to see Charlotte.'

'Of course.' Moving from behind the desk, as Jack followed her through a door. He stopped and stared at his unconscious wife lying on a medical bed. Wires connecting her to sophisticated machinery, and food and drink tubes. If it hadn't been for the hardware surrounding her, anyone would've believed she was sleeping thought Jack.

'How's she been?' he said.

'Much the same.' Jen said. 'There's been a small reduction in muscle mass. The new electronic muscular stimulation equipment appears to have slowed it down, though. Charlotte mightn't be ready for a marathon when she gets out, but at least her body won't have withered away.'

Jack lowered his eyes. 'They've taken me off the program.'

'Why?'

'Insidious detected me. If I go back in, it'll know and try to kill me.'

'What're they going to do?'

'They're sending Richard in,' Jack said.

She put a hand on his arm. 'He's a good bloke.'

'It's just …'

'I know,' she said. 'Do you want a few moments?'

'If you don't mind.'

The nurse smiled again and left the room. Jack pulled a chair up next to his wife's bed and brought his hand up to her face, allowing it to linger. 'I've failed you, Charlotte.' Tears filled his eyes. 'I wish you'd just get out, somehow.' He leant forward and kissed her on the lips. He hated visiting this place. It brought home to him how much he missed her. He replaced the chair and waved at Jen, half-heartedly, as he left.

**2016** - Charlotte and Meg left the coffee shop after Meg arranged a date with the handsome barista.

'So,' Charlotte said. 'What's handsomes name, then?'

'Harry.' She smiled. 'Meal, then the pictures.'

'What are you seeing?' They reached Meg's car.

'Who cares? I'll spend most of the evening staring into his eyes.'

'I'm sure you will.' Charlotte climbed into the passenger seat, glancing across the road she saw someone looking at them, fumbling for her glasses she hastily put them on.

Meg started the car up. 'What are you looking at?'

'That guy over there. He was in the coffee shop earlier.'

'So?' Meg said.

'He was staring at me from outside the coffee shop, too.'

'Are you sure?' Meg said.

'Pretty much,' she said, as the man raced off.

Meg raised her eyebrows. 'Maybe he fancies you.'

'Maybe,' she said.

Meg drove home, the two of them putting any thoughts of the man behind them. Once back, Charlotte headed upstairs to try on her new outfits and write in her journal. She felt depressed. Dr Whitmore warned her she would have days like these. She thought about the man and wondered if she was imagining he was spying on her. Picking up her journal she wrote. *'I wish Jack was here. I miss him so much.'*

The man unlocked the door to the cellar and descended the steps. He stopped at another door at the foot of them, opening this too, before entering. The room dimly lit, had a musty smell to it. A large cage stood in one corner of the chamber. The man strolled across to the cage and kicked the front of it with his foot. The creature inside whimpered, the way a frightened animal would.

'Good news, Sarah.' His voice a low monotone. 'I've found someone new. Your torment will soon be over. I've only got to decide what to keep from you. Just think, you'll be immortalised with the others. He wandered across to the far side of the room, to a table. Looking at items of jewellery and locks of human hair. Scattered amongst these were bits of human existence. A purse, a picture of a baby, hair-slides, and a single glove. Above the table, shelves, rows of jars neatly placed along their length. He perused the jars and their contents. Within each, a preserved organ or piece of human viscera. In another, two eyeballs gently lay at the bottom. He touched the glass and allowed his fingers to trace along the jars. His excitement mounting as he remembered their former owners, closing his eyes he smiled. His tongue protruding lizard-like, as he licked the scar of his hair-lip.

'Her name is Charlotte.' He turned, his eyes taking on a manic stare. 'I'm coming for you, my dear,' he whispered. 'Soon.'

Charlotte jolted from her sleep, sat up in bed, sweating profusely, the image of her nightmare burning brightly in her mind. She rubbed her eyes, before closing them tight. Trying to shake the vision, but stubbornly it refused to budge. Jumping from her bed, she picked up her laptop and ran a search on the internet. Multiple available pages on the screen jumped out at her. Devon Wicken - serial killer, said one. She pressed the Wikipedia entry and stared in astonishment at his face, as the man from her nightmare stared back at her.

# CHAPTER EIGHT

**2021** - Harmby summoned Jack, or at least that's how it appeared to him. Harmby, along with Richard Lewis, stood in the room making fine adjustments to the equipment.

'Ah, Jack,' Harmby said. 'Have you got a moment?'

'Of course.' He followed Harmby towards his office. Lewis shrugged and smiled, apologetically as he passed.

Harmby pointed at a chair and forced a smile. 'Take a seat. How are we today?'

'I don't know how *we* are, George, but *I'm* all right.'

'Good. Good.' He rubbed his chin. 'Can I get you a drink?'

Jack sat back in his chair. 'It would be better if you got to the point.'

'Quite,' Harmby said. 'I know we had words yesterday. I know you think we've made the wrong decision, but—'

'You'd like me to help Richard,' Jack said.

'Well, yes. It'd help greatly.'

'I can't believe you thought I wouldn't. Of course, I'll help. She's my wife, for God's sake.'

'I know, it's just—'

Jack put his hands up. 'George. I said things yesterday that were out of order. We've been friends for a long time, and I wouldn't want anything to spoil our friendship.'

'I appreciate that. If you could give Richard all the help you can. We intend to send him in around 18.00.'

Jack stood. 'I'll go along now.'

'We'll get her back,' Harmby said. 'I promise.'

'I know you will.'

Jack entered the lab. Lewis, with one of his assistants helping him, readied the equipment. Jack stopped inside the room and waited.

'Jack,' Lewis said. 'Come in.'

'Harmby said you needed my help.'

Lewis smiled at his assistant. 'Can you give us a moment?'

She nodded at Richard and left.

Jack wandered across to the machine. 'You're going under at 18.00.'

'Yeah, that's the plan.'

'What can I help you with?' Jack said.

'Take a seat.' The pair sat. 'The thing is, I'm a little nervous.'

'You'll be ok,' he said. Sensing that's what Lewis wanted to hear.

'What's it like?'

'You were there when I completed the briefings,' Jack said. 'I told you how it works.'

'I know, but I was hoping you'd give me a few extra insights.'

'I'll be honest,' Jack said. 'It won't be easy. You won't remember any of this. Your memories are gone. The persona the game assigns envelops you. Totally.'

Lewis rubbed his chin. 'Is there no hint about your real life?'

'None. Except …' Jack paused for a moment.

'Except?' Lewis said.

'Jamais vu,' Jack said.

'Jamais vu?'

'A feeling that although something's familiar, it feels somehow strange. As if what you're experiencing isn't real. You have no point of reference, so you tend to ignore this. If I'm honest, though, *it will save your life.*'

Lewis stood and peeked outside into the corridor, satisfied, he sat down. 'Just making sure nobody overhears this.' Jack frowned. 'I need to tell you something,' Lewis continued. 'Insidious is showing signs of breaking down.'

'Breaking down?' Isn't that good news for Charlotte?'

'Not really. Quite the reverse. Charlotte and Insidious are so intrinsically linked now, the thought is …' He paused, looking for the right words. 'If it fails, we could lose Charlotte.'

Jack got to his feet. 'Lose?' You mean she'll die.'

'She may not die, but she will suffer severe mental damage. We've run scenarios, and they don't look good.'

'What do you mean by that? Come on, Richard. For Christ's sake.'

'Jack, please sit down. I'll be in serious bother for telling you this. I was sworn to secrecy, by Harmby and the director.'

Jack slumped back in his seat. 'Yet you told me.'

'I'm looking at the only person who can save her.'

'What?' Jack said.

'I'm probably throwing away my career here, but I think you should go back in. I'll be honest. I'm scared shitless.'

'But I thought Insidious had recognised me?'

'It may have. I've got a possible solution, though.'

Jack leant in closer. 'What?'

'I can cover your persona. I've developed a programme we can introduce into Insidious. It'll cloak your image with a false one.'

'Why haven't we used this before?'

'Insidious would've cottoned on straight away. Because it's compromised, we have a better chance. I can't promise too much, though. You'll be up against it, time-wise.'

'How long?'

'I've no idea. Insidious will realise it has an alien programme and attempt to eradicate it. If that happens, it'll blow your cover. I've also incorporated some help along the way.'

'What sort of help?' Jack said.

'It's a complicated algorithm. I'm not entirely sure what form it'll take in the game. Hopefully, though, it'll be of some help. Something you may find familiar. That's if Insidious doesn't recognise and eradicate it first.

'How long?' Jack repeated.

'Hours, days, possibly weeks. It's a sophisticated program, but Insidious is an incredibly clever device.'

'I can't let you throw your career down the pan like this. Harmby will sack you when he finds out.'

Lewis reached into a black bag next to him and pulled out a small case. 'That's why I've got this.' He opened it, revealing a syringe.

Jack took it from him. 'What's in it?'

'It's a fast-acting sedative. I'll tell Harmby you over-powered and drugged me.'

Jack laughed. 'I'll be finished after this.'

'But you could have her back. And you do want her back?' Lewis said.

'More than anything.'

Lewis stood. 'Get here at 17.30, and we'll do it. I'll concoct a story.'

'What about the programme you're introducing?'

'That's between you and me. No one else knows.'

Jack closed his eyes as the machine fired up. He took a deep breath and uttered a prayer as the memories of who he was, and who he'd been, were replaced by someone new. Someone unfamiliar. Within seconds he was subsumed by the character. The machine whirred, as the prone form of the unconscious Lewis, lay on the floor.

**2016** - Charlotte finished her meeting with Dr Whitmore. She'd told him about her nightmare and that she believed someone was watching her.

Whitmore managed to assuage her fears. Telling her dreams like hers, were likely. The length of time she'd spent within the game could have profound effects on her. He arranged for additional counselling sessions. Enabling her to discuss these problems in more depth. She left feeling much better and descended into the underground car park, in a more positive frame of mind.

She stopped at her car, threw her handbag onto the passenger seat, and got in. She started the engine up, but spotted an elderly gentleman, his left arm in a sling, struggling to put a box in the hatchback of his car. She got out and strode across to him. 'Can I help you?'

'That's kind of you. It's this damned arm.'

'How'd you do it,' she said.

'A fall at home. I'm not a sprightly as I once was.'

Charlotte picked up the box. 'Let me.' Sliding it along the flat back seat of the estate car.

As she turned, the man brought the cosh down hard on her head. Charlotte slumped across the boot, not quite unconscious. The man lifted her legs and in one quick movement, pushed her inside. He reached and opened a bag to the side of the boot, and pulled out a rag which he placed across her mouth. Charlotte looked up, and noticed the man's false moustache had become dislodged. Beneath it, a scar from his hair-lip surgery was visible before darkness enveloped her.

# CHAPTER NINE

Detective Inspector Alex Robinson sat in his office. The remnants of the lunch he'd eaten, scattered across his desk. He took a large swig of his coffee, as the only other person in the room looked on.

'Your diet's terrible,' Detective Sergeant Russ Elwick said.

'Who are you? My mother?' Robinson said.

Elwick smiled. 'Doesn't bother me. I'll have that seat when you have your coronary.'

'It's all yours, bonnie lad.'

Robinson's phone sounded, the handset loudly vibrating on his desk. He sighed and glanced at the clock. 'Robinson,' he said. Listening, he grunted now and again. 'On our way.' He hung up. 'Get your coat, Russ. Possible abduction.'

Elwick rolled his eyes. 'Why'd we always get them near the end of the shift?'

Robinson grabbed his coat. 'Shit happens.'

Robinson and Elwick drew up outside *The Monroe Medical Facility* and were met by another officer, as they exited the vehicle.

'Possible abduction?' Robinson said to the officer.

'More than possible, Guv.' DC Wells said. 'Almost certainly. Her name's Charlotte Richmond, twenty-seven. She was attending an appointment.'

Robinson marched towards the building, closely pursued by Elwick and Wells. 'What have we got, then?'

'Some CCTV footage from the car park,' Wells said. 'One of the staff found a car with its door open.' The officers made their way inside and entered a room with *Security* marked on the door. A uniformed guard stood as the three men burst in.

Wells pointed at the guard. 'This is Phillip Smith, Guv. Can you show the Inspector the film, Phillip?

Smith complied, pressing a button on a console as the footage began. It showed a woman getting into her car. After a few seconds, she got back out and headed out of view. A few moments passed before a red vehicle was seen driving from the car park. The driver of the car not visible.

'Is that it?' Robinson said. 'What happened to the woman?'

'We believe she was in the car.' Smith said. 'One of the car park security men found her car with the door wide open and the keys in the ignition.'

'Who does the red car belong to?' Elwick said.

Wells peered at his notepad. 'A doctor Stephen Wright. Somebody stole it this morning. We think that's how he was able to get into the car park. He used Wright's security pass.'

Robinson stared at the guard. 'Haven't we got a better view of the driver?'

The guard shook his head. 'No.' That's the best footage.'

Robinson blew out hard. 'I don't know why people install these cameras. They show bugger all.' He stomped out of the room, followed by his officers. 'Who was she meeting here?'

'A Doctor Whitmore,' Wells said.

Robinson stopped. 'Right. Take me to this doctor. I want CCTV footage of the surrounding area. Let's see if we can find out where he went, and what he looks like.' Robinson resumed his march.

Robinson and Elwick sat in a room as Whitmore entered. 'Sorry to keep you waiting, gentlemen,' he said. 'Can I get either of you a drink?'

'Not for me,' Robinson said. Elwick shook his head.

'Charlotte Richmond?' Robinson said.

Whitmore sat. 'She's a patient of mine.'

'Can I ask the nature of her appointment this morning?' Robinson said.

'I'm not at liberty to disclose that information, Inspector. Client confidentiality.'

'We've reason to believe Miss Richmond was abducted after visiting you. We need to know if the reason she was here, had anything to do with that.'

'How awful,' Whitmore said. 'Yes of course. I'll assist in any way I can.'

Robinson sat back, nodding slowly. 'What can you tell me about her?'

'Have you heard of *Insidious*, Inspector?'

'Yeah,' Robinson said. 'It was the game the authorities outlawed a few years back.'

'Charlotte Richmond was liberated from Insidious three months ago. She'd been in the game for two years.'

'Really?' Robinson said.

Elwick looked up from his notepad. 'Could her being in this game have anything to do with her disappearing?'

'I don't see how. The appointment this morning was to evaluate Charlotte's progress. Being trapped in this game for that long comes with unique problems.'

'What sort of problems?' Robinson said.

'Charlotte was progressing well, but she was concerned someone was watching her.'

'Did she say who?' Robinson said.

'No. However, Charlotte did complain about a bad nightmare. In her dream, she saw Devon Wicken.'

Robinson glanced at Elwick. 'The serial killer?'

'The same. Devon Wicken played Insidious a few years ago. We believe his persona caused the problems with the game in the first place.'

Robinson scoffed. 'Bit sci-fi, this. In any case, one person we know didn't abduct her is Devon Wicken.'

'Quite,' Whitmore said.

'Was there anything else she told you?' Elwick said.

'No. That was it.'

After concluding their interview. The officers visited Charlotte's family and headed back to the station. Robinson marched into his office, followed by Elwick and Wells. 'Shut the door, boys.' He slumped into his seat.

'It's him, isn't it?' Elwick said.

Robinson nodded. 'Looks that way. Same M.O.'

'Anything on Sarah Trent?' Robinson said. Looking at Wells.

'Not yet, Guv. If he follows the same pattern, it shouldn't be long.'

Robinson stood. 'Well. There's nothing else we can do tonight, boys. We'll sleep on it. See what tomorrow brings.'

Elwick's mobile phone sounded. 'Elwick,' he said. '... Ok, let me know what forensics come up with.'

'Who's that?' Robinson said.

'They've found the car. They're going over it now.'

Robinson reached for his coat. 'Yeah. Like they'll come up with anything. Let me know if they manage to change water into wine,' he shouted over his shoulder, as he left.

Charlotte woke and reached for her head touching the spot where the man struck her. It was tender, and she could feel a large bump there.

She blinked her eyes against the gloom, her vision slowly coming into focus. She was in a metal cage. The ones large dogs are kept in. She tried the door at the front of it, more in hope than anything. The door was locked, a large padlock securing it. A shuffling movement to her left caught her attention, and Charlotte listened carefully. Her heart-rate rising appreciably.

'Hello,' she said. 'My name's Charlotte.'

She could see a form, housed in a cage like her, but she couldn't decipher its contents.

'What's your name?' Charlotte said.

'Sarah,' whispered a voice.

'Where are we, Sarah?'

'Hell,' she said. 'We're in hell.'


Robinson and Elwick sat opposite each other as DC Wells entered.

'You were right, Guv. There weren't any prints in the car. There are DNA matches with the owner and his family. We found DNA from Charlotte Richmond in the boot, though.'

'And?' Robinson said.

'It's his DNA,' Wells said.

Robinson leant back in his chair, placing his hands behind his head. 'We've got ourselves a copy-cat killer.'

'He has to have known Devon Wicken,' Elwick said. 'The first girl we found had all his trademarks.'

Robinson rubbed his chin. 'Yeah. I'm going to meet the copper who led the case into Wicken's murders. DI Robert Hayes. He may have some insight into this.'

Elwick picked up a file. 'There was no mention of an accomplice in the case notes. Maybe something was missed.'

'Get your things together, Russ,' Robinson said. Elwick nodded. 'There's no time like the present.'


The two of them drove from Durham to Peterlee. Arriving at Hayes' last known abode. A flat in a tower block, on the outskirts of the town. The lift which was out of order forced them to climb the three floors to his flat. They stopped outside his door. Elwick knocked as the two of them recovered their breath and waited. The door opened an inch.

The unshaven features of a man peered through the gap. 'Yeah.'

'Robert Hayes?' Elwick said.

'Who are you?'

Robinson held out his credentials. 'DI Robinson and DC Elwick. Can we have a chat?'

The door opened fully. The two officers followed the man through a short corridor, and into the kitchen.

'Tea?' Hayes said.

'Not for me,' Robinson said. Elwick shook his head.

Hayes picked up the kettle. 'So? What can I do for you two?'

'We'd like to ask you about the Devon Wicken case.'

Hayes stopped briefly with the kettle poised in his right hand. He trod across to the sink, half-filled the kettle, and placed it back on its stand. He pressed the button to start it boiling and turned.

'What about it?' he said.

'We were hoping you'd give us an insight into him,' Robinson said.

'Devon Wicken, gents, was the evilest man I ever met. He cost me my career, marriage, and kids.'

'I'm sorry to hear that,' Robinson said. 'I know it's probably hard talking about it, but—'

'I descended into hell when I, when we, discovered his cottage. Everything you want to know is in the case notes. I can't tell you anything more.'

'We may have a copy-cat,' Elwick said.

Hayes rubbed his chin with his right hand. Shakily, he lifted the kettle and poured the boiling liquid into a cup. Droplets of the hot liquid splashing either side of it.

Hayes blew out hard. 'The world didn't merit a bastard like Wicken. It certainly doesn't deserve another. I can't help you, though. I can't go back there. I've been dry for six months now, and I've no desire to dive into a bottle again. Wicken filled my head with so much shit, no amount of booze could obliterate it.'

'I understand—' Robinson said.

'No. You don't!' Hayes said. 'You really fucking don't. I was a copper, and in the job you expect to come up against some awful people. But Wicken went beyond that. His cellar was like an abattoir. Bits of those poor girls in jars. Can you imagine trying to speak with their parents, while all the time, knowing what he did to them?' Hayes lurched towards the sink and vomited into it.

'Are you ok?' Elwick said.

'I'm all right.' Waving the officer away.

'I'm sorry,' Robinson said. 'It's just … We wondered if there was ever any suspicion he had an accomplice?'

Hayes ran the tap, splashed water onto his face, and dried his face on a hand-towel. He turned to face the officers, glanced at Robinson, and fixed Elwick with a stare. 'I don't think so. We assumed he was a lone attacker. Nothing he did, led us to suspect he had help.' Glancing at Robinson again, and then back at Elwick.

'Sorry to bother you,' Robinson said. Nodding first to Elwick, and then the door. 'It was Wicken who died?' Robinson paused at the threshold.

Hayes sneered. 'Of course it was Wicken. His DNA matched.'

'No facial identification?' Robinson said.

'Tom, my DS, was first on the scene. He was attacked by Wicken and fatally stabbed. Before he died, though, he got a shot off obliterating Wicken's face. They couldn't do a face match. All this is in the case notes, Robinson.'

'I know,' Elwick said. 'But they're huge. It'd take us months to trawl through them.'

Hayes sighed. 'Murdering more than sixty women tends to do that.' He slumped down at the table with his cup.

'Thanks for your help,' Robinson said. 'We'll let ourselves out.' Turning, he marched towards the door.

'Watch your back, Elwick,' Hayes whispered.

'What?' Elwick said.

Hayes picked up his cup and turned away. Elwick frowned, turned, and followed Robinson out.

Charlotte tried to continue her dialogue with Sarah, but she seemed reluctant to speak. Any noise from the floor above would have her moving to the back of her cage, whimpering. Charlotte listened to what she assumed to be the front door shutting, and the sound of a car engine starting up.

'Sarah?' Charlotte said.

'Yes,' Sarah whispered.

'How long have you been here?'

'Seven or eight weeks, I think. I can't be sure.'

'Have you always been on your own?' Charlotte said.

'No,' she said. 'There was another girl. Helen.'

'What happened to Helen?'

Sarah let out a sob. 'He killed her.'

'How'd you know?'

'He killed her in this room, in front of me. He made me sit in a chair and watch.' Her sobbing increased. 'Helen screamed, but I couldn't watch. I tried to block it out, but I couldn't.'

Charlotte crawled to the front of her cage. 'Can you see me,'

'No,' Sarah said. 'When I wouldn't watch, he …'

Charlotte frowned, pushing her face against the cage. 'What do you mean?'

'He'll make you watch when he kills me. You mustn't look away, though,' Sarah said. Sarah's head appeared towards the front of her cage. A bandage wrapped around the place where her eyes should've been. 'He doesn't like it if you look away.'

# CHAPTER TEN

Robinson and Elwick attended a briefing with the Chief Inspector, explaining the case to him. They now believed someone was copying Devon Wicken's crimes. Helen Philby's mutilated body had been discovered three months earlier. The copycat appeared to be following the same M.O. as Wicken. Wicken took a new victim approximately every two months. Once he had a new victim, he'd murder and dump the body of the previous girl. Sarah Andrews had been missing for almost two months now. Charlotte Richmond had just been taken. If it continued in the same vein, they expected to discover Sarah's body soon. They had nothing to go on, though. Robinson and his team dug into Wicken's past to establish a link. So far, they'd been unsuccessful. Fearing as with Wicken, this killer could be months and a countless number of murders from being caught. The Chief Constable told them of his intention of giving a press conference. He wanted the women out there to know they were in danger, and not to allow themselves to go unaccompanied. Robinson and Elwick agreed with this and left him to draw something up.

Elwick brought the car to a halt outside the house. A mid-terraced property, its front garden massively overgrown. The gate to the building hanging on one hinge.

Robinson glanced at his notebook. 'This is it.'

'She probably won't be happy with us turning up,' Elwick said.

'Well. We've nothing else to go on, so we'll have to start somewhere.'

The two officers got out of the car and headed up the short litter-strewn path. Elwick knocked on the old front door, its paintwork peeling from years of neglect. There was no answer, the curtain in the downstairs window twitched. Elwick knocked again, much harder this time. Someone headed towards the door and began undoing bolts and chains.

The door opened a couple of inches. 'What do you want?' said the voice from inside.

Robinson flashed his credentials. 'Can we talk, Mrs Wicken?'

The door opened further. The two officers following the elderly woman through into the lounge. The room was a mess, months of newspapers strewn all over the living room. Old cups and plates, with remnants of food scattered randomly on almost every table, chair, and sideboard. Unopened post lay around the many dusty surfaces.

'We're sorry to bother you, Mrs Wicken. I'm Inspector Robinson, and this is DS Elwick. We'd like to ask some questions regarding your son.'

'Mrs Jones,' she said. 'I haven't used Wicken since ...' Her voice trailed off. 'My son is dead. It's the best place for him.' She slumped into one of the armchairs. 'He was evil.'

'The thing is,' Robinson said. 'We'd like some background information. Friends of his.'

'Devon didn't have any friends.'

'Have you any photos of him?' Elwick said. 'From his past?'

'I burnt most of them. I kept one album.' Pointing to the sideboard. Elwick walked across and picked up the book, brushing the dust away from it with his hand.

She picked up her handbag. 'I kept it because there were pictures of him when he was a boy. Before he turned into a monster. Before he turned into ...'

Elwick held the book aloft. 'Can we have a look?'

'Why? My son's dead. Your lot shot him when they found all those poor girls.' She started crying. Robinson handed her a dusty tissue box. 'Why can't you leave the past where it is? I gave birth to him. If I'd known what he'd grow into, I would have killed him myself.'

'It's something we're working on,' Robinson said.

'Is this about those missing girls?' she said.

Robinson nodded. 'We've reason to believe someone's copying your son's murders. We're hoping there's a link between the two of them.'

Mrs Jones reached into her bag and removed a packet of cigarettes, shakily lighting one. She took a deep draw on it and sighed.

Elwick flicked through the album. The photos of Wicken were of him as a baby up to about the age of twelve or thirteen. All the pictures, except one, had Wicken captured on his own. This one, though, had him and a smaller boy. Standing on a beach somewhere. 'Who's this other kid?' Showing her the photo.

Mrs Jones took it from him and putting on her glasses, viewed the snap. 'He was a boy who lived down the road from us. His name was William Morris. He and Devon knocked around together for a while. I think his family moved away.' Handing the photo back to Elwick. 'I've no idea where.'

'Is it ok for us to keep this one?' Elwick said. Mrs Jones nodded.

'Were there any other friends?' Robinson said.

'None I remember. Devon was a loner. They got on because they both got bullied. Devon because of his hair-lip scar, and William because he was small. They formed a sort of bond.'

'Thanks for your time,' Robinson said.

She grunted as she accepted the photo album from Elwick, and clutched it to her breast. Opening it she smiled, leafing through the pages as the two officers left.

They climbed into the car. 'What do you think, Guv?' Elwick said.

'Bit of a long shot, I know, but we haven't anything else to go on. See if you can locate this William Morris.'

Charlotte sat in the cage as she listened to the footsteps descend the stairs to the cellar. Sarah pushed herself into the corner of her cage, curling into a ball. The door opened, and he walked in. Charlotte squinted at him in the gloom of the room, trying to see his face. He strolled across to her cage and squatted in front of it. She stared up at her jailer, the features of Devon Wicken staring back. But the face wasn't real. Something appeared false.

'Hello Charlotte,' he whispered.

She said nothing, her attention captured by a whimper from Sarah's cage.

'Ignore her. She used to be my favourite, but not anymore. You're my number one now.' As he pushed his face closer to the front of her cage, she realised what it was. He wore a mask. The man was dressed in a Devon Wicken mask. She stared at it, puzzled. The man who'd attacked her in the car park wasn't wearing a mask. Had it been Wicken, though, or had she only imagined it was him. She wasn't sure now, her mind whirring.

His eyes stared at her through the mask. 'I'm not sure I like your hair.' Sarah let out another whimper. 'Shut up!' Walking across to her cage, he kicked it. 'You need teaching a lesson.'

'Please don't hurt her,' Charlotte said.

'Compassion?' the man said. 'Compassion is a weakness, Charlotte. Compassion is what got you here.'

'Hasn't she suffered enough?'

'I'll decide when she's suffered enough. I hope you're not going to be difficult?' He returned to her cage. 'I may have to do something about that.'

He strode to the other side of the room and picked something up. Charlotte watched as he squatted and unlocked the door to her cage.

She readied herself to lunge at him, but as the door swung open, something hit her. Unable to move, as the voltage from the taser discharged itself.

Robinson and Elwick sat sifting through a mountain of paperwork. Elwick had never seen as much for any one case.

The door to the office opened, and a young female DC entered. 'I've got some information on William Morris, sir. His family emigrated for a time but returned in 1990. They moved to Sandsend, near Whitby. William Morris still lives there.'

'Have you Morris' address?' Robinson said.

'Yes, sir.' She handed him a piece of paper.

'Well done, Sally,' he said. 'Grab your stuff, bonnie lad. We're off to the seaside.'

Charlotte came to. She sat in a chair, her arms, legs, and torso secured with tape. She glanced over her shoulder, craning to look at Sarah's cage. The girl huddled in one of the corners.

'Hello, Charlotte.' He said, pushing his face near to hers. The eyes, the only piece of his face visible behind the mask. Charlotte jumped as he pulled a pair of scissors from behind his back. 'Time for a haircut.' Menacingly he held them out for her to see. He picked up a piece of her hair and cut it off, carrying it across to the table he deposited it along with his other trophies. Returning to cut some more. His clipping, moving from slow and meticulous to deranged within seconds. Wielding the scissors, wildly. Charlotte yelped as she felt the tip of them strike her forehead. A trickle of blood ran past her eye. He paused to inspect his work before resuming. Finally satisfied, he stepped back to view his finished creation. Charlotte's shoulder-length hair reduced to tatters.

'Now, that's much better.' Touching an index finger to her bloodied forehead. He viewed the blood on it. Turning, he lifted his mask momentarily and tasted her blood.

'You're mine, now Charlotte.' He replaced his mask, turned, and pressed a cloth across her mouth. She fought to stay awake, her body quickly losing the battle.

# CHAPTER ELEVEN

Robinson and Elwick reached the address in Sandsend. The property an old Victorian-built detached house, perched up on a hill. Parking, they headed along the driveway. Elwick pressed the bell, the name Morris printed below it. A few seconds passed before the door opened. A middle-aged, attractive woman, stood there.

Robinson showed his card, 'Mrs Morris?' Elwick did likewise.

'Yes,' she said.

'Is your husband in?' Robinson said.

'Yes. Would you like to come in?' Moving aside, allowing the officers to enter. 'Billy!' she shouted up the stairs.

A man appeared at the top, peering over the bannister. 'Yeah?'

'There are two policemen here.'

The man trod his way downstairs, stopping at the foot of them. His eyes narrowing. 'Oh yes?'

'It's nothing to worry about,' Elwick said. 'Just routine stuff.'

'Should we go through into the lounge?' Morris said, as he led the way. The officers and Mrs Morris following. He motioned for them to sit, which they did. Morris and his wife sat opposite.

'Can I ask you about Devon Wicken,' Robinson said.

Morris sat back in his chair. 'Bloody hell. That's a blast from the past.'

'Devon Wicken, the murderer?' his wife said.

Robinson glanced at her. 'Yes.'

'When did you last speak with him?' Elwick said.

'The last time I spoke to Devon Wicken was thirty-years ago. I was twelve when I last saw him. Why? Devon Wicken is dead.'

'I know, but …' Elwick paused, and looked across at Robinson who nodded. 'There have been abductions of young women. There are similarities to his crimes. We believe we may have a copy-cat.'

'How does this involve me?' Morris said.

'We're looking into his past,' Elwick said. 'We believe whoever's doing this, knew Wicken.'

'I can't help you, gentlemen. I only knew Devon as a boy. Before he turned into a monster. As I said, I haven't seen him in years. I've never told anyone about knowing him. You can imagine what the press would be like if they found out. I'm a solicitor, and I can't afford any bad publicity.'

Elwick handed Morris a piece of paper. 'We appreciate that. Could we ask where you were on the following dates?'

Morris studied the paper. Disappearing, he returned shortly after with his diary and showed it to the officers. Elwick jotted down the information he provided.

After asking one or two more routine questions, he and Robinson left.

Elwick stopped at the car door. 'What do you think, Guv?'

'We won't know until we investigate his alibi's. If they check out, we're no further forward.'

Charlotte woke, her head banging. A pounding headache, caused by the taser she supposed.

Pushing herself into a seated position. 'Sarah,' she said. 'Are you there?'

'Yes,' Sarah whispered.

'Has he hurt you?' Charlotte said.

'No. He told me my suffering would be over soon.'

'When?'

'Tonight.'

'Oh, God,' Charlotte said. She'd never felt so helpless.

Robinson and Elwick were back at the station when Robinson's phone rang. He sipped his coffee, placed the cup down, and picked up the phone in one swift movement. 'Robinson.' He listened to the caller. 'I'll be along shortly. Show him into one of the interview rooms.'

'Who's that?' Elwick said.

'William Morris is here. He wants to speak with us.'

'What about?' He drained his cup of tea.

Robinson rolled his eyes. 'The weather. What do you think?'

The officers made their way downstairs and into one of the interview rooms. Morris sat cradling a cup of tea in front of him. He forced a smile at the two of them, as they sat opposite.

'Well?' Robinson said.

'I thought I'd better come in, Inspector. I have more information.'

'Such as?' Elwick said.

'What you need to understand is I …' He paused, rubbing his chin.

Robinson smiled. 'Look, William. Just tell us what you know.'

'When I said Wicken and I hadn't contacted each other, it wasn't strictly true.'

'Go on,' Robinson said.

'After I moved away, Wicken and I corresponded for a while.'

'How long?' Robinson said.

'Until about a week before he was killed.'

'And you didn't think to tell anyone?' Elwick said.

'After he was killed, and his crimes came out, I was in shock. I couldn't believe what he'd done. My business was struggling at the time, and a scandal would've finished me.'

'So, you kept quiet?' Elwick said.

'I knew nothing about any of his crimes. I've never seen him since we were kids. I couldn't see the point.'

'You couldn't see the point?' Robinson said. 'The point was. Your friend killed sixty women, and possibly more.'

'I know. I know.' Morris brought his hands up to his face.

'Why did you continue your correspondence?' Elwick said.

'We shared a hobby. Coin collecting,' he said. 'We'd write initially. And later, email each other.'

Elwick stared at Morris. 'And you're sure you didn't meet him?'

'Yes.'

Robinson scoffed. 'I find it hard to believe, Mr Morris. You lived fifty miles from him, and never met.'

'Inspector, you have to believe me. We never met.'

'Why not?' Elwick said.

'As a kid, I'd been a little bit in awe. Devon had this overwhelming personality. He had a way of manipulating people. It was a little disconcerting. That's why.'

'So why keep in contact with him?' Robinson said.

'Wicken travelled extensively. He'd obtain coins from around the world. I was interested in the coins, you see.'

'And Wicken never asked to meet you?' Robinson said.

'He'd ask from time to time, but I always managed to put him off. We'd send coins through the post to each other.'

'He knew your address, then?' Elwick said.

'No. I used a private postal box.'

Elwick smiled. 'It appears you were frightened of Wicken.'

'A little.'

Robinson leant forward. 'Did you think he had something to do with those missing girls?'

'Come off it, Inspector. There's a world of difference between believing someone's weird, and someone's a serial killer.'

Robinson slowly nodded. 'Maybe.'

'Look, officers,' he said. 'The Wicken I knew wasn't the type of person you'd want to sit with, in polite company if you know what I mean? My clients would drop me like a stone if they thought I knew him. As I said, if it hadn't been for the coins I would've had nothing to do with him.'

Elwick drummed the desk with his index finger. 'Would you be able to give us your whereabouts when Wicken's victims were abducted?'

Morris sneered. 'Please. You're not trying to link me with those, are you?'

'Just routine,' Elwick said.

'As it happens, I've diaries covering that time. I'll be only too willing to let you have a look at them. I will, of course, help in any way I can.'

Robinson stood. 'I'm sure you will. We'll be in touch, Mr Morris.' As he and Elwick left.

'What do you think?' Elwick said.

'Not sure. Morris could've said nothing, and we'd be none the wiser.'

'Maybe he was worried we'd find out about him and Wicken trading coins. It's got to leave a trail.'

'He's a solicitor,' Robinson said. 'He'll know the ropes. You'll need a spade, bonnie lad. We're going to have to dig deep on this.'


Charlotte watched from the rear of her cage as the masked man erected a table in the centre of the room. She knew what this meant, but tried to push thoughts of what would occur later to the far corners of her mind. The masked man's phone sounded in his pocket. He stopped what he was doing and reached for it. 'About time.' He paused and listened to his caller. 'Tonight … I need you here to film it … Watching it live is something else … I promise you. The feeling is exquisite.' He rang off. 'That was a friend of mine, Sarah.' He wandered over to her cage. 'He's looking forward to meeting you.'

'Please,' Charlotte said. 'Don't hurt her.'

'Charlotte, Charlotte, Charlotte.' Moving across to her, he squatted in front of her cage. 'You have to be the centre of attention, don't you? Your time will come soon enough. I'm going to enjoy our bonding. Forget Sarah. You should worry about yourself. When you see what we do to Sarah tonight, you'll understand what we have in store for you. Your death will be the pinnacle.' He moved back across to the table and began his work again, as Charlotte desperately tried to think of a way of getting out.

# CHAPTER TWELVE

Elwick entered Robinson's office. The team had been looking into dates and times of Wicken's victim's deaths. Trying to link them with Morris. They'd been unsuccessful. Unable to find one instance where he and Wicken met. The pair had either been very careful, or incredibly lucky. Robinson and Elwick were now beginning to believe Morris wasn't involved in any way.

Elwick sat and blew out. 'Nothing, Guv. Can't find anything to link the murders to Morris.'

'Have you checked everything?' Robinson said.

'Not everything. The team's still working on it. Morris' diaries are accurate, as far as we can see. He's quite meticulous.'

'Too meticulous?'

'Maybe it's his nature. Some people are like that.'

'Back to square one, then,' Robinson said.

'If I'm honest, I don't think we ever got off square one.'

'What about his friends and colleagues?' Robinson said.

'They all say he's a decent bloke. Does his bit for charity. Good family man.'

'I think we may have to look for other lines of enquiry, then. The brass won't be happy.'

'They never are,' Elwick said.

Charlotte came around. The same pain and numbness from the last time she'd been shot with the taser, apparent. She was seated. Her arms, legs, and torso taped against the seat. Her head restrained, secured to a piece of wood. The wood crudely fastened to the chair. In front of her was a table, and atop the table, Sarah. Her arms and legs clamped. She wore nothing but a pair of briefs. A gag placed across her mouth and a bandage across the empty eye-sockets on her head. Charlotte glanced to the right as two figures drifted into view. Both wearing Devon Wicken masks.

'Hello, Charlotte,' the familiar voice said. 'This is a friend of mine.'

The other voice sniggered. 'We thought we'd film this for prosperity.'

Charlotte watched as the second man moved out of sight. A noise behind grabbed her attention, as if he was setting something up. She assumed he was adjusting some photographic equipment, as the man in front of her nodded towards him.

'Can you remember a game from your childhood, Charlotte? *Operation*.'

Charlotte said nothing as the man strolled across to a bench on the other side of the room, and picked something up. He wandered over and stopped in front of her. 'You must remember it?' Fanning the cards in his hands.

Elwick sat at his desk. A tap on the door as DS Sally Wainwright entered.

He smiled. 'Sally. What can I do for you?'

'I've got the phone records for Morris. There doesn't appear to be anything unusual, sir. Nothing to link him with Wicken.' She popped some A4 sheets in front of him.

'Thanks,' he said. 'Robinson's looking at other avenues. If Morris was, is, involved, he's keeping it well hidden. I don't think he'd have come to us about Wicken if I'm honest. If he was involved, I mean.'

Sally raised her eyebrows. 'Some of the guys are checking into the background of the girls, but so far there's no link.'

'The women Wicken killed weren't linked either. He took them randomly.'

'We'll keep trying,' she said. And left.

Elwick picked up the pieces of paper and flicked through the row upon row of numbers. Next to them, the length of time the phone conversation took. And next to this, the date. One number jumped out at him. A number he recognised. He began looking through them again. Hi-lighting the same one, with a bright marker as it appeared. He counted them up. Astonished to see there'd been twenty-five calls to, and from, the same number. Elwick opened his drawer and pushed the pieces of paper to the bottom of it, covering it with folders. He sat back in his chair and closed his eyes deep in thought.

The door opened, and Robinson entered. 'What're you up to, bonnie lad.' Tossing his coat on the stand.

'Not a lot, Guv,' Elwick said. 'No headway yet.'

'Cuppa?' Robinson smiled. 'I'm parched.'

Elwick stood. 'Yeah. I'll get you one.'

'Bloody hell. Wonders never cease,' Robinson said. 'Russ making me a cup of tea. You remember where the kettle is, do you? It's the white thing hanging out of the wall.' He laughed, as Elwick left.

Charlotte sat silently. The masked figure stood in front of her. 'Pick a card.' Holding them out for her to see.

'I'm not going to play your sick games,' she said. 'Please, let Sarah go. She can't identify you.'

'Maybe I should cut out her tongue as well.' He hissed. 'So she can't tell them what happened either.'

'She's just a girl.'

'This isn't about her, Charlotte. It's about you. It was always about you.'

'What do you mean?' Tears rolled down her face.

'No matter.' Wandering across to Sarah. 'It appears, Sarah, Charlotte wants you to suffer.'

'No, I don't,' Charlotte said.

'Well, pick a card,' he repeated. Moving close to Charlotte again. 'Give me a number, and we can finish this quickly. Don't, and I'll make you watch all night as Sarah suffers.'

Charlotte glanced past the man at Sarah. She wanted to shut her eyes and wake from this nightmare. She wanted Sarah's suffering to be over. 'I'm sorry, Sarah,' she mouthed. 'Three,' she whispered.

'Number three,' the man said. Picking up, and placing the first two cards to the bottom of the pile. He took hold of the third one, studying it.

'Take out the patient's liver for £250.' He turned the card around for Charlotte to see.

Elwick made his way along the corridor and stopped at the threshold of the incident room. Officers, both plain-clothed and uniformed, milled about. He looked around and spotting Sally, shouted her over. Sally put down the paperwork and headed across.

'Sally.' Taking her by the arm, and gently pulling her into the corridor. 'I need a favour.'

'What sort?'

He glanced up and down the corridor. 'The list of phone numbers you gave me? I need you to check one of them.'

'Are you following a new lead?' she said.

'I'm not sure. Probably not, but we're struggling just now.'

Elwick handed her a piece of paper. 'Yeah sure, Russ.'

'One more thing,' he whispered. 'Keep this between us. Don't tell anyone else.'

'Not even Robinson?' Sally said.

'Not even Robinson.'

'No problem,' she said.

Elwick glanced over her shoulder at DC Wells, who was watching them. When he met Elwick's stare, he turned away. 'Cheers,' he said. Sally turned and returned to her desk.

Charlotte stared, as the masked man loomed over the helpless Sarah. Desperately wanting to look away, but she remembered what she'd been told. Her eyes viewed the scalpel in his hand as he lowered it towards Sarah. He turned to face Charlotte again and raised his mask. The face of Devon Wicken stared at her, but there was something wrong. It was his face, she was sure. But it didn't appear real, the edges blurring as his manic eyes gawped at her. Her head swam, visions of people and places she didn't recognise swamped her mind. One name drifted into her consciousness.

'Jack,' she murmured

The man glared at her. 'What was that?'

'Nothing.' Sensing the mention of his name was somehow wrong.

'He can't save you.' Moving closer to her. 'Jack's gone. There's only you and me.' He ambled across to the table and held the scalpel inches from Sarah's body. 'Don't you dare look away, Charlotte,' he said. 'I'll have those eyes if you do.'

Charlotte watched a surreal event unfold in front of her. She saw the man draw the blade across Sarah's body, wanting desperately to cover her eyes against the aberration happening before her. As tears tumbled down her face, she heard the muffled cries of the girl. The man continued his grisly work as the red liquid flowed freely from Sarah. Trying to ignore the terrible sight, as blood dripped sickeningly onto the floor. He continued. His hands stained red with Sarah's blood, as he reached inside her and pulled something free. She fought against the rising vomit as it pushed its way into her throat. Swallowing hard as the man hoisted Sarah's liver aloft. Blood dripped onto the floor and ran the length of his arm. The man behind her giggled. Wicken, or what appeared to be him, crept towards her. Charlotte stared at a point in space, seeing but not seeing. She looked past the man at the inert body of Sarah, now beyond suffering. He pushed the organ under her nose, so near, she smelt the blood. Charlotte couldn't stop herself. Gagging, as the vomit spewed from her onto the floor below. He turned away, disgusted by her. Moving to the other side of the room, he deposited the liver in a waiting jar. She heard running water, as he filled a bucket and threw it over her. The cold water causing her to gasp.

'I hate it when they puke,' he said to his companion. 'You've let me down, Charlotte,' he whispered. 'I thought you were stronger than this. I can't look at you now.' He moved to the other side of the room again, searching for something. Finding it, he strode across to her and pushed the plastic bag over her head. Charlotte struggled to breathe, the plastic sticking to her face. Her head swam, and she thought of Jack again. His face drifting into her mind before she descended into a dark-well of blackness.

Elwick sat in the canteen, eating a sandwich and reading his paper. Wells sat opposite him and placed his tray on the table. Elwick lifted his head and glanced at him.

'Anything new, Russ? Wells asked.

Elwick took a sip of tea. 'Like what?'

'I saw you speaking with Sally earlier. Any new leads?'

'Not really. A bit of a long shot.'

'Maybe I can help.'

'Has Sally said anything?' Elwick said.

'No. I'm just sick of sifting through endless paperwork, that's all.'

Elwick shrugged. 'That's what being a copper's all about.'

'Yeah, I know, but I thought maybe.'

'I'll keep you in mind,' Elwick said. 'If I need another helping hand.'

'Thanks.' Wells picked up his tray and headed for another table.

Elwick watched him leave, his eyes following him as Wells sat with two uniformed female officers.

'Jamais vu,' Elwick said to himself. The feeling loitering briefly before receding into nothingness.

Charlotte lay on the floor of the cage. Shivering, her clothing damp from the dousing she'd received. She had no memory of being deposited in the cage. Which wasn't unusual, but the customary ache in her muscles from the taser wasn't present this time. Maybe she had passed out when he covered her head with the plastic bag? Charlotte tried to push the memories of this, and what happened to Sarah, away. The harder she tried, the more difficult it became. Cold, hungry and alone. She curled into a tight ball and mingled unwillingly with her nightmarish visions.

Robinson was out of the office as Elwick sifted through his ever-growing mountain of paperwork. Sally entered, closing the door behind her.

'The mobile number,' she said. 'It's registered to DI Robinson.'

Elwick's eyes widened. 'I thought it was. I only recognised the number because it's almost identical to mine. There's a couple of digits different. I checked my phone, but I've deleted his number. I'm certain he said he'd lost it, or something.'

'What's Robinson doing telephoning Morris?' she said.

'Why, indeed.'

'Should we tell the Chief Inspector?' she said.

'No. Keep it under your hat for the moment.'

'Are you sure, Russ?'

'Yeah. If you don't mind. There could be an innocent reason for this. I'll investigate further and then, when we know more, speak with the Chief.'

'No, I don't mind.' she said. 'Tell me what you find.'

'I will.' Elwick's phone rang. 'Yeah.'

'I've tried ringing DI Robinson, sir.' Wells said. 'But he's not answering. Another body's been discovered. We believe it's Sarah Andrews.

'Right,' Elwick said. 'I'll get in touch with Robinson.'

'Yes, sir. We'll need a positive ID.'

'Her mam or dad?' Elwick said.

'There's a problem with that. The body we found was missing its eyes.'

'I see,' Elwick said. Glancing towards the door as Robinson entered.

'Morning, bonnie lad,' Robinson said.

'Hold off on that for the moment,' Elwick said. 'I'll speak with you later.' And hung up.

'Morning,' he said to Robinson. 'Where have you been?'

'Why, what's up?' Hanging his coat on a hook.

'They've found Sarah Andrews.'

'Oh,' Robinson said. 'Let's go then.' Picking up his coat again.

They made their way downstairs to the incident room. Robinson stood, deep in conversation with one of the team. Elwick took out an old mobile he'd retrieved from the drawer in his office and headed into the corridor. He located the stored number Sally had checked for him and called. Elwick observed Robinson as it rang. Robinson didn't move as the phone continued to ring before it went to answerphone.

'Hi. You've reached the mobile of Andy Robinson.' Elwick hung up.

# CHAPTER THIRTEEN

Robinson and Elwick stood in the lab, next to senior pathologist Dr Stephen Borrowby.

'We'll need a positive ID,' Elwick said.

Robinson stared at Borrowby. 'What about her missing eyes? Were they removed after death?'

'I'm afraid not,' Borrowby said.

'Christ!' Elwick said. 'He's one sick bastard.'

'I could use prosthetic ones. Her eyes will be closed. So no one would know.'

'That's a bit unethical,' Robinson said. 'It may be best if we use DNA. To save her family from seeing her like this.'

'And if they insist?' Elwick said.

'We'll cross that bridge when we come to it,' Robinson said. 'How did she die?'

'Massive blood loss. The liver was removed,' Borrowby said.

'While she was alive?' Elwick said.

Borrowby nodded. 'While she was still alive.'

'Fucking hell.' Shaking his head.

'Anything else?' Robinson said.

'Numerous minor injuries. None life-threatening. Malnourished. I suspect she was only fed a minimal amount to keep her alive.'

'Water?' Elwick said.

'The same. Just enough to keep her alive.'

'Cheers, Steve,' Robinson said, and turned.

'One other thing. There's a tattoo on her back. I only mention it because it's new.'

Robinson spun around and looked at Borrowby. 'New? Do you mean the murderer tattooed her?'

Borrowby nodded. 'It looks like that. It's quite crude. It wasn't an expert tattooist who did it.'

'What is it?' Elwick said.

Borrowby handed Elwick a photo. *'One word. Insidious.'*

Robinson took the photo from him. 'Insidious?'

Elwick considered this for a moment. 'Insidious.' Something stirred deep within his mind, hopelessly out of reach.

Charlotte was losing track of time. The man appeared sporadically, leaving food and water for her but never spoke. She wasn't even sure it was the same man who killed Sarah, or someone else. She spent most of the time huddled in a ball in the corner of her cage, lost in dreams and visions she didn't recognise.

Elwick stood outside Sally Wainwright's flat. He pressed the bell and waited. Sally opened the door and smiled broadly at Elwick. 'Russ. This is a surprise.'

'Can I come in?' he said.

'Yeah, of course.' She moved aside, allowing Elwick to pass. He paused in the hallway as Sally closed the door and beckoned him into the living room.

'Drink?' she said.

'What have you got?'

'Whisky, Vodka, Jack Daniels.'

'Jack Daniels with coke,' he said.

'Jack Daniels it is.' Removing the bottle from a sideboard, she disappeared into the kitchen. Returning moments later with his drink, and one for herself.

'So?' Sitting opposite Elwick. 'What can I do for you?'

'Straight to the point. I like that,' Elwick said. 'Robinson.'

'What about him?' she said.

'I've been thinking about the number. I can't think of any reason Robinson would ring Morris. Especially on his personal mobile.'

'Could it be related to the case? Maybe he was making enquiries?'

Elwick took a sip. 'That can't be. Some of the calls go back before the first girl was abducted.'

'Did he give any indication he knew Morris when you interviewed him?'

'None. But if I'm honest, I wasn't looking for any.'

'What're you saying, Russ?'

'I don't know. I've racked my brains about this. I can't imagine Robinson's involved, though.'

'But,' she said.

'Yeah, but,' he said.

'What do you want me to do?'

'I need your help. I'm going to dig deeper into Robinson's life. I want you to assist me.'

'Of course, but why me?'

'I don't know why, but I trust you. I can't explain it any better than that.'

She smiled. 'I'm flattered.'

'I'll ring tomorrow and discuss our plan of action. I'm going to speak with a friend who worked with Robinson a few years back. During the Devon Wicken murders. He may be able to help.' Elwick drained his glass.

'I'll wait for your call,' she said.

Elwick stood and moved towards the door, pausing. 'Thanks for this,' he said, and left.

Charlotte woke as footsteps descended the cellar steps. She watched as the masked man trudged across to the other cage. He had something in a sack slung across his shoulders. Dropping it onto the floor, he bent and opened the door. He pulled a knife from his pocket, and cut the tape securing the sack around whatever was inside. He rolled the bundle open, revealing an unconscious woman. The masked man unceremoniously bundled her into the cage. Closing and locking the door, he strolled across to Charlotte's cage and bent down. 'Not long now, Charlotte,' he said. 'He'll have to come now.'

She frowned. 'Who?'

'Jack, of course. Insidious is getting closer. It senses him.' He stood, and disappeared up the stairs as a puzzled Charlotte looked on.

Elwick, woken from his sleep by his mobile, groggily grabbed for it in the darkness, and viewed the name. It said DI Robinson.

He sat up. 'Yes, Guv.'

'Get yourself ready, bonnie lad. Meet me at Sally Wainwright's flat.'

'Sally's. Why?'

'She's missing. A friend of hers went around there and found the door open. There are signs of a struggle. There's something else too.'

'What?'

'On the living room wall, someone's painted *Insidious*.'

'The same as the last girl?'

'Yeah. Quick as you can, Russ. She's one of our own and the clock's ticking.'

Elwick turned the light on, catching his reflection in the mirror. His face momentarily not his own. Blinking, he rubbed his eyes and looked again. The features of Russ Elwick stared back at him.

'Jamais vu,' he whispered.

# CHAPTER FOURTEEN

Elwick reached Sally's flat moments after the DI. Jumping from his car, as Robinson disappeared into the house. He marched towards the property, flashing his ID at a uniformed officer stationed outside. Elwick carried on through into the living room, Robinson and Wells turned to face him as he entered. Elwick stared at the chimney breast above the fireplace. *Insidious* written out crudely in red, streaks running away from the letters and down the wall. Elwick gasped.

'Paint,' Robinson said. 'I thought the same as you when I saw it.'

'What happened?' Elwick said.

Wells joined him. 'The neighbours said they heard a commotion around nine last night. The guy from next door looked outside, but didn't see anything suspicious.'

'We think she put up a struggle,' Robinson said.

Elwick's eyes darted between the wall and wells. 'Any signs of injury?'

'None,' Wells said. 'The crime scene boys haven't gone over it properly. But they haven't found anything yet.'

Elwick moved closer to the wall. His eyes following the streaks downwards. 'How'd they get her out without someone spotting them?'

'Through the rear door.' Wells said. 'A neighbour, a bloke a couple of doors down, saw a dark-coloured estate parked out back. The man turned into the alley and couldn't get down because of it.'

'Make and model?' Elwick said.

Wells shook his head. 'Nope. Possibly a Ford, but he's not sure.'

Robinson stepped forward, handing Elwick a card. 'And there's this.' Elwick studied the card. On the back was typed, *Operation,* and on the reverse, *Remove the patient's heart for £300.*

'From the game—' Wells said.

'Operation,' Elwick said.

'Yeah. What's the significance?' Wells said.

'Sarah Andrews' liver was removed. It appears her killer's playing some sick operation game,' Elwick said.

Wells nodded towards the card. 'The card refers to Charlotte Richmond?'

'I think the card's self-explanatory,' Robinson said.

Elwick headed outside, pursued by Wells. He stopped at his car and putting both hands on the side, exhaled loudly.

'What's going on, Russ,' Wells said.

'What 'd you mean?'

'You and Sally were up to something, and now she's missing.'

Elwick turned to face Wells and shrugged. 'Sally was following a lead for me. That's all.'

'Does the Guv know?'

Elwick glanced at the flat. 'Can you keep something to yourself?'

'Of course,' he said.

'William Morris was a childhood friend of Devon Wicken. Morris claimed he'd never been in touch with him for over thirty years. Then he came to the station and admitted he'd kept up a correspondence with him. Claimed they both collected coins.'

Wells nodded. 'And you believe Morris has something to do with the girls disappearing?'

'We've done thorough checks and found nothing. Here's the interesting thing, though. A check of Morris' phone records came up with a number.'

'Whose?

'Elwick rubbed his chin. 'The Guv's private number. Or a number he used to have.'

Wells glanced back towards the property. 'Are you sure it's the DI's?'

'Yeah. Robinson hasn't to my knowledge used it for over a year. I deleted it from my mobile when he told me he'd lost the phone.'

'Maybe he did, and the killer found it,' Wells said.

'Bit of a coincidence, don't you think? The man investigating a crime lose his phone. Fails to block the sim card. It's found and used by someone who's in regular contact with the primary suspect.'

'I see your point. What're you going to do?' Wells said.

'Not sure. I spoke with a friend of mine who knew Robinson when the Wicken case was being investigated. He told me Wicken always appeared one step ahead of the police. The rumour was.' He paused. 'Someone on the force, or maybe even on the case, was assisting him.'

Wells raised his eyebrows. 'I never heard anything about that.'

'Nothing concrete was found. After Wicken was killed, it was assumed he did it alone.'

'What about the senior investigating officer?' Wells said.

'DI Hayes. We visited him, and he said he didn't think Wicken had an accomplice.'

'I take it the Guv went with you?'

'Yeah.'

'Maybe we should return without him.' Wells said. 'If Hayes knew about these rumours, maybe, he'd be more forthcoming if Robinson isn't there.'

'Good idea. We'll go this afternoon. I'll make some story up so we can get away.'

'Shall we say two-thirty?' Wells said.

Elwick patted Wells on the arm. 'Yeah. Two-thirty's fine.'

Elwick and Wells arrived outside Hayes' flat at three in the afternoon. They ascended the stairs and stopped at the threshold as Elwick knocked. There was no answer. Elwick knocked again, much harder. Crouching he peeked through the letterbox. Standing straight, he barged the door with his shoulder. The door giving way as it flew open. The two officers could see the legs of someone, Hayes, Elwick presumed protruding from out of the kitchen. Elwick and Wells moved closer and on reaching the kitchen, pushed open the door. Hayes lay on the floor, a large pool of dried blood surrounding his head. Next to him, a piece of bloodied metal pipe. He'd apparently been dead for some time. Elwick covered his mouth and nose. The body omitting the familiar smell of decomposing flesh. He took out his phone and made a call.

Elwick and Wells stood outside Hayes' flat as forensic operatives milled around inside.

'What do you think?' Wells said.

'Seems strange. Hayes is murdered not long after we visited.'

'Could be a coincidence. Maybe it was a burglary.'

'What burglar locks the front door and puts the key through the letterbox?'

'Maybe he panicked?' Wells said.

'I'm not convinced.'

'You think this could've something to do with Robinson?' Wells said.

'I don't know. I can't believe the Guv has anything to do with this. Maybe someone followed us here. Worried what Hayes would tell us.'

'Possible,' Wells said.

'What's possible?' Robinson said. Elwick and wells turned as Robinson came up the stairs.

'We were just saying, Guv,' Wells said. 'Maybe Hayes knew something, and someone followed you and Russ here.'

Robinson glared at Elwick. 'Maybe. What were you two doing here, anyway?'

'We just thought another talk with Hayes would help,' Elwick said.

'Running your own investigation are we, Russ?'

'Of course not, Guv.'

'In future, boys, anything involving this investigation is run past me first. Have we got that?'

'Yes, Guv,' Wells said.

'And you, Russ?'

'Absolutely, Guv,' Elwick said.

Charlotte listened intently, hoping to hear some sign of life from the other cage. Finally, there was a groan.

'Hello,' Charlotte said.

Sally heaved herself into a sitting position. 'Hello. Where am I?'

'I've no idea. I'm—'

'Charlotte Richmond,' Sally said.

'Yeah, how'd you know?'

'I'm Detective Constable Sally Wainwright. I was working on your abduction case.'

'Oh.' Was all Charlotte could muster.

'Do you know who's keeping us here?' Sally said.

'No. The man wears a mask to hide the face. I was abducted by an old man, or at least he appeared old. He wore a disguise so I couldn't tell you what he looks like. He wears a Devon Wicken mask. He's being helped by someone else, too.'

'Right,' Sally said. 'Are they here now?'

'One comes and goes. The other was only here when Sarah …'

'Was killed,' Sally said.

'Yeah.'

'Tell me everything,' Sally said. 'When they come, how they treat their prisoners, everything. We need a plan to get out of here.'

# CHAPTER FIFTEEN

Elwick and Wells sat in their car, parked near to William Morris' house and waited.

Wells glanced at Elwick. 'Are you sure we're doing the right thing, Russ? Robinson will be livid if he finds out.'

Elwick shrugged. 'He's got to be hiding something. Why would he have made all those calls to the DI?'

'I suppose,' Wells said.

'We don't have a lot of time to save Charlotte Richmond. If Morris is involved, following him may reveal where she is.'

'And Robinson? What if he's involved?'

'Two birds, one stone,' Elwick said.

Elwick's phone sounded in his pocket. He viewed the name on the screen, DI Robinson. Glancing at Wells and holding his index finger to his mouth, Elwick answered. 'Evening, Guv.'

'Where are you, Russ?' Robinson said.

'At home. Why?'

'Are you sure? I'm outside your flat now. Your car's not here, and I've knocked twice.'

'Ah,' Elwick said. 'Banged to rights.' He laughed. 'Having a few pints.'

'I was thinking about Morris,' Robinson said. 'Maybe we should have him watched. I'm not entirely convinced he isn't involved.'

Elwick glanced at Wells, again. 'Morris. What're you thinking?'

'We should follow him. See what he's getting up too. If he's not guilty, we'll soon know.'

'Good idea, Guv. When?'

'I'll speak with the Chief and ok it with him. Then we can start straight away.'

'Fine. I'll see you tomorrow,' Elwick said.

'Yeah, bonnie lad. One more thing, Russ,' Robinson said. 'Jamais vu.'

'What?' Elwick swapped his phone to his other ear. He glanced at Wells who looked on.

The phone went dead. Elwick stared at the screen, before depositing it in his pocket.

'What did he say?' Wells said.

Elwick rubbed his chin. 'He wants to follow Morris. He's going to speak with the Chief about it.'

'What else did he say?' Wells said.

'That's it.'

'Are you sure?'

Elwick narrowed his eyes, surreptitiously taking a sideways glance at Wells. 'Of course I'm sure.'

Charlotte explained to Sally what happened when the man came. Telling her how difficult it would be to do anything when he opened the cage, as he used a taser. Even if Sally could attack him, she'd have trouble overpowering a man. Sally agreed, but felt they had no choice but to try. She had nothing to use as a weapon, the man having gone to the bother of removing her shoes and belt. However, she'd impressed on Charlotte the importance of taking the opportunity when it arose. Sally would be ready for him. The two of them settled back and waited.

Elwick and Wells sat for two hours outside Morris' house. There had been no coming and goings in that time. Elwick glanced at his watch again. 'Maybe we should call it a night?'

'Wait,' Wells said, as Morris exited the house and got in his car. Elwick waited for him to go out of sight around the corner, and set off after him.

Morris headed towards Saltburn. The two officers followed him as they passed through several villages along the way. Within sight of Saltburn, Morris turned away from the main road and trundled along a farm track. Elwick, allowing him to turn-off, passed the track and continued along the main road. Stopping a quarter of a mile away, he turned the car around and halted at the turn-off to the track.

'We'll walk from here,' he said. Wells nodded in agreement.

They crept along the track to the farmhouse ahead. Morris' car parked in front. Elwick moved stealthily around to the front door, Wells followed closely. Elwick stopped at the door and held up his hand as Wells joined him. He tried the door. It was locked.

'We'll try the back,' Elwick said.

They reached the back-door, and Elwick tried the handle, the door opened with a groan. He stepped through, reaching into his pocket as he did. He allowed Wells to pass him, and move through from the kitchen into the hall. Wells stopped and turned, his mouth open, about to speak as Elwick hit him hard across the head with his gun. Wells stumbled backwards, the blow sending him crashing into a table in the hall. He attempted to get to his feet, but Elwick sent him reeling with a thud of his right boot against the side of his face. The officer slumped to the floor unconscious.

'Who's that?' shouted a voice from upstairs.

Elwick glanced about, spotting a mask on the floor he'd knocked off the table, he put it on. Ascending the stairs, he reached the top as Morris came out of one of the bedrooms.

'Oh, it's you,' Morris said. 'What's all the noise?'

Elwick raised his gun, slowly removing his mask as he did. Morris stared back at him.

'Surprise,' Elwick said. And fired. Morris smashed against the wall as the bullet exploded his chest. He slid to the floor, his head drooping to one side as he came to rest, half-kneeling and half-sitting. Elwick raced over to him, lifted his head, and viewed his lifeless eyes. He bounded downstairs, stepping across the prostrate Wells in the hallway, and quickly searched the rooms. They were empty, but continuing his search, he spotted the door under the stairs. Carefully he opened it, switched on the light near the top, and descended. On reaching the bottom, Elwick scanned the room. Two cages located in opposite corners. He hurried across to Sally's grabbing hold of the lock.

'I knew you'd end up here, bonnie lad.' Elwick spun around. Robinson pointing a gun at him stood there.

'I knew you were involved,' Elwick said.

'You shouldn't have knocked out Wells. He's an innocent party in this. He may have been able to assist you. I knew you'd fall into my trap.' Robinson stepped from the shadows. 'Jamais vu, indeed.'

Elwick felt for the gun in his pocket. 'What now?'

'I'll have your weapon for starters.' He raised his pistol higher.

'And your part in all this?' Elwick threw his gun at Robinson's feet.

'Devon Wicken and I go back a long way. Birds of a feather, and all that. Let's just say Wicken and I, had similar tastes. I won't bore you with the details.'

'You helped him?'

Robinson grinned. 'Of course. No one's that lucky. I'd procure the girls for him, and Devon would allow me to watch.'

'What about Morris?'

'We'd send Morris videos and photos. Quite a little trio we had going. Until Hayes cottoned on, of course. When Wicken was killed, I decided to resurrect him. I took over where Devon left off. Morris would fill in for me, and I'd ... Well, you get the picture.'

'Why did you kill Hayes?' Elwick asked.

'Hayes suspected someone on the force. It'd only have been a matter of time before he put two and two together and blabbed.' Robinson lowered his chin to his chest, lifting his head, he gave it a shake. His features altering. Robinson's face slowly fading, replaced with Wicken's. He smiled at Elwick, a knowing smile. 'Hello, Jack.' He grinned. 'You just don't give up, do you?'

Elwick frowned. 'Who's Jack?'

'Let's not play games,' Wicken said. 'I know why you're here. You've come to save the lovely Charlotte.'

'I don't know what you're on about,' Elwick said. Even as he'd said the words, a realisation crept into his mind.

'See. It's coming back. Clever of you, to disguise yourself. Not clever enough, though.'

Elwick's mind flooded with memories of Jack as Elwick was slowly and inexorably expunged. Something was missing, though. He was Jack, but not completely Jack. It was as if he was only a percentage of Jack.

Wicken stepped closer. 'You can't have her back. Without her I'm nothing. I'll cease to exist, and that'd never do.'

'You're dying in the real world,' Jack said. His transformation from Elwick now complete.

'You won't escape,' Wicken said. 'I almost killed you last time, at the bridge. Wicken moved within a few feet. 'Let's have some fun,' he said. He fired into Jack's shoulder. Jack fell backwards onto the floor, clutching his injury. Wicken fired again, hitting Jack's knee, the bullet ripping through bone and sinew. Jack screamed again in pain, the noise from the gun reverberating around the cellar.

'No!' a female voice shouted. Jack unsure if it was Charlotte or Sally, crawled towards the nearest cage. It was Sally's.

'Does it hurt, Jackie-Boy?' Wicken said. Towering over the stricken Jack, he laughed. 'The coup de grace.' Raising his gun a third time, he pointed it at Jack's forehead. 'Game over,' he said.

# CHAPTER SIXTEEN

Wicken's finger slowly pressed the trigger. Revelling in the moment, he grinned. Jack glanced across at Charlotte, her ashen face pressed against the front of the cage, her eyes full of tears. He stared across at the foot of the stairs as he heard a noise. Wells launched himself at Wicken and the gun fired with a terrific bang. Jack flinched, the bullet whistling past his ear. Then a crash as Wicken and Wells collided heavily. Jack stared at the gun as it fell from Wicken's grasp. The weapon spun across the floor, tantalisingly close. He crawled towards it, his injuries hindering him. Wicken screamed, he and the bloodied Wells grappling on the ground. Jack reached the gun and sitting against the wall, levelled it at the two of them. He fired wildly, missing Wicken with the first, but hitting him in the stomach with the second. Wicken fell back, fatally wounded, and slumped to the floor. Jack watched his features return to those of Robinson. Instantly, Wells transformed into Wicken, an insane grin filling his face. Jack raised the gun again as Wicken launched himself at him. The firearm blasted as the pair of them crashed into a heap. Wicken grabbed Jack by the throat and squeezed. Jack fought for his life, his uninjured arm holding the gun lashed out wildly, as he tried to manoeuvre the weapon so it was pointing at Wicken. Wicken, although he had been shot through the side, still fought with the strength of a madman. The two of them wrestled with the weapon as slowly Wicken pushed the muzzle at Jack. The gun sounded again. Jack groaned with pain as the bullet tore through his side. The recoil of the weapon momentarily pushing the two combatants apart. Jack summoned his last bit of strength and turned the pistol towards Wicken, who launched himself at him. The gun blasted. The bullet hit Wicken in the head, his inert form landing on Jack. He tried to extricate himself from the dead body. Slowly, painfully, he struggled free.

'Jack!' Charlotte screamed.

He crawled towards Sally. Motioning her to move to the back of the cage, and shakily raising the gun again, shot at the lock. The lock blasted apart as he slumped against the cage. Sally kicked at the door, finally opening on her third attempt. She climbed out and moved to Jack, a large pool of blood had formed around him. She grasped hold of his hand, and as he stared into Sally's eyes a smile played on his lips. 'Jamais vu,' he said.

'Jamais Vu,' Sally whispered.

Jack's head dropped forward, and he drew his final breath. Sally allowed his hand to fall from hers, as she searched around frantically for something to force open Charlotte's cage. Finally, locating a mallet she began to hammer manically. The lock gave up its resistance and opened. Sally threw open the door as the exhausted Charlotte crawled free.

'Jack?' she said, staring at the body of Elwick. 'Jack was here. My Jack. I saw him.'

'He's gone,' Sally said. 'We need to get away from here. Grabbing Charlotte's hand, the two of them climbed the stairs. They reached the top and headed out of the rear door. The chilly breeze catching Charlotte by surprise as she involuntarily gasped. They raced around to the front of the property and stopped as sirens sounded in the distance. Sally paused for a moment as memories, familiar ones, flooded her mind. She grabbed Charlotte's arm again and pulled her forcefully, dragging her across the garden.

'This way,' Sally said. The puzzled Charlotte followed in her wake.

They reached a fence at the bottom of the garden and climbed over, Sally assisting the struggling Charlotte.

'Where're we going?' Charlotte asked.

'We need to go,' Sally said. 'It's here somewhere. I can sense it.'

'What?'

'Our way home.' Pulling Charlotte along with her.

'Who are you?' Charlotte demanded, standing still, refusing to move.

Sally turned to face her. She took hold of Charlotte's head within her hands and stared deep into her eyes. 'It's me.' As Charlotte gazed at the face of Jack.

'But ...' she said.

'No time to explain. It will try to stop you from leaving.' He pulled her along.

'What will?'

'Insidious,' he said.

They stumbled their way across the ground, heading for the cliff edge. The sirens in the distance, growing louder. Above them, a helicopter came into view. Jack dragged the exhausted Charlotte on, towards a fence five metres off the cliff edge.

'Stop them!' Someone shouted. But Jack continued, pulling the struggling Charlotte behind him. They reached the fence, and Jack pushed the almost spent Charlotte over it. Pulling her towards the edge they stopped.

Holding on to Charlotte's hand, he turned. 'Don't come any closer.' As several people headed towards them. 'We'll jump if you do.'

'Don't be silly, Jack,' the resurrected Robinson said.

Charlotte stared at Jack. 'Didn't he die in the cellar?'

'None of this is real, Charlotte.' He gazed at her. 'Insidious can't afford to let you go.'

'Insidious,' Charlotte said. 'I remember now.' The memories piling up, concertina-like, in her mind.

'Let her go, Jack,' Robinson said. Others joined him. Charlotte's sister, mother, father and Dr Whitmore.

Placing a hand on Charlotte's face, he smiled. 'You have to trust me.' She nodded. He scanned beyond the cliff edge. 'Look,' he said to her. 'Can you see it?'

Charlotte gazed at the sea below them, gently lapping onto the rocks. On the surface, an emblem of the **Freedom Foundation** appeared.

'I see it.' Smiling at him. 'What do we do?'

'Jump,' he said. 'It's a leap of faith.'

They turned to face the water, Jack holding on tightly to Charlotte's hand.

'Please don't go, Charlotte,' Wicken said. 'I'm nothing without you.'

Charlotte and Jack briefly glanced at him. The couple smiled at each other and pushed themselves off the cliff, leaving terra firma way behind as they hurtled towards the sea. And as they did, oblivion threw open its arms and welcomed them.

Jack opened his eyes as he heard the door click on the machine, pushing it open he jumped out. Harmby and Lewis following him as he sped off along the corridors. Pushing impatiently past people who got in his way. Jack stopped outside the suite, took a deep breath, and entered. Charlotte was sat up in bed as he tentatively entered the room. Walking over to her, he hugged his wife. 'I love you.' Tears filled his eyes.

'I love you too,' his wife said.

Jack and Charlotte told Harmby and Richard of the events. Jack thanked Richard for his help, making sure Harmby was out of earshot when he did. Harmby had just about forgiven Jack for going against his, and the foundation's wishes. In truth, he couldn't be mad at his friend.

Jack and Charlotte resigned with immediate effect. Setting off home to their house, a long and lonely journey he had made without her so many times before. On arrival, they kissed passionately. The way only people separated for so long, kiss. Taking hold of her hand, they headed to bed.

# OBFUSCATION - CHAPTER ONE

Charlotte stood in the kitchen, rubbing at the bump with her right hand as the baby inside stirred. Moving across to the window, she peered into the garden as bright sunshine bathed it in warmth. Jack entered and seeing his wife deep in thought, wandered across.

Putting his arms around her, he kissed her on the cheek. 'Penny for them?'

'How do we know any of this is real?' she said.

'Any of what?'

'This.' Pointing out of the window.

'Looks real enough to me,' he said.

'But isn't it a little perfect? And this,' Charlotte turned and faced him. 'It seems so familiar.'

'It's déjà vu. That's all. I have it all the time.'

'No, it's not that. It's just … I can't remember how we got into this situation.'

'Well.' Smiled Jack. 'Far be it from me to teach you the birds and bees, but surely you remember.' Jack patted her bump.

Charlotte lowered her eyes. 'I'm serious.'

'You are, aren't you?'

'Look at the sky. Isn't it a little too blue?'

He pointed outside. 'There's a cloud.'

'Only one of those wispy ones,' she said.

'And the grass needs cutting. Those shrubs need a prune, as well. Not what I'd call perfect.'

She sighed. 'I'm serious, Jack.'

'So am I. Look at these.' Moving towards the table he picked up pieces of paper, holding them aloft. 'Bills. Lots of them. In a perfect world, there wouldn't be bills.'

'You don't understand what I mean.' She sat at the table. 'I can't remember yesterday, last week or last month. I can't remember how we met. Nothing.'

Jack sat next to his wife, taking hold of her hand. 'What's wrong?'

'What do you remember? You're normally the cynical one. Scully to my Mulder.'

'Well, I …' Jack paused, mid-sentence. In truth, he couldn't remember anything either. He thought deeply. But the harder he thought, the more out of reach his memories seemed.

'You can't remember either.' She squeezed his hand.

'No, I can't.'

'Who are we, Jack? Where have we been?'

Jack couldn't answer. He was as confused as Charlotte, standing he pulled her into an embrace.

The rest of the day limped by, without Charlotte or Jack mentioning their early morning conversation. They'd gone about their business the way two ordinary people might. The phone didn't ring, and no one visited. For some reason, the pair of them were reluctant to venture outside. Although neither mentioned this to the other. They spent the afternoon watching a film on TV. Jack cooked around seven pm, and the couple sat down to enjoy Spaghetti Bolognese and a drink. Their muted conversation taking on a surreal feeling. Speaking to each other became increasingly demanding. After watching the usual early evening TV, they retired to bed around nine. Jack lay awake as Charlotte cuddled up to him. The two of them not saying a word, as they drifted into something resembling sleep.

Jack and Charlotte flopped onto the bed, panting from their exertions. Charlotte gazed across at Jack and smiled.

He grinned back. 'Wow!'

'Wow, indeed.'

'Ok?' Winked Jack.

'I've had better,' Charlotte replied, mischievously.

'Really?'

'Really,' she said.

'Maybe I need more practice?'

'Maybe you do.' She stuck out her tongue. 'Practice can only ever improve your performance.'

He blew out his cheeks. 'Give me a minute, and I'll be right with you.'

Charlotte frowned. Looking at the ceiling. 'Déjà vu,' she said.

'What?'

'Why's this feel so familiar?'

'Maybe you've done this sort of thing before,' Jack said. 'With a string of other blokes.'

'If I have, I can't remember them.'

'Ah.' He winked. 'Drunk, eh?'

'Where were you yesterday?' Her face full of seriousness.

'Yesterday,' he thought. 'Yesterday … I've no idea.'

'This flat. Who owns it?' Charlotte said.

'Us, I suppose. If not, the owners won't be happy with two strangers shagging in their bed.'

'Mmm,' Charlotte said.

'Come to think of it.' Joining in Charlotte's train of thought, 'I can't remember much. I'm not even sure of my age.'

'Where're your trousers?' She climbed out of bed.

Jack peered around the bedroom and jumping out of bed, ventured into the living room. There was no sign of their clothes. He continued into the kitchen, more out of hope than anything else. This too was empty. Opening one cupboard after another. These were empty as well. He opened the fridge, the oven, and even the pedal bin. These also had nothing in them. He returned to the bedroom. Where a puzzled-looking Charlotte stared at the vacant wardrobes.

'Hey,' he said. 'All the cupboards are empty. And the fridge. Shame, that, because I could've done with a drink.'

'Same here,' she said. 'No clothes, nothing. The bathroom's empty as well. No toiletries or anything. Not even a bog roll.'

'Maybe this is a show-house?' he said. 'You were showing me around and well … We got a bit frisky.'

She pouted. 'I suppose I was showing you around naked. And you were naked too.'

'Maybe we're on a nudist farm?'

Charlotte raised her eyebrows. 'Was there any food in the kitchen?'

'No.'

'So, we're on a nudist farm, where no one eats?' she said.

Jack sat next to her, nudging her gently. 'Fair point.'

'How do we get home?' he said.

'Where's home?'

'Another good point.'

'We can't just sit here, though,' she said.

'Why not?' he said. 'If we do go outside. And this place isn't some naturist community, we'll stand out like a sore thumb.'

'Yeah,' she thought out loud. 'Us two walking around in public, bollock naked.'

'Strictly speaking, I'll be the only one who's bollock naked.'

'Good point.' Nudging him back.

The doorbell sounded. Jack and Charlotte stared at each other.

'Now we're buggered,' she said.

'Why?'

'This could be the owners.'

Jack rolled his eyes. 'Owners don't generally press their own doorbell.'

'Maybe they've forgotten their key?'

'Yeah, perhaps,' Jack said. 'And they're ringing the bell hoping there are two naked burglars inside, who'll let them in.'

'We're not burglars. There's nothing to burgle,' Charlotte said. 'Except for the bed. And I can't see us getting it in our swag bag.'

'If we had a swag bag,' Jack said.

'Exactly. Maybe.' Leaning back on her arms. 'It's the dry cleaners with our clothes?'

'Of course.' Jack smiled. 'Why didn't I think of that? Or, maybe it's a food shop with the provisions we ordered online.'

The doorbell sounded again.

'What about …' Charlotte said. 'A new online shop, catering to all your needs. Maybe it has clothes, food, and anything else we require.

'A one-stop shop,' Jack said.

Charlotte nodded towards the door. 'Well?'

'Well what?' he said.

'Aren't you going to answer it?'

'Me? Why me?' he said. 'What happened to sexual equality?'

'It disappeared along with my underwear.'

'Emmeline Pankhurst would be proud of you,' he said. 'Well, I'm not particularly keen on opening the door to a stranger without any clothes on, either.'

'Why not? You've nothing to be ashamed of.' She winked at him. 'I could fluff it up a bit for you if you like. Make it more impressive.'

'And probably get me arrested as well,' he said. 'What happens if it's a woman?'

'I can think of worse sights opening a door.'

'Why don't we both go?' Jack said.

The doorbell sounded again.

'They're persistent,' Charlotte said. 'What about flipping a coin?'

'We haven't got one.'

'Can't we imagine we had one, tossed it, and I won?' she said.

He stood. 'Yeah because that'd be the sensible thing to do. They're clearly not going away.'

'Go on, Big-boy.' She grinned at him.

Jack headed towards the door, pausing for a deep breath before opening it.

A young man in uniform stood outside. 'Morning, sir,' the man said, seemingly unfazed by Jack's nudity.

'Morning.' Trying to appear casual, and struggling to adopt a relaxed stance. Jack hadn't spent a lot of time standing around nude. He wasn't sure what would be considered appropriate in polite company. He was roused from his musings by the man.

'I didn't get you out of the bath, did I, sir?' he said.

'No.' Jack said. 'My girlfriend and I were having wild sex when you rang. We tried to ignore it, but you were so persistent.'

'Oh, I'm sorry,' the man said.

'It's my girlfriend you need to apologise too. She was mid-orgasm.'

'Ah.' The man nodded. 'I have a telegram for Jack and Charlotte.'

Jack frowned. 'A telegram? Who the hell sends telegrams these days?'

'I've no idea, sir,' he said. 'Can you sign here?' Handing Jack a pad. Jack scribbled his signature and gave it back.

'Thank you,' he said. Giving Jack the telegram.

'I would give you something for your trouble, but, as you see.' Pointing to himself.

'That's ok, sir,' the man said. 'I hope you manage ...'

'Oh, you've ruined the moment now.' Slamming the door. He smiled to himself and meandered back into the bedroom.

'Well,' Charlotte said, sitting cross-legged on the side of the bed. 'Food, clothes, or both?'

'Neither.'

Charlotte smiled. 'I never thought. You could've wrapped a sheet around yourself.'

'Bit late now.' Fake smiled Jack.

'Well,' Charlotte said. 'Who was it?'

'A telegram.'

'A telegram? Who the hell sends telegrams?'

'That's what I said to the man,' Jack said.

'So, it was a man. Good job I didn't go.'

'Yeah,' mumbled Jack. He eyed the message.

'Who's it addressed too?'

'It says, Jack and Charlotte.'

She clapped her hands together. 'That's us.'

He smiled. 'Unless the owners of this flat happen to be called Jack and Charlotte.'

'Jack,' Charlotte said. 'Just open the telegram.'

Jack tore it open and viewed its contents.

Charlotte tugged at his arm. 'Well?'

'It says,' Jack said, putting on a posh voice, 'To Jack and Charlotte. Stop. Time to come home. Stop. From Christian Gainford. Stop.'

'Christian Gainford? The billionaire?'

'Apparently.'

'I would've preferred clothes,' Charlotte said.

'I would've preferred food.'

Jack and Charlotte stood at the front door of the flat. With a bedsheet, toga-like, around themselves.

'What did you see when you opened the door?' Charlotte said.

'Nothing.'

'Nothing.'

Jack shrugged. 'I wasn't looking.'

'Why not?'

'I was speaking to the telegram guy, that's why.'

'Oh, all right,' Charlotte said. 'You're still mad because I won the toss.'

'The imaginary toss?' Charlotte nodded. 'The toss that never took place?'

'That's the one,' she said.

'I'm always like this when I lose make-believe games of chance.' Adopting a fake sad face.

'Well.' Nudging him with her shoulder. 'Let's go home. Wherever home is.'

Jack pulled open the door, and the pair of them stepped onto the landing outside. As they did so, the scenery changed. They were standing on a cliff-top, the roaring sea crashing onto the beach and rocks below. They turned to where the door had been, but it had vanished.

Jack pointed over Charlotte's shoulder to a house in the distance. 'Should we head for there?'

'Why not,' Charlotte said. 'My diary's empty.'

'Look.' Pointing at Charlotte's clothing. She was now wearing jeans, a sweater, and a pair of Doc Martin boots. Jack similarly dressed.

'How weird,' she said.

'Yeah. I'd never pick a jumper with this pattern and colour. It looks an outfit my dad would wear.'

'Have you got a dad?' Charlotte said.

'Possibly.' Not knowing if he had or not.

'Does any of this appear familiar?' Jack asked, as they headed for the house.

'All of it, and none of it.'

'Is this you being enigmatic?' he said.

'Maybe, maybe not.' Skipping ahead of him like a happy schoolgirl.

They reached the rear of the property and darted through a hole in the hedge, into the garden. As they did, it became night.

Jack glanced across at Charlotte. 'Someone hasn't paid their bill,' he said.

'Why's none of this surprising?' Charlotte said. The pair stopped at the rear door of the property. 'I mean, one minute it's day the next it's night. Bit strange don't you think?'

'Time-lapse.' Taking hold of the handle.

'Time-lapse?' she said.

Jack smiled. 'Maybe the hole in the hedge was deeper than we thought.'

'Yeah. Makes complete sense.'

Jack pushed open the door, and the couple stepped inside. They found themselves in a pub. A bar was to the side of them, numerous tables scattered around the room. Jack ambled behind the counter, picked up a glass and pushed it under one of the optics a few times. half-filling his drink. He put the glass to his lips and took a large swig.

'Well?' Charlotte said.

Jack screwed his face. 'It doesn't taste of anything.' He sniffec at the glass. 'It doesn't smell either.'

'Now this pub looks familiar.' She performed a slow pirouette.

'Oh, yeah?' Jack filled a second glass.

'I think I met my ex here.' Stopping, she turned to face Jack.

'Ex,' Jack said. 'What was he like?'

'Not sure.'

Jack put down the glass. 'None of these drinks taste of anything.'

'Good.' Moving towards the door. 'We haven't got time for you to go on a bender. We're on our way home.'

'Have you considered clicking your heels together,' Jack said.

'Not sure it'll work with Doc Martin's, and don't they have to be ruby red?'

'They're oxblood.' Raising his eyebrow's a little.

'Come on, empty head.' Beckoning him towards her.

Jack vaulted the bar and joined her at the door. Charlotte reached for the handle, stuck out her tongue at him, and turned. The pair stepped outside and found themselves in a large dining room. A huge table in the middle, with two place settings taking centre-stage.

Charlotte strolled across and plucked the white card from the table. 'It looks as if we're expected.' Showing Jack the card with her name on it. 'Look, there's one for you too.'

'Great. We may get fed.'

'Is that all you're bothered about, food?' she said.

'Why not, considering how far we've travelled.'

Jack sat and picked up his knife and fork, smiling at her

Charlotte frowned at him. 'Come on. We haven't time to indulge your epicurean urges.'

'Wow!' Jack said. 'Epicurean. I bet you've been on a hair-trigger, waiting for an opportunity to shoehorn that into a sentence.'

Charlotte stopped at the door on the opposite side of the room they'd entered by. Jack traipsed across to her, feigning disappointment.

'I'll buy you a pizza when it's all over.' She gently tapped his cheek.

Jack shook his fists in mock excitement. 'Will it be a meat feast?'

'Of course.' Taking hold of the handle. 'Ready?'

'Ready,' he said.

The door swung open, and they stepped through into a foyer of an eerily-empty, palatial hotel. They ambled across the marble floor, stopping in the middle of the room. Jack strolled over to the reception desk and rang the bell. No one answered.

'I don't know how this place stays open,' Jack said.

Charlotte pointed to some doors. 'Outside. Unless you'd like to check out the dining room?'

'Nah.' Joining her. 'I've got my heart set on a pizza.' He clasped hold of Charlotte's hand and squeezed it gently.

'Holding hands, are we?' she said.

'I've a feeling.' Putting his mouth close to her ear. 'We're nearly home,' he whispered.

'I hope so,' she whispered back. 'These boots are killing me. Nancy Sinatra clearly didn't have these in mind.'

The two of them stepped forward, and as the electronic doors opened they strode outside.

Jack viewed the empty street. 'Bit disappointed if I'm honest.'

'Yeah,' Charlotte said. 'Maybe we have to walk from here.'

A large black limousine turned the corner and pulled up outside the hotel. The windows were dark, stopping the pair from seeing inside

Jack made his way over. 'Your carriage awaits, Madam.' Taking hold of the handle.

Charlotte pinched his bottom. 'Thank you, Wolverston. I'll see you later in the potting shed.'

He opened the door, and the two of them jumped in. Jack glanced across at Charlotte, who motioned for him to shut the door. Which he did with a resounding clunk.

# CHAPTER TWO

'They're waking up,' a voice said. 'Go and fetch Mr Gainford.'

Jack opened his eyes, along with Charlotte. The pair seated on reclined leather chairs. A headset sat on a table next to each of them and in the corner, a giant electronic machine. The room was bright, blindingly so. Jack and Charlotte shielded their eyes against it, allowing more time to become accustomed.

'Hello, Jack. Hello, Charlotte,' said a man dressed in a white lab-coat.

'Where are we?' Jack said.

'You're at the Gainford Foundation. My name's Professor Devon Wicken.'

Charlotte and Jack viewed each other, exchanging worried glances.

'Don't worry,' he said. 'I'm not some demented serial killer. The programmers like to have a laugh and use names of people they know.'

'What're we doing here?' Charlotte said.

'I better let Mr Gainford explain. He's on his way. If you'd like to follow me, we'll take you to the recovery suite and get you some refreshments.'

Charlotte and Jack followed the professor and one of his assistants into another room. The room had a table with comfortable chairs arranged around it. A lifeless monitor on one wall, and pleasant paintings adorned the others. It resembled an up-market doctor's or dentist's waiting room. Jack and Charlotte sat on two of the seats and waited.

'Please help yourself to drinks and snacks,' he said. Indicating towards a table at the far end of the room. 'I'll be back shortly with Mr Gainford.'

As he left, Jack jumped up and helped himself to a coffee and a couple of sandwiches. Charlotte did likewise. The two of them sitting quietly, unsure of what to say.

The door opened. Vanessa, along with Gainford entered.

Gainford smiled and offered his hand. 'Hello, you two.'

The pair stood shaking it in turn.

'Take a seat,' Gainford said. 'And we'll begin. You remember Vanessa, pointing at her?' Jack and Charlotte nodded.

'I'm sure you have lots of questions?' Gainford said.

'A few thousand,' Charlotte said.

Gainford chuckled. 'What's your last recollection?'

Jack and Charlotte glanced at each other. 'The limo,' they said in unison.

'The one at the station or the one outside the hotel?' Gainford said.

'The one at the hotel,' Charlotte said. Jack nodded his approval at her answer.

'That limousine wasn't real.' Indicating for Vanessa to continue.

Vanessa smiled. 'Everything that happened after you got into the car at Kings Cross, isn't real.'

Jack put a hand on Charlotte's arm as she was about to speak. 'Wait a minute,' he said. 'What do you mean, not real?'

'It was all part of a game,' Gainford said.

Charlotte frowned. 'Game?'

'Yes,' Vanessa said.

Jack rubbed his chin. 'But surely we'd remember putting on the headsets and that. We saw them in the other room.'

'Ah,' Gainford said. 'Bit of a confession here. For you to give yourself up entirely to it, it was vital you weren't aware you were in a game.'

'No way,' Charlotte said. 'We'd know.'

'The Champagne,' Vanessa said.

Charlotte frowned, again. 'The Champagne? What—'

'You drugged it,' Jack said. 'You bloody drugged us.'

'I know what you're going to say,' Gainford held up his hands in defence.

'No you don't.' Charlotte got to her feet. 'That's against human rights or something. I'm sure. Isn't that right, Jack?'

'Please, Charlotte,' Gainford said. 'It was all above board.'

Jack stood too. 'How can it be above board. You pick us up on the pretext we've won a competition, and abduct us.' He glanced at Charlotte, who nodded approval. 'Bring us to God knows where …'

'You agreed,' Gainford said. 'You signed a waiver.'

Charlotte scoffed. 'I never did. I wouldn't. I could've been violated.'

Vanessa opened her bag and took out two pieces of paper, handing one to Jack and one to Charlotte.

Jack sat. 'What' are these?'

'You both signed them in the limousine,' Vanessa said. 'It was in the small print.'

'Oh, come off it!' Jack said. 'No one reads the small print.'

'I do,' Gainford said. 'Always.'

Charlotte slumped back down. 'I do, usually. But when I saw Jack sign it, I assumed it was ok.'

Jack snorted. 'So now it's my fault?'

'No. I'm not saying that but ...'

'Kids, kids,' Gainford said. 'Let's not fall out over this. You two are unique. You're the first to play a multi-platform scenario. None of my people who tested it did that. You two are famous.'

'Multi-what?' Jack said.

Gainford folded his hands. 'Normally when we run the game, in testing, the participant only chooses one genre.'

Charlotte and Jack stared back vacantly.

He continued. 'Do you remember the forms Vanessa emailed you? The ones you were asked to fill in?'

The two of them nodded in unison.

'Well, in those forms you were asked what genre of games you liked to play. The form told you to tick one box only. Jack picked three, and Charlotte—'

'Four,' Charlotte said. 'Is that why there were so many variations?'

'Yes,' Gainford said.

Jack stared at Charlotte. 'Who're you going to blame for that, Charlotte,'

Charlotte looked away, but not before giving Jack her middle finger.

Gainford laughed. 'Let's not fall out again.'

Vanessa opened a folder. 'Jack picked intrigue, chase, and horror. Charlotte picked love interest, spirituality, mystery and—'

Charlotte sighed. 'Horror.'

'It appears you both love horror,' Gainford said. 'We couldn't wake you and ask you to limit your picks, as this would've let the cat out of the bag. So, we went ahead with your choices.'

'The serial killer bit was scary,' Charlotte said.

Gainford laughed. 'We think it was heightened by the fact you'd both chosen it. A sort of double espresso.'

Jack sat back in his chair. 'Wow.'

'Wow, indeed,' Charlotte said.

Gainford held up a finger. 'It appears, though, the game can only handle a maximum of two choices each. Which is why it started breaking down towards the end. It's why the game became erratic.'

'So how long were we in this game for?' Jack said.

'Two hours eighteen minutes,' Vanessa said.

Charlotte's eyes widened. 'No way!'

'How can that be?' Jack said.

'But it seemed like months,' Charlotte said.

Jack nodded his agreement.

Gainford grinned. 'It's fantastic, isn't it? Without getting technical. The game's super-compressed. Like a zipped computer file, only more so. The brain's a remarkable thing.'

'What now?' Charlotte said.

'The game's getting launched at the end of this week. The media are assembled, and you two are the main attraction. My people will assist you in getting the best financial deals out of this. You're going to be very wealthy, very soon.'

There was a tap on the door, and a young man popped his head in.

'Sorry to interrupt, Mr Gainford. Graham Norton's and Jonathan Ross's people are on the line. They desperately want Jack and Charlotte to appear this weekend.'

Gainford smiled. 'And so, it begins.'

Jack looked across at Charlotte, a broad grin on his face. Charlotte stared back open-mouthed.

Charlotte leant in close to Jack. 'If this is a game, I hope I never wake up.'

Jack and Charlotte enjoyed a whirlwind two weeks of non-stop interviews. They'd appeared on just about every TV chat show available, as well as several radio shows. A well-known publisher offered them a book deal, and Hollywood was sniffing around about the possibility of making a movie. Gainford had been right, though. Their bank accounts snowballed, as company after company threw money at them. The pair realised their fame wouldn't last forever, of course. They joked that when it did wane, they'd go on I'm a Celebrity. Their families travelled to London to spend a week with them. Giving Jack and Charlotte an opportunity to get to know each other's relations. Finally, after a month of media work, they decided to take a hiatus from the hectic lifestyle and go home. Gainford's new game, 'Duplicity,' was outselling any in the history of gaming adding more to Gainford's billions. Charlotte hadn't minded this, though, Gainford's philanthropy and altruism being well-known. He'd offered to have one of his cars take the two of them back north. The pair decided to travel by train, albeit first-class. They both had, for some strange reason, developed a phobia about Gainford's cars. A fact Gainford found amusing.

They sat opposite each other on the north-bound train from Kings Cross station. Charlotte gazed across at Jack. It was the first time since they'd played the game they'd been alone together. Charlotte couldn't help but think about what they'd gone through. She smiled to herself.

Jack noticed her smile. 'Penny for them,' he said.

'I was thinking about the game.'

'Oh, yeah?' Leaning in closer. 'What part, exactly?'

'Have you got an anchor tattooed on your arm?' she asked.

'An anchor?' he laughed. 'Do I look like Popeye?'

'I thought not,' she said. 'Any tattoos at all?'

He grinned. 'Well, you'll have to wait and see.'

'Who says I want to?'

'No one, but the offer's there. By the way,' he said. 'You haven't got a heart-shaped birthmark on your bum, have you?'

'You're making it up,' she said. 'You'll have to wait and see, too.'

Jack nodded along the carriage. 'Fancy showing each other our tattoo and birthmark? Or join the mile-high club? We have been married.'

She leant forward. 'Only in the game.'

'True,' he said.

'Haven't you got to be on a plane for that? The mile-high club, I mean.'

'Probably. Whatever it's called on a train, then.'

'Aren't you frightened of planes?' she said.

Jack sighed. 'That was in the game. I don't mind flying. We don't know much about each other, do we?'

'Well, there's no time like the present.' Taking hold of his hand and pulling him up. 'Follow me.'

'If this turns out to be another game, I won't be pleased,' he said.

'Me neither.' Heading along the corridor.

'What happens if we're caught?' Charlotte said.

'We'll be all over the papers again,' he said. 'Bothered?'

'Not in the least.' They stopped outside the cubicle.

Charlotte frowned. 'Jack? How can we be certain this is real?'

'We can't.'

Charlotte rubbed her chin. 'Six weeks ago, we'd never met. And now we ...'

'And now, we're on a first-class north-bound train. Having spent a month appearing on all the top shows on telly.'

'With bank accounts large enough to sign an average premiership footballer. It does seem surreal.'

'Yeah,' he said. 'When you think about it.'

'Look!' Pointing out of the train window.

'It's a bird,' Jack said.

'Not any bird. It's a humming-bird.'

'So?'

She rolled her eyes. 'You don't get hummingbirds in England.'

'Maybe it escaped from a zoo.'

'Do you remember when we entered Gainford's game, *Broken*,' she said. Jack nodded. 'And you had to choose a mental prompt? If you got

215

stuck in the game. It'd alert you to the fact it was a game you were playing?'

Jack sighed. 'Yeah.'

'Well, mine was a humming-bird.'

'It's probably a coincidence,' he said.

'Really?' she said. 'What was your prompt?'

'An elephant.'

'An elephant?'

'Yeah. I thought if we had to have a mental prompt, what better than a huge elephant. You wouldn't mistake that, would you?'

'Look,' Nodding behind Jack as a young man, wearing a t-shirt with a picture of an elephant on the front, walked by.

'Oh, come on!' he said. 'Bit of a stretch.'

'Well, it seems strange to me.'

Jack shrugged. 'Maybe.'

'What's behind this door, I wonder?' She nodded towards it.

Jack raised his eyebrows, comically. 'A basin and a bog. I hope.'

'There's only one way of finding out, Jackie-Boy.' Adopting a false seriousness.

Jack grabbed hold of the handle. 'There certainly is.' Clasping her hand with his other hand. 'Ready?' He grinned at her.

'Ready.' She grinned back.


## THE STORYTELLER

Are we any clearer on the nature of reality and fantasy? No? Well, let me try and help. Just as Jack and Charlotte can't be sure if what they are experiencing is real, can we? Next time you look up at the sky ask yourself, is it a little too blue, a little too perfect? Look around the edges. Those sly glances from your peripheral vision we allow ourselves. The dreams and reveries we indulge in. Are they our imagination, or maybe something more substantial? Taking everything on board, though. There's only one question you need to ask yourself. Just one question requiring an answer. ***Who's writing the narrative of your life?***

## THE END…?

# THE AUTHOR

John Regan was born in Middlesbrough on March 20th, 1965. He currently lives in the Acklam area of Middlesbrough.

This is the second book he's written and fulfils a life-long ambition of his. At present his full-time job is an underground telephone engineer at Openreach and, has worked for both BT and Openreach for the past fifteen years.

He's about to embark on his third novel and hopes to have it completed sometime next year.

June 2016.

Email: johnregan1965@yahoo.co.uk

# OTHER BOOKS BY THIS AUTHOR

**THE HANGING TREE** – Even the darkest of secrets deserve an audience.
Sandra Stewart and her daughter are brutally murdered in 2006. Stephen Stewart, her husband, is wanted in connection with their deaths, having disappeared on the night of Sandra's murder.
Why has he returned eight years later?
And why is he systematically slaughtering apparently unconnected people?
Could it be the original investigation was flawed?
Detective Inspector Peter Graveney's catapulted headlong into an almost unfathomable case. Thwarted at every turn by faceless individuals, intent on keeping the truth buried.
Are there people close to the investigation, possibly even within the force, determined to prevent him from finding out what actually happened?
As he becomes ever more embroiled. He battles with his past, as skeletons in his own closet, rattle loudly. Tempted into an increasingly dangerous affair with his new Detective Sergeant, Stephanie Marne, Graveney finds people he can trust, rapidly diminishing.
But who's manipulating who? And as he moves ever closer to the truth, he finds the person he holds most dear, threatened.
Graphically covering adult themes 'The hanging tree' is a relentless edge of the seat ride, exploring the darkest of secrets and the lengths people go, to keep those secrets hidden. Culminating in a horrific and visceral finale, as Graveney relentlessly pursues it to its final conclusion.

**"Even the darkest of secrets deserve an audience."**

## THE ROMANOV RELIC – The Erimus Mysteries

Hilarious comedy thriller!

Private Detective, Bill Hockney's murdered while searching for the fabled – Romanov Eagle, cast for The Tsar. His three nephews inherit his business, setting about, not only discovering its whereabouts but also who killed their uncle.

A side-splitting story, full of northern humour, nefarious baddies, madcap characters, plot twists, real-ale, multiple showers, out of control libido, bone-shaped chews and a dog called Baggage.

Can Sam, Phillip and Albert, assisted by Sam's best friend Tommo, outwit the long list of people intent on owning the statue, while simultaneously trying to keep a grip on their love lives?

Or will they be thwarted by the menagerie of increasingly desperate villains?

Solving crime has never been this funny!

31045139R00129

Printed in Poland
by Amazon Fulfillment
Poland Sp. z o.o., Wrocław